Marion Halligan was born in _____ the sea. She is rather surprised to find herself living in Canberra, instead of on the coast. She always believed she was going to be a writer, though took a while to get started. Halligan has now published some nineteen books (including a children's book, *The Midwife's Daughters*) and has written short stories, articles, book reviews and essays for various publications. Her most recent book is *The Taste of Memory*, a memoir about food and gardens, travel and home. But she believes that it is fiction that illuminates our lives, and for this reason she loves to read it as well as write it.

Also by Marion Halligan

The Taste of Memory
The Point
The Fog Garden
The Golden Dress
Cockles of the Heart
Wishbone
The Worry Box
Lovers' Knots
Eat My Words
Spider Cup
The Hanged Man in the Garden
The Living Hothouse
Self Possession
The Midwife's Daughters (for children)
Out of the Picture
Collected Stories

marion HALLIGAN

the apricot colonel

ALLEN&UNWIN

First published in 2006

Copyright © Marion Halligan 2006

All rights reserved. No part of this book may be reproduced or transmitted in any form or by any means, electronic or mechanical, including photocopying, recording or by any information storage and retrieval system, without prior permission in writing from the publisher. The *Australian Copyright Act 1968* (the Act) allows a maximum of one chapter or 10% of this book, whichever is the greater, to be photocopied by any educational institution for its educational purposes provided that the educational institution (or body that administers it) has given a remuneration notice to Copyright Agency Limited (CAL) under the Act.

Allen & Unwin
83 Alexander Street
Crows Nest NSW 2065
Australia
Phone: (61 2) 8425 0100
Fax: (61 2) 9906 2218
Email: info@allenandunwin.com
Web: www.allenandunwin.com

National Library of Australia
Cataloguing-in-Publication entry:
Halligan, Marion, 1940-
The apricot colonel.

ISBN 1 74114 766 2.

I. Title.

A823.3

Edited by Rosanne Fitzgibbon
Text design and typesetting by Midland Typesetters
Printed in Australia by McPherson's Printing Group

10 9 8 7 6 5 4 3

For my beloved Lucy

who read this novel and asked excellent questions

> Man thinks, God laughs.
>
> JEWISH PROVERB

> It pleases me to think that the art of the novel came into the world as an echo of God's laughter.
>
> MILAN KUNDERA

This story happens in that last overheated sinister summer, in a space of time beginning with the fires that in a day burned over five hundred houses and the Police Academy and the animal hospital and the great telescope at Mount Stromlo, so that for a short while people who lost their houses were giddy with a strange excitement, that fate had marked them but not for death, they were still gloriously alive. It ends with the announcement that our country was at war with Iraq.

From the sixteenth of January to the twenty-second of March, in that year of little grace, 2003.

The summer is over now, the garden is sharp with autumn, dry still, the sun benign and the air remembering that frost will come. The cat has vomited up a fur ball and is asleep in a warm corner of the wall as though it had never been.

Chapter 1

The puncture happened on one of those long straight stretches of highway where the land seems to fold back from the road. It is the rind of the earth and you are a small creature clinging to it; what you mainly see is sky. Except that today it wasn't sky. The sky was an invisible lid and what I saw were sinister layers of smoke trapped thick against it. Bushfire smoke, from hectares of burning national park. The sun was a quivering disc; sun and smoke coated the countryside in sulphurous yellow light.

I don't know how to change a tyre. Maybe the service manual would tell me, but it wasn't in the car.

Nobody stops for people broken down by the side of the road.

I bent over and looked at the tyre. I thought if I touched the ground the dirty yellow light would wipe off on my fingers like grease. At least the tyre hadn't blown and sent me spinning into the culvert.

The speed of cars seems normal when you're there doing it with them. But when you stop and stand just out of their passage they are going so fast the noise and the rush buffets you. In a minute you'll be an empty plastic bag tossed and flapping in the dust. I was wearing a skirt and sandals, comfortable for driving. But when I bent over the skirt whirled around me and my hair blew out from my head as though I was already tumbling through the empty landscape.

I had my phone but it was out of range. I looked at the long ribbon of road. Which way was the nearest blue phone?

It could be kilometres in either direction. The temperature was forty degrees. I could collapse with heatstroke before I got to one. I could collapse with heatstroke staying with the vehicle, as they warn you should do in the desert.

A car stopped, needing a while to do it, and backed up fast until it was just in front of mine. Out got a man, not tall, with brush-cut hair and mirror sunglasses. He had on one of those dazzling white T-shirts that mould bulging muscles and in his case a small football of a stomach. Of course anybody is sinister, on a lonely road with only an occasional car blazing past.

Got a flat, love, he says. Jack?

I think this is his name and wonder why he asks it as a question. So I'm looking puzzled. He shakes his head and makes tch-tching noises. Opens his boot and gets out, of course, his jack, and a tool kit.

These little buzzy-bee buggery cars, only take a minute, he says. Hardly need a jack, in all truth.

He makes a gesture of lifting it up with his hands.

I say how kind of him, and all that, I was feeling desperate, then stop; shouldn't say this, I think. I look at his car. It's a bronze colour, gleaming, burnished, all massive outside with a little cabin enclosed in huge slabs of metal. It looks new but somehow I know it isn't.

Nice car, I say.

Yup, he says. She's some hot baby.

I see that this is the name on the numberplate. Hotbaby. What kind of car is it, I ask.

He stands up. Puts his hands on his hips. Slides his sunglasses up his forehead and gazes at me. His eyes are the sharp pale blue colour of ice, the irises seem made of little chips of glaciers. They glitter. He can't believe his ears, this look says.

She's a Monaro. Best bloody car ever made.

A kind of Holden, isn't it?

The best. She's the best. Not just Holden, of any car. Spare?

It doesn't take long to fix. He puts his tools away. I open the car door. He leans on it. Well, he says, what's that worth?

I look at him, reaching in behind me for my handbag.

Not money. Why would you think money?

No, not money, I say. I pull out my little case of business cards and take one out. I step towards him so he steps back and put it in his hand. There, I say. That's more than money. You have my fair words and thank yous and a name and address.

He looks at the card, holding it at arm's length, squinting. I jump back, into the car, slam the door, lock it, reverse, and roar off. Well, not roar. Buzz. He's still holding the card in his outstretched arm but staring after me, last I see.

I was late, but not very. I'd left myself extra time, I always do where a job is concerned. In case I had a puncture or something. Or couldn't find the house. The colonel was waiting for me. Come in, he said. A wash, or a glass of wine? Both, in either order? I recommend the sunset, shortly.

To get to the house I'd turned off a country road on to a rough track that led over a hill. On either side were cattle yards, enclosed in painted wooden rails, with after a while a white gate and a sign saying Private Road. There was a row of pines and behind it a small wooden house; beyond that I knew would be the sea but how far beyond or below I couldn't tell. In fact the little wooden house was just the beginning, a pretty painted cottage, small rooms, small windows. We passed through it like a passageway and stepped down into an enormous room hung on the edge of a low cliff which plunged down and then spread out into green slopes, their tilted shapes patched together with dark hedges and beyond them the sea a silvery shimmer filling the horizon.

Wow, I said.

Yes, he said.

This is Colonel Marriott, A.M. Marriott, Al. He has written a book about his experiences in the Gulf War. I'm a freelance editor. He rang and offered me the job of fixing it up. It'll need work, he said. A lot. He suggested I come to his house and do it there. On the south coast, just by Tilba. A pleasant spot.

My wife and I would be delighted if you would come and stay, as many days as needed, he wrote. Indeed, as many days as you want. We could work in the mornings and you could be free in the afternoons. I would pay a daily fee, plus an hourly rate for the work put in. I wish to be generous.

I don't know, I said. I'm not sure if I'm free.

In fact I was, but I didn't fancy the job. I don't like going to strange people's houses. But I did need the money.

Please, name your fee.

I thought of the most I could normally charge and doubled it.

If you are sure that's enough, he said.

So there I was, being led out on to a deck that wrapped three sides of a big glass box hanging off a cliff, to see the red rags of a sunset strung across the western sky. I had waited until the worst threat of the fires seemed to have passed, when I thought it was safe to leave my house, nowhere seemed at those moments very safe, when the ribbons of bush that were the beauty of the city turned into fuses that could bring fire to its heart. The sky was still full of smoke, that ruddiness wasn't usual.

Do you like sauvignon blanc? he said.

Two glasses, big generous curves, even a third full they used a lot of the bottle. I looked at him as he poured, a tall man, well moderately tall, slender, with wide shoulders and a flat stomach. A shapely head, his blond-grey hair long enough to curl a little. I noticed he had long thin well-kept hands, I like good hands in a man, and that he took the moment's pleasure in the shapes they made in the air as he talked.

Is your wife joining us?

He passed me a glass of wine and I took a sip. Excellent.

Alas, there is no wife.

He waved the glass at the sunset. Married to a sunset? Gone off into?

I didn't think you'd come unless there was a wife.

I can go, since there isn't one.

Please don't, he said. I promise not to pounce. Not until the work's done.

I took some more mouthfuls of wine. I'd better not drink too much if I was driving back.

I lied, he said. But it was a strategic lie, not a moral one.

A lie is a lie.

Surely that's a strangely simplistic idea. It was as I say a strategic lie. Designed to get you here. But not bad, or immoral, or cheating. Because I shall behave as though I had. A wife. I've told you I have a wife, and I don't, but my behaviour will be exactly as if I do and she is by my side, watching, not critically or with evil expectation, watching with affection my behaviour to you.

But since you lied about having a wife you may be lying about behaving as though you do.

He looked closely at me. The colonel has deep blue eyes, not icy but indigo, even perhaps violet, a dimple in his chin and teeth so white they dazzle. I put down the wine and picked up my bag to create the impression I was about to go.

Again, he said, that would be simple-minded. And not useful. The first is a lie of strategy. But were the second to be a lie it would defeat my purpose. My intention is to treat you with impeccable professional reserve. With courtesy, and kindness, of course, and to give you pleasure, I want you to be comfortable so you can work happily. Why would I jeopardise my whole enterprise by cracking on to you?

How do you know it would? I thought but did not say. His words fascinated me, at the same time as I wondered if they should make me nervous. I drank more wine.

Are you a bachelor?

Fine old word. Yes, at the moment. Can one be a bachelor at a moment? Or is it a state, like virginity, once lost never regained?

That's a very good question, I said. I wonder. Can a man become a bachelor again? Maybe not. So, you are telling me you have been married?

Oh, I was speaking metaphorically. Now I am a writer I think a lot about words.

I did consider it a good question. I'm a sucker for a good question. I was thinking about it when he came back with Volume 1 of the *Shorter Oxford* and a small hessian sack. He passed me the dictionary and shook the sack gently open, over the slatted wooden table. Oysters slid out, and he took up a knife like a fat-handled dagger. He opened one and passed it to me.

Wine, oysters, dictionary. I didn't leave. Of course I didn't.

Turns out, bachelor comes from *bacca lauri*, laurel berry, as in being crowned with. Why? Who knows. Presumably this is where the Bachelor of Arts idea comes from. The word originally meant one of the stages of knighthood, then later an unmarried man, usually of marriageable age. But whether it is a condition that once discarded is never to be retrieved I could not ascertain.

Chapter 2

My name is Cassandra Travers. An elegant name, I think, I always admire it when a grateful client writes in the acknowledgments *And thanks to my editor Cassandra Travers* . . . I wasn't christened Cassandra, it's not my mother's kind of name. Sandra, she called me, still does; then she thought it was glamorous, now she persists with her choice. People sometimes call me Cass. It feels like a voyage, from Sandra to Cass. I chose to lengthen it because I wanted something with more syllables than my surname, something solider, more musical, more I suppose, in my own terms, glamorous. It's a good name for an editor: Cassandra the princess of Troy, who told the truth, and was not believed.

And Travers: even that is its own small fiction. Not mine. My grandfather was Traverso. Traverso to Travers: Italian to English, migrant to native. Drop one letter, add three: you are a different character in a different narrative. You edit your name, you edit the person you might be.

Some people don't believe that names have any power. More fools they.

Some people think that an editor is a dull dry little

person. Mimsy, pedantic. Living at second-hand. Boring. Nearly as bad as a librarian.

No. An editor is a person of power. Of grandeur. I look at a manuscript and see the scope, the structure. Grand things. This takes vision. Very few people have it.

I'm not a copyeditor. I turn words into books.

Imagine: a house, large, spacious. But somehow the windows and doors are bricked up. There is no light or air inside, however palatial the rooms. No way in from the outside. Blind and inaccessible. Or: a building of fine quarried sandstone blocks. How beautiful they are. But no rooms inside, no passages, just beautiful sandstone blocks all cramped together. A deception, appearing to be a noble edifice, but instead a set of facades with no internal life.

I will turn them into spacious and elegant dwellings where people—writers, readers—can walk in and out, in contentment, and pleasure, even bliss, taking account of the rooms, the handsome furnishings, the amenities, the courtyards, the vistas. Holding conversations like intricate dances of which miraculously they know the steps. All this done by magic: the claustrophobic stones, the excluding bricks, all moved by words, the choice and placement of careful black marks on a white page, so the intended spaciousness of these edifices may have its being.

My mind is good at structures, on all scales: sentence, paragraph, chapter, book. Writers can turn out some fine things, but they can't always structure them.

There's terror, too, always we must have terror, but not of the walling in or out kind. Terror is the most subtle and difficult of all. Terror we will come to later.

I'm not a writer, no way. I'm a reader. It is other people's writing that I know about, that I can see whole and clear, laid out like the plan of an architect. A window here, move this wall, those steps are too steep. And I'm good at grammar. (When I need to be. Choose to be.) Being good at grammar isn't something this society values. It thinks it doesn't. Won't teach it to its children. It may find out one day how wrong it's been. If George Bush had known more grammar . . . but no, let's not go that way.

I said I'm not a copyeditor. I can do you commas and colons. Em dashes and whom is who. I can do keeping the protagonist's eyes the same colour all the way through. Standardising the T-shirt, dehyphenating the tea bag. Removing the metaphorical watch from the wrist of the heroine, striking out the anachronistic aubergine. But it is turning the inchoate mass into a civilised book that is really my thing. I know the different ways of cricket autobiography—there's a laugh, having your life written for you by a ghost—and your Booker Prize winner. Who am I kidding, haven't cracked one of those yet. But I do get some good novels, better often than the Bookers; novels are the best.

A good novel: it's the apotheosis of the book.

And you know, the marvellous thing about this job: it's the perfect alibi for reading. The more you read the more you know, about words and books and *things*. See Cassandra lying on the sun lounge reading. What a life, one long holiday that girl.

Not a bit of it. See Cassandra lying on the sun lounge working hard, reading.

Actually I don't care for sun lounges. Prefer a table and

chair any day. Or a good sofa. But sun lounge's got a good ring to it.

So that's established. I'm not mimsy or boring or a dull dry little person. And here's what I look like: average height, average weight, okay breasts, small bottom, shapely legs, excellent ankles but not a great waist. Not the sort of body that makes strangers gasp when you walk down the street, but those who have desired to get to know it have found it beautiful. Ah yes but isn't that the least we can all hope for. When I was twenty-seven my hair went white which was an awful shock at the time but now I think it's great, I see myself as a pure white dazzling blonde. It's thick and silky, I wear it shoulder length and it falls like a thirties film star's in a swoop across my brow. My skin is pale brown and my eyes dark brown. I am thirty-six and think of myself as a young person with so much to do and a lot of life ahead of her in which to do it. Of course I understand that other people might not see me like this.

I should have got someone else to describe me: old school friend, ex-lover, sister: what would they have said? Would any of their accounts be recognisably the same person?

It has to be said, too, that I have not always been so good at life as I am at books but life does not sit quietly there and let you edit it.

Oysters. The sea mysteriously made flesh. A small morsel of fleshy seawater, edible as the sea never is.

I have never eaten my fill of oysters before. When I went down to my room which hangs under the main room with some of the same view—it has as its back wall the rock of the cliff—I felt the calm content of enough oysters as well as the good wine I had drunk. The colonel sat on the deck and played a guitar, not particularly well, but with a sweet melancholy human sound in the quiet night. In bed I can hear the murmur of the ocean, its endless lullaby roar.

In the morning I start reading. 'Her Privates We: A Memoir of the Gulf War'. That title will have to go. It's been done before. And anyway he's a colonel.

We're at a long table in the big room. I've read fifty pages. Terribly boring, I say.

What have I done, he says. A trollop, a baggage. Am I paying you for this? No I am not.

This should offend me, bringing my sexual morals into it, but it just sounds funny, he rolls the words so unctuously round his mouth. You've been reading too many archaic texts, I say. You are paying me for the truth. Somewhere there is a story. It's interesting. Vastly. And moving. Important, even. But not here.

You've only read fifty pages. It gets better.

Nobody will get that far to find out.

How can you say boring, it's full of the most terrible events.

That's not the point.

With respect, madam, I was there and you weren't. That is how it was.

With respect, Colonel, we are not talking about the Gulf War, we are talking about you writing the Gulf War. I know about writing.

And I don't.

Not yet, no. I want to get you to write it down so your readers are there, with you.

That's what I've done. Written down what happened. The truth. Surely that's pretty simple.

Simple is the hardest. What you have there isn't simple.

I was being hard on him but it was the right thing. His hardness was showing too, bare and blunt. Editing is like training puppies. You have to show authors who's master. Of course they are, like puppies, but you can't let them think that, not at the beginning.

To begin with, I said, lose the first fifteen pages.

I know this is like telling a mother to kill her firstborn. The colonel went white.

Start here, I said, page sixteen, with the death of your companion. Not all this prosing-on explanatory stuff. Okay, don't lose the earlier stuff, hang on to it, you might want to put it in later. You might not, you'll probably find you don't need it. But at least wait until you've got us hooked on a great story.

What a struggle this was for him. No gain without pain, as they say; distastefully, I think, but people like these pat little adages. They see deep and powerful truths in them.

Next, I said, try leaving out all the adjectives and adverbs.

Adjectives and adverbs . . .

The words you've stuck on to the nouns and verbs.

That's where all the colour is . . .

You think you're making them more intense but you

aren't. Those words are winding us up. Rabblerousing. We don't like to feel we're being wound up.

I jabbed my finger on a sentence and passed him a purple pen. *The shocking scarlet shreds of deadly tracer fire ripped hideously through the sinister darkness of the inky-black night.* Go on, I said, cross out every adjective and adverb.

It used to be a blue pencil, but in these days of computer manuscripts I like a purple pen; it's symbolic I suppose, using purple to get rid of purple.

It took him a while. Keep going, I said, keep going. He ended up with *The shreds of tracer fire ripped through the darkness of the night.* I'll let you have tracer, I said. But I don't know that you need both darkness and night . . . *ripped through the darkness* . . . see, the words have value. Rare is precious.

He looked like a man under fire himself.

See how it's colder, I said, and so much stronger.

You're tough, aren't you.

I think I detected a certain admiration in his voice.

When you've taken out all the adjectives and adverbs I might let you put some back, I said. Plain is good, is powerful, is what touches the heart. Leaves us nowhere to hide. But maybe, sometimes, a little colour.

We went through the printout with the purple pen and did this for a while.

It's exhausting, editing. I told Al this, not to be surprised. I told him it would get easier, and better still, he could learn not to fall into the various traps in the first place. I didn't tell him that empurpled prose is just the beginning of his troubles.

In the morning we had breakfast on the veranda, looking out over the folded green of the fields, so vividly emerald that it might have been another hemisphere. Dairy country, once. Not any more. Rich person's second-house country now, said the colonel. With acreage and water. Pop down in the plane for the weekend. Foreign film stars paying millions on the say-so of a brother-in-law dropping in by helicopter.

Working places turning into pleasure palaces.

Indeed, said the colonel, that's good. I like that.

His coffee was black and rich, the milk hot and frothy. We drank for a while in silence.

Whose book will this be, he asked.

What do you mean?

Well, will I have written it, when it comes to the crunch?

Too right.

Not you—?

Got a minute, I said. I'll tell you a story. Of when I was a baby editor. Very baby, it was actually a kind of work experience, I was still at university but I knew what I wanted. With a small independent publisher, good reputation, did some marvellous books, discovered some terrific writers. Paid attention, the book was the thing, not the marketing, the hype, not like these days.

Are you old enough for this?

Plenty. A manuscript came in. Written by an unknown writer. The editor, the boss, I'll call her Evelyn—

Not her real name?

Not her real name. We editors are discreet. She recognised its potential, that she could turn it into a brilliant book. I went in to her office one day, it was the drawing room of a once-grand terrace house in Darlinghurst, and there it was, pages spread everywhere, and she was doing this huge cut-and-paste job. Not a computer cut-and-paste, the literal thing, with scissors and glue pot and wastepaper basket. And pen and ink.

That long ago, it was, I said, before people offered manuscripts on disk.

She totally remade that book—Evelyn, not an editor beginning with the premise, see how *you* can do it, asking questions, pointing out problems, suggesting, helping the writer to work out how to do it, *she* did it. And the writer, we'll call him Theo, he so much wanted a brilliant book, he let her do it. But then it wasn't his any more.

It really was successful?

Oh yes, won heaps of prizes, published overseas, international acclaim, short-listed for the Booker, et cetera. I thought about this a lot, and I realised that I had seen at first hand the working out of a Faustian temptation, both of them wanting the amazing book, selling their souls to get it. That's when I, baby editor that I was, I figured it out, that the book must always remain the writer's. You must leave him his—her—integrity. His dignity. Theo has written a number of books since, but none of them has done as well.

Does he know they're no good?

Interesting question. Probably he doesn't. Maybe he doesn't want to believe they are not as good. Maybe he doesn't have good judgment. But he must know that none of them have had the stunning success of the first. And as for Evelyn, what does she care that she robbed a writer of his work. She saw a chance to make a clever book and was too greedy, too vain, not to take it.

Well, said the colonel. I can see how one of the signers of the pact with the devil gets his comeuppance—sad Theo, one good book, never another. But what of the other, the publisher, Evelyn? Does she get the sharp end of the stick somewhere?

Oh, by no means. Goes from strength to strength. Honours upon honours. Becomes a pundit, a guru. People hang upon her every banal word. A most interesting case of power-mongering in a world famous for it. But I think I know why. In the Faustian pact, poor Theo was the victim, the Faust figure if you like; Evelyn was the devil.

Ooh. The colonel whistled, then his mouth widened in a smile of pure delight. Oh, how superb. I think I shall enjoy this new world you're taking me into.

But you get my message? *Your* book. *Your* integrity. I am not the devil. No pacts with the powers of darkness.

No ma'am. No, indeed not.

Chapter 3

After lunch the colonel said he was leaving me to my own devices. He was going up the coast, he had some business. I read for a while and fiddled around, then got in my car and headed south. I drove along the coast roads, in and out of the hot summer bays, the blue water with its tantalising dreams of seaside living, the seductive headlands where the waves beat in drifts of spray. So beautiful, and I coveted it, but knew I would never do anything about possessing it. A small shack was a nice thought and so were the serious riches needed to fund it. Though when I came to a little pub with a balcony overlooking the water I didn't resist the temptation to pretend all that vast blueness belonged to me for a little while. Both of us, the pub and I, turning our backs on the tidy streets of Canberra-on-the-coast, where retirees bring their suburbs with them.

The pub was on a point, with sea on both sides, and a tall pine tree. I saw dolphins surface far out. And there were sea eagles hanging and swooping in the blue air; four of them.

The terrace was quite crowded, with groups and couples, though there were spare tables. I was the only person on my own, but I rather like that, it makes me feel strong. And when I came back with a light beer, a wimpy drink I know, but it's the driving, I saw there was another woman sitting quite grandly by herself.

I know I have a habit when I'm in a place on my own like this of selecting someone to look at, to stare at really, though I try to do it subtly, someone to observe and wonder about. Guess at stories for them to inhabit. This woman sat three-quarters turned away. I could see she was quite tall, and well built, a gym-toned body, with shoulder-length blonde hair, rather stiff as it starts to get after a lot of dyeing. (Not like my soft white mane. Bear with me, it's my one vanity.) I could see she had sensational legs, long and slender but shapely, with sharp anklebones, and tanned that wonderful biscuit colour you want to nibble.

But, and this is the thing, she was wearing a dress—as women do, you'll say—but this was the kind called a shirtwaist, with a collar turned up round her neck, bracelet-length sleeves, buttons down the front, and a swinging skirt cut on the bias. It was made of some slippery sort of fabric, every now and then she settled into a different posture, recrossed her legs, leaned back with an arm draped over the chair, or forward on one elbow, and I could see how the dress slid over her limbs and yet clung. The fabric was white with a pattern of scarlet poppies and yellow wheatears and blue cornflowers. I recognised it as art silk. It was the kind of dress that used to be known as an afternoon dress. Women put on a cotton house dress in the morning, tidy and clean, for doing the housework and all that, and then in the afternoon they would have a pretty dress, for going out, visiting mother, or sisters, going to town, maybe playing bridge or taking afternoon tea. In some levels of society you'd change again, for cocktails, dinner, but this was the afternoon dress of ordinary women, and handmade. Beautifully. An anthropological item in the narratives it offered of a vanished life.

She had a little white hat on her head, tilted to one side, with a small brim that swooped down over her nose. Women only ever wear sunhats these days, and I suppose it came into that category, but only by stretching it. She was drinking something that looked like Pimms, tallish and brownish, fizzy and vegetable. When did I last see someone drinking Pimms?

Shirtwaist, afternoon dress, art silk—short for artificial silk—how do I know these words? They're well before my time. They're my gran's era. I got one of those oral history kits from the National Library and did it with her. She loved it. I've got stacks of tapes of her talking. You start off with questions, and the idea of the kit is that they're the right questions, so you find out what it's important to know, but Gran took off pretty fast. She loved remembering her youth, her heyday she called it, and the time when her kids were small. She'd been trained as a dressmaker, went to tech, learned to draft patterns and all that, but once she was married she made clothes just for herself and her daughters. Her sister Muriel was a milliner, she made the hats to go with them. Gran sent me to get out the photos, she was by that stage pretty much confined to bed, but she knew where everything was. She said she wished she'd kept a photographic record of every dress she'd ever made, instead of just odd pictures of the occasions they'd been worn. She sent me for the boxes of patterns, Butterick and Women's Home Journal and Simplicity. I wore that to May's wedding, she said. That was Bill's twenty-first. Later her daughters got on to Vogue Couturier designs, such fancy things, and complicated. But it was her dresses, her youth, she liked to talk about, and how when she met Jack she'd been wearing a dress of eau-de-nil satin-backed crepe with a skirt cut on the bias that fell in scallops round the hem, and when she danced it flared out and showed her ankles, that's what got Jack interested, he always said she had such pretty ankles. She knew about seduction and desire, my gran, and I will be forever grateful that I understood that about her. We need to realise that our generation has invented nothing in that line. The old woman sat in her bed and her face lit up with secret pleasure when she remembered Jack admiring her ankles. Ankles, she said, it was more like knees, but Jack was always a discreet man.

The dress of this woman on the pub veranda was very Butterick. And her ankles as fine as Gran's. I got another beer and thought of all these things. Sometimes I gazed at the sea but my eyes kept coming back to the shirtwaist woman. You know how people reckon that if you keep looking at someone they'll eventually turn round, to see where the gaze is coming from? This woman didn't. At one point she stood up and walked to the edge of the balcony and stood like the models in those same Butterick patterns, weight on one hip, legs in a Y-shape, looking over the balustrade. Her shoes were the only contemporary thing about her, white strappy sandals with no backs and kitten heels. They gave her that slippy-sloppy slightly awkward walk that's rather sexy and I could tell from the way she shimmied her hips that she knew it. She stood for a while, looking down into the street in front of the hotel, then sashayed back and sat with her legs crossed, leaning picturesquely on one elbow. But at no time did she look at me, or any one else, and it suddenly occurred to me that she was an installation, she was a piece of performance art. Was she waiting for someone? Was it a bet? Was it an assessment for an art class? Did she charge a fee for her appearance? She sat there, an object for contemplating. Not that anybody was, the whole terrace was too busy in its own conversations even to notice. There was something surreal about the scene, this woman displaying herself with such gorgeous and accurate anachronism and nobody watching her. I wanted to stay and see what happened, but I got sick of waiting. On the way out I thought of passing her table with its sticky remnant of Pimms and orange slice and cucumber peel and murmuring, A brilliant performance, well done. But I didn't. The whole of life is made of totally insignificant choices, so you suppose, but what consequences they may have.

When I got back the colonel wasn't there but in a while he came rushing in with a fish for dinner. He asked me about my afternoon, and I told him about driving south along the bays and he said South? Mm I said. See anyone you knew? he asked. No, I said, you're like my gran, she was always asking me did I see anyone I liked better than myself, and was going to tell him about the shirtwaist woman but he started yapping on about the fish, whether to cook it in a French manner or some sort of Thai style, and the moment passed. But all night I kept thinking about her, and the antique theatrical nature of her costume, and how Gran would have been intrigued by it all. I felt that her ghost had visited me, or rather, not the ghost of Gran but of her clothes. Her clothes as a young woman. Her heyday.

Chapter 4

Of course I had to read the whole manuscript through, but my fifty-page assessment was accurate, as I knew it would be. It was going to be a big cut-and-paste job. The colonel was right. There was a good story in there. Somewhere. But it wasn't exactly kicking and screaming to get out. It needed a good infusion of the will to live, if not quite the kiss of life.

Oh shut up Cassandra. You always did get carried away by metaphors.

Anyway, we'd done a lot of work. The colonel was what my father would have called a quick study. Even though I could see it broke his heart he slashed away with the purple pen. With the delete button on the computer. I'd told him to keep the original on the hard disk, to edit on a copy. The thing I hate about computers is the way they destroy manuscripts. In the old days the whole journey of the book was there, documented, the handwriting maybe, or just a typescript, annotated, retyped, annotated again. I remember seeing a photo of Proust's manuscripts. He pasted bits in and pasted on to the pasted-in bits and then pasted more again—he never seemed to cut—so that the whole thing cascaded out, a metre and a half, two metres, long. He did the same with his proofs. In some ways an editor's nightmare, in others the perfect editee. (I know, but edit is a verb formed from a noun, a little licence is allowable.) Imagine, these days, you wouldn't get away with changing proofs like that. Publishers threaten to make writers pay if they make any changes beyond the correction of faults. But Proust had these marvellous concertina sheaves of pasted-on pages, falling to the floor and fanning out across it.

Anyway, days passed, the colonel was doing well, so I suggested he spend time working on the book on his own, and I'd come back in a while and we'd have another bout. He could always ring me, or email.

This is costing a fortune, I said. Give yourself a break.

I don't care about the money, he said, and I knew I'd offended him.

I know, I said, that was crass of me. But seriously I think it would be a good thing to work on it, in your own time, without me hanging over you. Give yourself time to think.

Stay a couple more days, he said.

Al had told me to make myself at home in his house, and so I did, in my own room and the big room he called the cliffhanger, which was sitting room and library, study and kitchen. But there were other rooms I'd no reason to go into. One led off my bedroom. Its door was locked. You could get into it off the deck outside and I sometimes saw the colonel doing this but I could hardly follow him. Then there were the rooms of the small wooden cottage. I'd only walked through it as a passageway. Some of the doors had Yale locks on them. I'd said I'd like a tour of the house and he replied of course, but it never happened. I had a feeling

I should not insist. I'm not sure why. I lay in bed and listened to the sea and thought of Bluebeard. Not very seriously. Still, sometimes having your head full of fairy stories doesn't help.

I didn't actually know anything about the colonel. I know I was editing his memoir, his autobiographical account of his Gulf War, but it is surprising how little autobiographies reveal. You can read a hefty volume and still know little of the person writing it. I know the literary fascisti tell us that's where post-modern truth lies, in the memoir. Ho ho. If you want true confessions, give me a novel any day. That invites you into the head of the writer, to stroll around, make yourself comfortable, have a conversation, be charmed, overwhelmed, surprised, appalled, terrified. You don't need to worry about whether or not it is fact, you know it is true. And a novelist can't hide the way a memoirist can.

The colonel, his house: wanting to know about them might look like unseemly curiosity on my part. But remember I'm an avid reader, and these were unfinished stories: unfinished, unbegun, simply fragments. I wanted the whole narrative. Of course you never get that, in life or in art. The shape, though, the adumbration; you can go on yourself from there.

It is the desire for the story that keeps us living.

I got a bit more on the last evening. I'd been sitting on the veranda looking across to the west, the low sun shining through folds of sea mist so the mountains were dim shadowy shapes. The light falls upon the rounded nearby slopes making deep shadowed clefts, there are ponds and dams, this late light like a veil laid gently over the land still glitters on them, their water ripples in glowing stripes. There are occasional stands of rainforest, tall trees with slender trunks which cast long shadows in marvellous complicated patterns. So green and misty and rounded, this country. The soft curves mean it is fertile soil, it doesn't weather in rough craggy shapes. The hills are quite steep in their roundness but the cows still gently graze on them.

This landscape is my Picasso woman, says Al. You know how he rearranges his nudes? All the breasts and buttocks and long curving flanks, all the moist crevices and soft shaded lines all there, just rearranged.

And green . . .

Yes, green. Mossy, fecund, moist. And the luminous sea-misty light, making love to them.

And after that, yes, I did see his landscape, according to Picasso, I always will, it's his gift.

He'd been to Bateman's Bay and brought home a quantity of small red prawns caught in the Bay that morning. Not quite so tiny as school prawns, sweet and intensely flavoured. We ate them with lemons from the old tree that grows against the wall of a tumbledown barn, with rye bread and sweet butter and more of his fragrant white wine, a lovely honey-dry riesling this one.

I don't always cook, he said, though I like to, but I never eat badly. I have eaten more than enough bad food in my life. Never again.

Wasn't your mother a very good cook?

Not my mother! I'm not speaking of my mother. The army. That famous gastronomic experience.

Oh, I said. Bully beef and all that.

Yes. All that. He was quiet for a minute. The food of my childhood was wonderful, he said. In its way. Very local, very pure.

He told me that he'd grown up in the old house, the wooden cottage. His father had been a farmer. Those green paddocks produced superb milk. The school bus stopped up on the road; he used to walk along the track every morning. He'd look back at the little house on its hill, the line of pines, the hidden sea, and think not how beautiful it was, but that life was elsewhere.

And so, one day, you set off to find it.

Yes, he said.

But told me no more. He fetched a bowl of peaches. From the Araluen valley. The best you've eaten, I reckon.

I'd eaten Araluen peaches before. But the colonel was right.

Do you know the Araluen Valley?

I do know it, but answered, Not very well.

It's a small Utopia. A little Eden. How does it go? Demi-Paradise. From such a place could Adam and Eve have been expelled. He sighed. They grow avocadoes there, you know. It ought to be too cold.

It's a microclimate, I said.

Oh, microclimate. I prefer Eden. We're so silly when we're young. We think life is elsewhere, but in fact it's all around us, never more intensely than in small remote beautiful little works of nature. But we have to go elsewhere and suffer before we find that out.

Suffer, I said, hoping he'd tell me more, but all he did was nod.

It's all in the book, he said. You've read it.

Well, I have. But the suffering he spoke of, that made his voice tremble, a tremble very faint but unmistakable, that suffering I had not read in the book I was editing.

Chapter 5

When I got back from the coast I went down to Tilley's. My local, I think of it, I often wander down there instead of brewing my own coffee. Or opening my own bottle. It was six o'clock, had been a stinker of a day, the air heavy with smoke laid like a close-fitting lid over the land, keeping steam and heat and anger and all the boiling muddle of life trapped in its tiny space. But the sea breeze had come in and even though the air was still thick and you had to think poisonous it was pleasant enough, sitting on the pavement underneath the umbrellas. You can usually depend on finding someone you know. Sally Dale was drinking a beer and sucking on a fag though she's given them up at least five times to my knowledge. Sally is one of those solid old acquaintances. We don't visit in one another's houses much, but we have a lot of conversations at Tilley's. We're not so much fond of one another as used to one another.

I go and get a glass of white wine and ask can I join her. She looks at me, avidly I decide is the word, though I can't imagine why. She takes a mouthful of beer. You've been away, she says.

I nod. Swallowing lovely cold white wine after a busy day and a long drive through the sad droughty landscape.

So you haven't heard about Tamara?

No. Should I have?

Murdered.

What?

Murdered.

Such a greedy word it was in Sally's mouth. Like rare meat she was chewing on, its bloody juices. Watching me to see if I was appreciating its sticky savoury bite between the teeth. I felt sick. I didn't know Tamara well. I talked to her occasionally, but she was mostly with another crowd. But just recently she'd sat beside me and asked about editing. She'd written a book, she said.

Oh no, I thought. But at least she'd written it. Most people are only going to, one day, when they have the time. She said she knew I was an editor, and wondered if I'd be interested in working on it with her. A purely commercial transaction, she said. Well, that was something. A lot of people who wouldn't dream of asking a doctor or a lawyer friend for a free consultation think that editing is different, as though we are all book lovers together in some grand scheme where money is irrelevant. She gave me her card. A slip of crimson pasteboard with white letters.

```
Tamara Sissons
   iTServices
```

In that punning way that IT people always seem to have to indulge in. Underneath her name it said:

Crashed? Let me rescue you.

Is the book about IT, I asked. Not really, said Tamara, sort of . . . hard to say. You'll see.

She was serious, she said, she'd been to creative writing classes to learn how to do it.

I could certainly think of more exciting things to do than editing a book about information technology, however sort of. But a job's a job, I'm as keen on eating as the next person and not fond of cheap wine, so I gave her my card in return. Get in touch when you're ready, I said.

And now Sally is telling me that Tamara has been murdered.

Sally's a plump dissatisfied woman who comes to Tilley's a lot one week and not at all the next, depending on whether it's a custody week for her kids. I say dissatisfied meaning superficially; she's always changing the colour of her hair and asking what you think of some new garment she's bought. Great, I say, but I know it's just like all the others, when it's not new she won't find it interesting. But I think dissatisfied in more serious ways as well. Life is not what she wants it to be. I can see she's upset by Tamara's death but excited as well, with that terrible fascination that other people's disasters have for us. I know. I can feel it in myself. It's as though murder is the ultimate story; just as it's the final narrative of a person's life, so it is somehow the most glamorous tale we can tell. I've spent a lot of time thinking about the stories we tell ourselves. I know that underneath I am just as greedy as anyone for the gruesome details. I just like to think I am a bit more elegant and a bit more sorrowful than Sally is.

She isn't much help with the details. Though she yaps on. She says it was in Tamara's apartment, she has one of those new ones, in O'Connor, more of a town house, pretty ritzy, Sally says, Tamara must have been doing very nicely thank you.

See what I mean about dissatisfied.

Well, until now, I said.

I had thought those apartments were supposed to be absolutely secure. Walls and gates, deadlocks and codes, your own little fortress in the suburbs. Loathsome signs of the times. But maybe it was someone she let in, someone she knew.

How . . . how was she killed?

Sally didn't know. I think the police are keeping that secret, she said. It happened several days ago, but she wasn't found till yesterday.

The terrace at Tilley's even in the shade is hot. We've had days of heatwave temperatures. And the sea breeze though itself cooler can't freshen the air. Breathing makes your lungs feel stifled, not refreshed.

I went and got us another drink, stood at the counter waiting as you do even when the place seems empty, glad of the chance to be alone, pondering this death. Wondered just how accidental, how arbitrary it was. Was it someone she knew? An old lover? Tamara had lived with someone for quite a while and I'd heard the break-up was acrimonious. Old boyfriends are always murdering people. In Canberra anyway. You read some frightful death and you wonder how could one human being do that to another, and then it turns out to be an estranged husband or an ex-de-facto. It's that old love-turned-to-hate thing. People are always quoting the second part of that couplet, *Hell hath no fury like a woman scorned*, but the powerful bit is the previous line, *Heaven has no rage, like love to hatred turned*. That's what kills these women: love to hatred turned. *Nor hell a fury, like a woman scorned* comes next. But you don't see them doing much murdering. Revenge, maybe, cutting up his suits, hiding prawn shells in the innards of his sofa, waiting till he's on holidays, soaking his carpets and sowing them with grass seeds. I like that. The two-timing hound coming home to a carpet lawn.

The couplet is from a play called *The Mourning Bride*. Congreve. A Restoration comedy, I imagine. Haven't read it, just checked the quotation in the *Oxford*. Fabulous title, *The Mourning Bride*.

For sure, it's the old lovers who do us in.

And of course I know I would want to think that. I'm remembering something else. The man who changed the flat tyre on my car. The man who'd seemed threatening in his request for some sort of return. The man I had given my card to. The thing is, it wasn't my card. It was Tamara's. The crimson pasteboard with *Crashed? Let me help you*. With her home address because that's her office too. Like me, she works from home.

There's no more of the Margaret River riesling left, says the waitress. I've got a Helms.

Yes, I say. Yes.

Most victims know their murderers. So they say. It is

intimacy that leads to the impulse to kill. But there is the odd rapist, serial killer, pervert, who kills for kicks. That man with his blue eyes like chips of ice. I was thinking of him as Jack though of course that was the tool not his name. Hotbaby was the car. I didn't ask him what he was called. Nor did I tell him my name. I recall taking out my little silver case, opening it, seeing Tamara's card (mine are white, classical, hers so red) and flicking it in his direction. Thinking if he did get in touch it'd be the wrong person and he'd just go away. Thinking I need to survive this encounter and any means is fair. Not thinking there would be anything like a murder. And of course it's foolish of me to draw any conclusions. Of course there's no connection between Tamara's card and her death. It's stupid to think that, just because I was made nervous by a man on a lonely road.

And what about her book, which had started all this? Dangerous things, books, they cause all sorts of troubles.

I mentioned the book to Sally, saying I didn't suppose it would happen now, there probably wouldn't be anybody to see it through. I said that I couldn't imagine a book about information technology being very exciting. Even allowing for the publicity value of its being posthumous to a murder.

Oh, it isn't about IT, said Sally, it's a sort of biography of her mother, who was a Bluebell Girl, in the sixties.

I must have looked rather stunned because Sally said, You know, one of those dancers, very high class, fabulous bodies, six feet tall, statuesque, wear dresses like peacocks that leave their bodies pretty well naked. In Paris.

I know Bluebell Girls, I said. That inheritance explained Tamara's looks, not quite six feet tall but slender and willowy and long-legged, all those things we all not so secretly want to be.

I felt a terrible dread sadness for Tamara, who was younger than me and bright and clever and interested in everything. Like me, I suppose you could say. Though she seems to have been a lot richer. And I don't have a brainy ex-boyfriend going mad when we split up. She'd lived in a glamorous town house with barred windows and deadlocks and codes to get in and out. I live in a scruffy old O'Connor duplex. When I bought it the kitchen had been pushed out on one side and done up a bit and it was newly painted a tasteful off-white and the wooden floors polished. I'd had all sorts of plans to do things with it but it was all right and I hadn't. I'd save up some money and think maybe this is the start of a new bathroom but then I'd go to an exhibition opening and buy a painting instead, or a ticket to Morocco or Hanoi or somewhere. The front door lock is one of those you can pick with a credit card, so they say, I haven't tried, and the back has a bolt. I work on the assumption that no burglar not even a druggy kid is going to think I'm worth bothering with. Though I do leave two twenties and a ten under a paperweight on the hall table (or what would be if I had a hall) so if they do break in they'll take the money and go, not wreck the place. Of course a serial killer is different, not that this looks like such a thing, it doesn't look random, not with that safe house and the mad boyfriend. Though I can't help thinking about the card I gave that guy. I also know that life has far more coincidences than literature; no novel could get away with the sort of coincidence that is commonplace in daily lives.

Of course nervousness is never rational.

Maybe it's the dog days, that time in summer when Sirius the Dog Star is in the ascendant and everyone goes mad with the heat. Perhaps that's where barking mad comes from.

I carry my dining chairs up the stairs and pile them up at the top. They're bentwood, very light, no barrier at all, but I pile them haphazardly so any attempt to move them will bring them crashing down. I put a cowbell gingerly on top. That will fall down and clang. I put my bed against the door and my mobile phone beside the pillow. I feel like an idiot. I feel unsafe. I wonder who I can invite to stay. Where are burly ex-lovers when you need them?

I slept badly. Every time the branch of the silver birch went scrawp against the window I twitched awake. That night I heard the dogs for the first time. Suddenly, a whole lot of them, not so much barking as wailing. The air is still full of smoke and the memory of the fires and it is as though these dogs are finding the sounds to go with it, crying, calling, their voices plangent and full of pain, making this twisted plaited rope of sound in the night. I can hear lots of different sorts of dog. Refugees, I suppose, come here because where they live was burnt, and what might they have seen, many of their companions perished in the fires. Suddenly they've arrived in my quiet suburb, and suddenly they start their sounding, plaintive yelps of fear, wild groans, eerie flutings, soprano songs, deep bell tollings. Just as suddenly they fall silent and then mysteriously all together they start up again, in this strange dissonant unison. It is a kind of music, mournful, despairing, terrified, all at once. An animal sound, and yet as I lie in bed, sliding in and out of faint sleep, it speaks to me of our human condition, it fills my heart with pain.

The helicopters on their dawn journey to the fires set them off. And who knows what warnings only they can hear.

About six I fall into one of those deep enervating sleeps from which you wake late and unrefreshed. Get out of the house, down to Tilley's, double shot coffee, raisin toast, the newspaper. Annie is tucked in the corner of a booth, also with a newspaper, her face pursed up and frowning. Opinion at Tilley's is divided on how gaga Annie is. Not particularly is my opinion. No more so than she finds useful at the moment. She lives on her own in one of those little wooden houses up in Baker Street and walks down to Tilley's most days. I'm not sure how old she is, but as a child she saw the Duke and Duchess of York open the first parliament, which was when? 1922 I think, and if you trust her vivid memories of the event she wasn't too tiny a tot. So that puts her well in her eighties. She chatters on in an inconsequential way about all sorts of things. There's a son turns up every now and then and threatens to put her in a home, and she comes down to Tilley's in a state of fury but with her mind wonderfully concentrated and so far she's managed to refuse. She's very fond of caffe latte and regulars like me offer to buy her one but she always refuses. I can still manage to buy my own lattes thanks love, she always says. You can put me away when I can't.

Some people call her Dirty Annie, which she isn't at all, she's a tidy and even glamorous old lady with a silky crumpled complexion and a fine frizzy head of white hair that she twists up with a comb. Nonchalant elegance she has. She smells lovely. I once said this to her and she winked. Chanel No. 5, love. It's about all that son of mine can manage. Christmas, birthday, mother's day. Chanel No. 5. So he doesn't have to think. Not that I'm complaining, mind. I just slosh it around. It's my signature scent.

What she does do is talk a lot about dirty tricks, and this might be the reason for the name. She often mutters, darkly, *Dirty tricks, oh yes, it's for dirty tricks all right. There's the fix.* Any difficulty or problem, and out it comes: dirty tricks. Makes her seem cynical and yet she's so cheerful with it.

I lean on the counter waiting to give my order. I wave at Annie but she doesn't see me. Engrossed she is in her newspaper. I go and sit on the terrace with mine.

There's a picture of Tamara's mother arriving from London. Her father is on a posting to Caracas and won't be here for a couple of days. No new details, except that the police have a man helping them with their inquiries.

I'm reading all the fill-in details, Tamara's job, her apartment, when a voice says: I hear you've been off with the Apricot Colonel.

What?

It's Daniel Mendheim, who does the news on one of the local television channels. He sits down with his coffee.

Ha, Daniel, I say. What do you know about this murder?

Tamara Sissons? What's the paper saying?

He turns it round to see. That her mother? The drop-dead glamorous type, isn't she.

She's a former Bluebell Girl.

What kind of flower fairy's that?

Honestly, the young. I'm only a couple of years older than Daniel but I'd be ashamed to be so ignorant. A person who puts together news for adults and knows nothing of general culture.

A man helping with inquiries, he reads. That'd be the ex-boyfriend.

Do you know anything about it?

Well, I heard . . . Daniel loves a gossip. He pulls in his chair, hunches his shoulders, bends his head to mine. There was a lot of blood. One of those places with white walls white carpets white sofas, and blood everywhere. And the murderer, presumably the murderer, had written words in blood on the walls. *Whore*, and *slut*.

Sounds like the ex-boyfriend.

Except that *whore* was spelt *hore*. He's a university lecturer, hardly likely to be him not being able to spell.

Or done deliberately to make people think it wasn't him.

Yeah.

That's the trouble with clues. They can go in all sorts of directions. Be accidental, mistakes, or deliberate red herrings. Even though I have decided not to, I think of Jack Hotbaby. Would he be able to spell whore?

It does seem to point to David Smeaton, I said. I mean, you'd think that an academic, and a philosopher at that, would be able to control his behaviour in public. But remember that time in the city market when he got into a huge argument and grabbed her basket, tomatoes and pears and avocadoes rolled everywhere and he ran about jumping up and down on them squashing the lot and shouting it was lucky it wasn't her he was squashing.

I didn't know about that. Did you see it happen?

No, but I heard about it, everybody was talking about it.

Might not have been as bad as people said. You know how things get blown up. Corrupted, like Chinese whispers.

Do you reckon the murderer might be a serial killer who thinks all women are sluts and whores and deserve to die?

Could be. Anyway, the police are keeping quiet about vital details, the way they do. They're not letting on about the blood. Or the murder weapon.

Do you know what it was?

He shakes his head. I can't tell whether he is telling the truth, or if this is a belated attack of discretion.

What a summer. He flips the paper shut. Bushfires and hundreds of houses lost. Eight people killed in a train accident. Seven dying when the space shuttle burns up. Bush determined to have a war. And poor Tamara.

What I hate, I say, is the way the death of seven astronauts is a national tragedy with the whole damn country in mourning whereas eight people in a train is merely a great pity. But the train is supposed to be safe, people just going to work, or home, ordinary daily stuff, whereas anybody in their right minds knows space travel is hugely dangerous and death quite likely. An occupational hazard, under the circumstances.

That's why, says Daniel. His voice goes all solemn and

pompous: They're heroes because they risk death. Noble people, incredibly talented, dying for their country.

Bollocks. That's Bush talk.

Yeah. That dumb voice quivers and he makes tragic martyrs out of them. But nobody can do that for a bunch of ordinary people in a train gone berserk.

I think of Tamara. If astronauts in a sense choose their death, what can you say of a murder?

Daniel goes for more coffee and I wonder what to do. I've got work, a book of essays by one of our leading intellectuals who'll have a fit if I change a comma, but there's no hurry. My lovely study with its view through a little grove of silver birches to the fountain all mossy with neglect doesn't have its usual charm, and not just because the moss has died in the drought. My study is the main room in the house, actually the living room, running from front to back; back is the desk looking out through the silver birches, front has armchairs and a sofa (I'm a keen horizontal reader) and would look at the street if it weren't for a high dense hedge of viburnum. French windows front and back, flimsily fastened, when you think about it, the other walls mainly books. The floor largely books too, in piles. I suppose you could say it's booby trapped with books.

The day is starting to hot up, even in the shade of trees and umbrellas on the terrace. Shade isn't what it was under this pall of smoke. I suppose I could bring the manuscript down and colonise a booth inside. Hardly ergonomic working conditions, those square lacquer red benches. Keep glancing out the window to see if Hotbaby cruises by. No, I'm not thinking about him.

The Apricot Colonel

Do you know how to find out the owner of a car from its rego, I ask Daniel.

Isn't it illegal?

I suppose. So nobody could find out where I live by checking my car rego?

Well, I'm sure there's ways. Legality doesn't count.

Out of the corner of my eye I see a ginger-gold Monaro gun past. I turn my head: it's one of those new glittering bronzed utes that I rather covet. Thirty-odd years younger than Hotbaby. I don't know why I'm so jittery. Tamara's death is having a bad effect, well I suppose it would, wouldn't it. And if she wasn't killed by a demented lover who of us is safe? In the dog days of the vilest bushfire summer on record.

I drink some coffee. It's all too hard.

By the way, I remember to ask, what was that about an apricot kernel?

The Apricot Colonel? I heard you'd been hanging out with him, down in the hinterland.

You mean Colonel Marriott? What's this apricot business?

He's a star. A champion. Bottles fruit. Wins prizes. *Stateline* did a segment on him. Hero of the Gulf War and of the local agricultural shows. Spectacular stuff. Following his mother, she was champion up and down the coast. His speciality is apricots, spiced, pickled, in conserves. He puts them in jars in fancy patterns. *Stateline* had a ball photographing them. The world through a jar of apricots.

Good grief.

He once challenged some guy to a duel. The guy said wasn't fruit bottling a pretty girly thing to do, and the colonel offered him a choice of weapons.

What happened?

Nothing. When the guy realised he was serious he got out of there fast. It was a pub and he wasn't entirely sober at the time. I gather the colonel looked him in the eye and he realised pistols at dawn wasn't just a manner of speaking.

Would he have done it, do you think?

The guy thought so.

I knew that what I really wanted to do was jump in my little car and drive back down to the coast. I'd be safe from the heat down there.

Instead I went home and did emails. I'd left one of those messages that automatically reply: Cassandra is out of the office, will get back blah blah. There was a stack to be got through. I'm quite fond of email. Beats writing letters on sheets of paper, putting them in envelopes, taking them to the post office. But it's also a chore.

My oldest friend Cleo wants me to go to a bushfire benefit. Dinner and concert, all donated, so all the money raised is profit. With her posh pals who bid large sums of money at fundraising auctions for things they don't need. I'll think of a subsequent engagement for that one. I love Cleo and support bushfire appeals but charity dinners aren't my thing. I send her an email saying there's a meeting of the Society of Editors I just can't miss.

Lots of missives are out of date. Too late for them. Delete, delete. A couple of interesting jobs, including a possibly very nice novel. Then there's a message from Justine.

She's coming to Canberra for a week. She would like to stay. Arriving tomorrow.

So, here is the burly old lover when I need her. And her coming illustrates yet again the ambiguity of granted wishes.

Justine, and that long warm winter. When I stayed home and edited some marvellous novels, running the central heating heedlessly, for Justine was my lodger as well as my lover, and money was okay. In the evening lighting the pot-belly stove, she working at one end of the table, me the other. Justine making hot chocolate, the way the Aztecs did she reckoned, whipping blocks of black chocolate into hot milk so they melted and frothed. The secret is the whipping, she said, her dark eyes gleaming, her strong wrist hardly moving as the fragrant liquid frothed. Justine from Auckland for six months' research at the National Library for her PhD. Justine my lodger and then my lover. Not so burly, but tall and broad and strong, with her kiwi accent and wide smiling mouth. I used to stroke my fingers over her cheeks and imagine them tattooed in intricate indigo patterns.

I knew she would go back after her six months, that she wouldn't stay, and I wouldn't go with her. I don't suppose she broke my heart. But it was tender and battered and aching for quite a long time after.

Did I want to see her again? A request to visit is a kind of command. I made up the bed in the spare room and bought bitter chocolate. Forgetting that it is a vile hot summer, not that cold winter of blissful warmth.

She arrived with a large carpet bag which would produce a surprising number of glamorous garments. And she didn't stay in the spare room. We ate salad and peaches and drank cold wine and talked till late and then she said, See you, and went off abruptly. I was a bit miffed. Was in bed reading when she came walking in, naked, gorgeous as ever. Not with the silky cello curves of your classical beautiful woman's body, French polished, highly wrought, but a figure more roughly carved, high-hipped and monumental, both newer in time and older. I never knew where her own musky scent and Yves St Laurent's Opium stopped and started, I just knew their intoxication.

I'm not actually gay. Just greedy, says Justine. And you don't say gay, you say lesbian.

I say pleasure, I tell her. Pleasure and comfort. And suddenly the strange music of the dogs starts up again. Shit, she says, what's that? Are they ghost dogs? She hangs on to me with her strong grip.

Ghosts, I say, don't you think they sound real?

It occurs to me: they are the voice of the dog days.

Justine when she isn't working on NZ–Australian trade agreements and the significance of the Closer Economic Relations Treaty or drinking hot chocolate or making love— she prefers women because she says her relations with men are always bomb sites—is into kickboxing. I was glad to have her in the house. She was there only at night, of course, but somehow daylight is less troubling.

I told her about the murder of Tamara. I mentioned my giving her card to Hotbaby. She looked at me intently; one of the best things about Justine is the way she listens to what you say and thinks about it. She frowned for a while after I had spoken.

Tricky, she said. I understand why you'd be worried. But it's also likely there's no connection. It's one of those things: how can you know? You have to suppose both. Hold opposite ideas in your head at once.

One evening, just before dinner—we ate quite late, Justine liked to stay at the library for a good day's work and would often cook—I came inside from picking the greengages the birds and possums had left. Cat Elspeth came in with me. Mary must be out, Elspeth wants company. And some food. Her sinuous silky body wreathes round my ankles. I am not sure how often she doubles up on meals. She's a plump contented tortoiseshell tabby, maybe not so fat as she would be if she ate all her meals in duplicate.

Elspeth's a funny name for a cat, a cute spitty mouthful of a name. I looked it up in my name book, one of my most valued texts, along with the Bible and the dictionaries and the quotation book. Names are immensely important. Naming is power. That's why calling him Hotbaby keeps that imagined killer in his place. Tries to. One of my novelists told me about writing a character called Elaine who just wasn't working. She chose it because she needed a lovely musical Welsh name, but it didn't suit. Her character wasn't much better than a wooden puppet. She changed her name to Molly and she came alive and danced with great energy on and off the page. Anyway, turns out Elspeth is a variant of Elizabeth, popular in Scotland; there's an Elspeth in three of Walter Scott's novels.

Lovely greengages for dinner, I said, trying not to trip over the wreathing cat.

I think your Hotbaby was here, said Justine, chopping parsley with sharp blows of the cleaver.

My heart lurched and dropped like a rock into my stomach.

Moderately tall, suntanned, ice-blue eyes.

Ice-blue eyes? I muttered. I'd have recognised those ice-blue eyes anywhere.

Sinister-looking. Though maybe that was because I knew who he was. Knocked on the door and asked for you.

Asked for me?

Yep. Is Cassandra home? he said. Cassandra, I said. No one of that name here. He looked extremely disappointed. Are you sure? he said. I lied again, assured him there was not, had not been, nor would be any Cassandra here. I must say he didn't look as though he believed me. I was all ready for him to try something. She flexed her leg.

I sat down on a chair, feeling stiff and quavery and a hundred years old.

He knows my name and where I live.

Looks like it.

In this flimsy house . . .

You should tell the police.

Yes, I said. Thinking it was time that my careless gesture with the business card came into their equation.

We always have pasta when Justine cooks. Tonight with olive oil, parsley and garlic. Wow. I got the phone book to look up the police number. Which one would be murder?

Did you see his car, I asked her. The bronze Monaro? Thirty years old?

Justine shook her head. The car was a Land Rover. Khaki. Gleaming.

I put down the phone. The colonel has a Land Rover. And I suppose his eyes are ice-blue. I'd thought, sea-blue, rather.

The colonel. I wanted to see the colonel.

This man—tallish, blue eyes. Hair . . .

Light brown, blond. Greyish maybe. Slight curl to it.

Pot belly?

Flat.

I'll be back in a minute, I said.

The pasta, it'll spoil.

Put it in the oven.

I got out the car and drove around. Tried Tilley's though I don't know why he'd be there. Justine said I'd missed him by five minutes or so. It was enough. I drove around but could catch no sight of the khaki Land Rover.

Funny, isn't it, said Justine. He matched exactly your description of Hotbaby. I could have sworn it was him. And yet you tell me the colonel is completely unlike him.

I can't imagine two men more different, I said. But of course that was in flesh, not words. Tallish, suntanned, blue eyes, light hair. Tick the box and it's Hotbaby. Or the colonel.

Hotbaby's sort of horrible, I said. You kind of don't want to touch him, as though he'd be a bit greasy, or something.

We went to bed. It was very comforting going to bed with Justine. But it seemed my heart was cured. Cured. It made me think of leather. Little dried up heart. Brown and leathery and tough. I wished I'd seen the colonel.

Chapter 6

I'm going to a meeting of the Society of Editors. I'm not going to the bushfire benefit. So why am I slipping into a dress like a petticoat, very Colette Dinnigan but of course it's not, which I am still thin enough and probably young enough to wear, and some rather killing sandals, in any sense of the word you like to use? Why is my hair blow-dried into the sort of slow-motion rolling swoop that you don't often see outside television commercials? (I said it was my one vanity.)

Because I am going to the bushfire benefit, that's why. I ought to have known Cleo wouldn't let a meeting of the Society of Editors stop her. Especially a fictitious one. Not that she knew it was fictitious, but I did. As an alternative engagement it lacked conviction. I keep thinking I'll learn to say no to Cleo but I never manage it. She's small and exquisite and everybody treats her as though she's a priceless china shepherdess who shouldn't be allowed off the mantelpiece when in fact she's about the toughest criminal lawyer in town and runs her family, handsome stockbroker husband and three adorable children, with all the precision and elegance and cut-throat timing of a fashion show, the parts you see. If I weren't so fond of her I wouldn't be able to stand her.

Daniel says she is a perfect model of second-generation immigrant syndrome. Her parents came from Turkey and set up an office-cleaning business. They prospered, but never very comfortably or easily, and because they worked alone and at night and never learned much English they always remained outsiders. Cleo was born when they decided they could afford her, later in their lives. But they never quite overcame their trepidation. They are lovable gallant people and their tentativeness breaks my heart. Cleo is a kind of mother to them, a respectful child mother who organises their lives for their own good. They're retired now and live in a big house in Chapman, and Cleo is the repository of all their hopes, the brilliant effortless creature who is reason, epitome, beneficiary and validator of the whole tragi-comic process. You see her dance with such grace and skill to this tune it all seems entirely carefree. But a dancer is no good if she lets you see the trouble and pain her performance costs her. Cleo's good; it's all radiant ease.

I have to come to the benefit, she says. She's got a gorgeous table. Just ten of us, very intimate. A lovely young man she wants me to meet. Cleo hasn't had a lovely young man for me to meet in a while. Not that he's a reason for going, they're always totally unsuitable. Hopeless. I tell her this and she says, Darling, this time I'm sure I'm right. He's thirty-three and a spunk. And definitely partner material. Partner, I say, whom for? The firm of course, Cass, don't be flip. A toy boy, I say, just what I have always wanted. Surely he's only a toy boy if you have to pay for him, says Cleo, this one is definitely self-supporting.

By this stage I know I'm not going to get out of going. But I stall a bit longer. And, she says, her pretty voice hushing—she went to the same school as me, for god's sake, and her parents can't speak an English sentence, where did she get those vowels?—Belinda's coming.

Belinda?

Belinda Sissons. Tamara's mother.

Bit soon, isn't it? Her daughter's only just been murdered.

She's staying with Molly Vander-Browne. Molly persuaded her it would do her good. Moping's no use. Sitting round being miserable won't help the police find the killer.

Tough, that's Cleo. And prurient, that's me. I was interested in getting a look at Belinda. Hello Belinda I'm the person your daughter's murderer really wanted to kill.

I don't think I believe that, not really. I haven't been to the police yet.

Anyway it's not every day that a former Bluebell Girl comes your way. I do believe I have a duty to experience what life offers. Makes me a better editor.

Cleo's looking amazing in a subtly pink dress, old rose Gran would have called it, or maybe ashes of roses, an affair of artfully crumpled silk taffeta that moulds her tiny waist and shows her breasts like pretty speckled eggs in a nest. It's simultaneously perfectly retro and day-after-tomorrow fashionable. Must stop using variants of the word perfect when I talk about Cleo. Where does she find time for this sort of shopping? My petticoat suddenly turns into a down-market copy of last year's dress. I thought it looked so pretty when I left home. With my necklace of Gran's little amethysts making interesting conversation with my hair.

The lovely young man is indeed that. Dermot O'Farrell. Tall, chin jutting and dimpled, porcelain-blue eyes, a mop of dark curls. Irish and all that goes with it. His mirror would have told him how pretty he looked before he left home and you can bet he still believes it. Kisses your hand, looks at you as though he has till this minute been desolate on a desert isle and you've just dropped from heaven to make his life. You know perfectly well that he won't normally look twice at a girl like you and would you want him to? I've never seen so guaranteed a ride to heartache.

I am sitting next to him with Cleo's husband Paul on the other side. I suppose if I had any money to invest I could find some fascinating stockbroking stuff to talk to him about. Belinda's on the other side of the table, dressed in something that looks like a man's dinner suit, but clearly designed for her figure, in a pearly black satin, worn without a shirt so its plunging neckline discreetly suggests the mounds of her breasts on either side of it. Black for mourning. But those breasts. Their message is perky. Her hair is pale yellow and looped into a chignon on the back of her head. Who was it said some lady's hair had gone quite gold with grief? Oscar Wilde I suppose, usually is. She looks beautiful and remote and melancholy. Far away and untouchable. Of course that might be more Bluebell Girl than grieving mother. But I can't help wondering whether

Molly Vander-Browne did the right thing in persuading her to come. Molly's sitting on one side of her and her husband Claude on the other. Belinda's husband still isn't back from Caracas. Claude doesn't say much. He tends to be absent, like so many of these men. The women sparkle, they charm, but the men—I think of them as in their counting houses, counting out their money. When the auction starts—a dozen bottles of wine, dinner for two at *Gingembre*, a Turkish carpet, a signed novel, a landscape gardening course, modest enough things, donated by locals—they are generous in their bidding. I imagine them going home afterwards, sitting on the slipper chair in the bedroom, while their wives chatter about the room divesting themselves of their finery, the man smiling a little, enjoying his rare possession, before, maybe, slipping into bed and making passionate love to her. I don't know any of this, it is a mystery to me, which is why I contemplate it.

There's another couple, called Pedro and Lyn, whose child seems to go to day care with one of Cleo's, and Philip, Cleo's gay bachelor she calls upon when she wants a single charming man. You don't have any trouble making conversation with him.

Isn't Cleo lovely, says Dermot to me. That dress, it's like a rose, like a bud opening around her, and she's an even more beautiful flower popping out of it.

I wonder if Dermot always talks like that. Rather tortuous metaphor, but pretty. He can get away with it because of his Irish accent. Dermot's Irish Cream. Hangover guaranteed.

You and Cleo are colleagues, aren't you, I say.

Colleagues—that's a bit grand. I'm a humble worker. She's a star.

Humble, I think. That's a good one. I remember Cleo saying he was partner material.

How long since you've lived in Ireland?

He looks at me, his face roguish, I think that's the word. He thickens his accent even further.

Oireland? Ah begorrah. Why would you be tinking Oim an Oirish lad then?

He's funny. I laugh. I can't imagine, I say.

And yourself?

Me? I'm a local. Born and bred. I always thought I'd leave. Well, I did. But here I am back.

Ah, it's in your blood.

And you, do you think of going back?

Oh, he says, in his ordinary voice, which is still pretty stagy, there's no going back, don't you think? There's only going on.

Food comes. People perform. Mostly singers. A harpist. A man who recites Victorian parlour poetry. People move around a bit. I don't, I hate working the room. People come and talk to you if you stay put. Daniel Mendheim stops to say hello, he's just arrived, after doing his mid-evening news. There are times when Canberra seems like a village. Claude is our wine waiter; when bottles are emptied he fetches more. There are more performances, some comic singers who aren't. Belinda sits quietly, speaking when spoken to. I wonder about Tamara's book about her mother the Bluebell dancer. One can see that profession in this grave woman, no problem, they always are stately and solemn above their nearly naked bodies. I just can't imagine making a book about her.

That's when I get my brilliant idea. If Tamara was talking about editing, maybe the book's done? Maybe Belinda would like it edited and organised, some tiny consolation in her grief? I bend towards her and say, I hear Tamara was writing a book about you . . .

She starts back, and stares at me, frigidly I have to say. Pardon, she says. I suppose my mentioning it was sudden, but it didn't seem a moment for small talk. How do you chitchat to a woman whose daughter's just met such an end?

Tamara's book. Your life story . . .

I could be a stage door Johnny trying to crack on to her.

I'm afraid I don't, she says, and stops, just stops. Claude comes back with a bottle of white and a bottle of red. Wine, Bel, he says, and pours some in her glass. She lifts it to her nose.

Maybe Tamara didn't tell her mother about the book? I bend back to my side of the table. The band starts playing for the dancing.

I remember when I was at university one of our lecturers talking about dancing. He was a lean and lugubrious man with a lean and lugubrious wife. He reckoned dancing was a poor substitute for fucking and why would you bother with dancing when you had fucking? At parties he would sit leaning against his wife and never join in.

I love dancing and I'm quite fond of fucking and I have no trouble telling the difference. Dancing may lead to fucking, it may be an enticing public kind of foreplay.

Dancers might be saying to each other, in another time and place we would make love, but now is not appropriate, let us take this polite public pleasure instead. And then there's dancing with people whom you wouldn't in a million fits fuck, it's just fun. But fundamentally dancing like flirting is its own thing and what happens next is quite a different matter. I often think of that couple sitting gloomily together instead of on their feet and carefree.

Dermot turns out to be a good dancer, attentive, elegant, skilled. And dancing is what we are doing. I am not thinking of fucking him. Though he does seem interested in me.

A lot of people have gone home. They've done their bit for bushfire victims. Like Pedro and Lyn who have promised the babysitter not to be late. But the diehard dancers stay on. The band plays on. I dance a lot with Dermot. Several times with Philip, which is a pleasure, you smooch around saying outrageous things about the other guests; gossip is an art with Philip. Once with Paul, who's very good in a punctilious way. Once with Claude, who tells me he has bought Molly a garden fountain for her birthday and is afraid that she will hate it and he won't know. Claude is one of those dancers who like every now and then to take you on a quick little whirl right round the edge of the dance floor, and on one of these I see Hotbaby sitting at a distant table, his hand on the neck of a woman with a big fuzz of red hair. Lucky Claude is also one of those men totally in control. I keep whirling instead of seizing up in panic. Twice more we go around, once Hotbaby is standing with his head bent over the redhead, the second time she seems to be on her own.

He hasn't seen me. Or he has, and hasn't recognised me. Or he has recognised me and is pretending he hasn't. I have been dancing, laughing, flirting, and maybe all the time those ice-blue eyes have been watching, watching. I'm pretty sure it's Hotbaby.

After the dance with Claude I'm sitting down, breathless in that exhilarated dancing way, when the colonel comes up. I hadn't even known he was here, the room holds a great many tables of ten, and anyway when I dance I don't notice anything much. Except possible Hotbabies.

He's looking terrific in a linen suit of a pale very faintly yellowish cream colour. And he turns out to be a good dancer. We dance a lot. I couldn't walk fifty metres in these sandals but I can dance all night in them.

When we sit down again there's nobody at our table. Sally mooches over, she usually does when you're with a halfway decent man. She's sitting at a table of work colleagues, mostly women, all terribly boring, she says, but I remark she hasn't gone home. She smiles under her eyelashes at Al. I don't call him colonel, just Al Marriott. Colonel would send her in all sorts of ratty directions. As it is she says, And where do you come from, Al, as though she's Oprah or somebody. He says he's a writer and her eyes go big. So maybe he's not my boyfriend but a client, I can see her thinking. She moves closer to him. Suddenly she says, By the way, Cass, they've arrested David, for Tamara's murder. David, you know, the ex-partner.

Ah, it's the old lovers that kill us.

What? Oh, yeah, it was a pretty nasty break-up.

It's evident that Al doesn't know anything about this so Sally launches into elaborate narrative mode, still masticating this grisly tale, her eyes wide with horror, her mouth trembling, her hand every now and then reaching blindly (I don't think) out and gently resting a few seconds on his hand, his arm. It's quite a performance.

Our table is full of diehard dancers. The band stops and they come back, mildly flirting still. Paul with Molly, Cleo with Claude, Belinda with Dermot. Sally has been going on about how the murder has been a terrible mystery. She describes the blood, the words *whore* and *slut* on the wall. I'm trying to kick her to get her to shut up, my pointed sandal hits Al in the shin. He looks at me with surprise. I can tell he's not liking Sally or her story. I can also see that Sally has drunk a lot of wine. She's holding the floor, oblivious to the returned dancers. *Whore* and *slut*, she says, written in blood.

Al says, Might not the words be true? Maybe she was a whore and a slut. Maybe that is why she was killed. Maybe she in her way asked for it?

These words fall into a silence. A bleak and icy silence. Everybody is staring at him, frozen. Then everybody starts talking.

I don't think we've met. I'm Cleo Paterson . . .

Shit, that's a bit . . .

Difficult sort of judgment . . .

Do you think the band's finished playing . . .

Belinda has been sitting taking quiet sips at her glass of wine. She stands up gently, walks around the table, and slowly pours the wine over the colonel's head. She's been drinking red, as do women of a certain age, believing it is good for them. It runs through his hair, down his face, all over the cream linen suit. I have a sudden image of raspberry sauce on vanilla ice-cream.

He jumps up, his body tense, as though he will fall upon this assailant, beat her, shake her, hit her. But turning he sees her standing there, not moving, not looking at him or anything, with tears in round drops sliding down her face.

Belinda is Tamara's mother, I say. And take his hand and pull him away. He resists for a moment, looking stricken, then bows formally, slowly, to her. Doesn't say anything, lets me pull him away, me babbling good nights. I'll take him off and clean him up, see you soon Cleo, thanks for a lovely night.

Are you a total dinosaur? I say to him. We've gone to his car, no point in trying to sponge this mess off. Whatever possessed you?

I know, I know. It was that Sally. She provoked me. She was so enjoying that horrible story. I did want to, I don't know, prick her, somehow.

He looks at me, his eyes are full of tears. How could I know that would be the girl's poor mother?

Of course you couldn't. But Al, you can't talk like that. Whatever the provocation.

Sally deserved it.

Maybe. But you can't, still.

I wanted to make her think. It was a kind of joke. And no worse than her licking her lips over murder.

Yes it was, it was quite different. You can't make jokes like that, not in our society, not anymore.

You live by a lot of rules, says Al. Is it being an editor?

We go to my place. So you do live here, says Al, with a kind of irritated satisfaction. I suppose anybody would be irritated at having his wonderful linen suit turned into an ice-cream sundae.

Mm, I say. Least said soonest mended, as Gran would have put it. I find a T-shirt and tracksuit pants, as large as possible, but he still looks as though they've shrunk in the wash. In fact he looks totally strangled in them. By this time it's quite a chilly night, normal for this time of year but so unusual in these times. I make us some hot chocolate, whipping and whipping with Justine's little whisk. I decide to tell him about Hotbaby. Though of course now they've arrested the boyfriend it's mainly a story.

We're sitting with our mugs, comfortable, when there's a creak from the staircase, which comes down into the study, which is also the sitting room. I call it the room. No such luxuries as halls. It's Justine walking down the stairs. Naked. Her rich body burnished in the dim yellow light of the one small lamp. One hand is on the banister, the other over her eyes, and she comes stepping down in a stately progress like some marvellous work of art.

I think you two have met, I say.

Chapter 7

Cleo's on the phone at some totally indecent hour of the morning. That terrible efficient life of hers. I did have several glasses of wine last night, I knew I would, which is why I didn't take my car. And sorting out the colonel and Justine didn't make for an early night. Justine claimed she was sleepwalking. You have to admire her gall. She came and sat down on the sofa all starkers as she was and asked for some hot chocolate.

Aren't you cold, I said, and she replied that she was a hot-blooded creature. Certainly not her voice, that was icy. I'm a hot-blooded creature, she said in frigid tones. Doesn't that work the other way? said the colonel. I got a wrap and gave it to her but she ignored it.

She simply sat there. Magnificent and grave as an idol. I'd started the Hotbaby story but didn't want to continue. So far it would have seemed to Al no more than an anecdote. He asked her why she'd told him I didn't live here when I did and she knew it and he knew it. Justine said she'd lied and would again because he didn't deserve to know.

Yes, but that was a mistake, I said.

Was it, said Justine.

Use every man after his desert and who should escape whipping? said Al.

Where does that come from, I asked. It was familiar but it was late and I was tired and I couldn't place it.

Hamlet, I believe. Telling Polonius to treat the players better than he might think they deserve.

Oh for god's sake, said Justine.

I met a man, said the colonel, in Baghdad, a sheikh he was, very cultivated, who told me that Shakespeare was an Iraqi. His works are all old Arab tales.

Was he being serious, I asked.

He was urbane, and elegant, and do you know I haven't the foggiest idea.

But all stories are old Arab tales, there's only so many stories in the world, nine, is it, or seven?

(I'm always quoting this, must check it.)

There's a subject for a PhD, murmured Al.

Justine snorted.

Since I seem to irritate you, dear lady, I shall take my leave. Al kissed my hand and bowed to her. I'll see myself out, he said.

I had to hand it to him, when he was irritated he was marvellously good at being irritating back. When he'd gone, looking a real dork in the shrunken tracksuit, Justine said, How could you, hot chocolate's our thing. How could you.

It seemed a nice warm drink. White wine's our thing too. I drink it with other people.

It was a betrayal.

Come to bed. You're cold.

No I'm not. Chilled to the heart, but not cold.

Come on, Justine.

But she was determined not to give in, and I got cross and said it was all very well for her swanning in but in a minute she'd go again and where did that leave me?

And so on. It was a long night.

So when Cleo rang so disgustingly early I was asleep and not happy to be woken up, still tired and headachy. Who was that frightful man, she asked.

The colonel?

Quite a hottie, but very rude. Are you an item?

Oh Cleo. He's a client.

So? That's as good a way to meet suitable men as any. If they are suitable. Dermot, now.

Cleo, you know very well, men like Dermot aren't for the likes of me.

Cassandra. What sort of defeatist attitude is that?

I sighed.

I expect you drank too much wine last night.

Cleo is a two-glass girl.

Did the bushfires make a lot of money?

I gather so. Everybody seems pleased. Cleo paused. I waited for what she was going to tell me. They've got David Smeaton in custody, she said.

The boyfriend?

Tamara's estranged boyfriend. Helping the police with their inquiries, as they say. He's in the philosophy department; Paul knew him at university.

The old assumption that it's angry lovers who kill.

I heard it was a dreadfully acrimonious break-up.

Mm. He's asked me to act for him. Defend him.
Did he do it?
It's Cleo's turn to sigh.
Given that it's usually the ex-boyfriend, I said.
Usually is not what counts with the law.
Do you think he did it?
The thing is . . .

Would you defend him if you did think he'd done it? I asked this knowing she wouldn't answer, she never has. I wouldn't have gone on if I'd been my usual self, I normally think it's proper that Cleo should be discreet, even if I wish she wasn't.

The thing is, said Cleo, I don't think I can. It would be very upsetting for Belinda.

If he's innocent surely it would be good for her. How's she going?

As good as can be expected, I suppose. Her husband's arriving today.

Will he be any help? Aren't they separated?

Oh, I don't think so. They live in different places, but they're still a couple.

Caracas and London. Not quite your usual commuting couple.

I believe they are very fond of one another.

Cleo drives me mad when she does this lawyer-speak to me. I want to shriek, I'm your friend, don't do this. I never do.

I remembered Belinda's odd response to my mention of Tamara's book. I started to ask Cleo about it but suddenly she had to go. That always happens with Cleo, you think you're in for a good talk, and she has to go.

Justine had gone off to work. She rides my bike, says it sets her up for a sedentary day among the records. I felt like turning over and going back to sleep. The phone rang again. I considered ignoring it, but I'm not good at that. Finally, too curious.

Hi, it's Dermot, said the familiar fulsome Irish voice. I hope you won't think me importunate . . . he paused.

Two lawyers on the phone and I haven't even had a cup of coffee. I muttered appropriately.

. . . but I did so much enjoy meeting you last night. So much that I'd like to see you again. Quite soon?

He paused again. I waited.

I was wondering, he said, his voice so warm, so cajoling, it was like loving honey oozing out of the phone. I held it a little further from my ear. I was wondering, he said, tonight, there's an exhibition, at Magpie, it's the opening, would you like to come with me?

Who is it, I asked, immediately recognising it was the wrong response. I could hardly dredge up a subsequent engagement now.

Garry Shead, you know, he does . . .

I know, I said.

It just so happens, I am a fan of Garry Shead. And I'd been feeling a bit less . . . poor, lately, thanks to the colonel, and the idea of going and looking at a new exhibition of his work with maybe enough money to buy one though I had no intention of doing so, I should get a locksmith in and make the place secure, for instance, or buy a clothes drier or get the house painted, but not buying a painting when you can is so much more fun than not buying a painting because you can't. You imagine you're doing it and you get a bit hot and breathless and excited and for a little while it's as though you have done it.

So I said yes to Dermot. Yes to Garry Shead, anyway. He'd pick me up at six, he said, Dermot that is.

I still hadn't got out of bed. The phone rang again. The colonel this time.

I am ringing to apologise, he said. I'm afraid I was the cause of a lover's tiff . . .

That made me speechless with rage. Tiff! I was spluttering and stuttering. He listened for a moment.

Please, he said, I am sorry for being so clumsy.

Do you set out to enrage on purpose or is it a natural gift? And do you bloody well have to talk like a well-made play? I feel we're being written by Somerset Maugham or Noel Coward or somebody.

I'm sorry. Perhaps I need you to edit my life as well as my book.

That's a different profession. They're called psychiatrists.

There was a silence. Do you think I need one of those? he said, with such hurt in his voice I felt contrite, against my better judgment.

It was a joke, I said. In a sulky voice, I wasn't ready to give in entirely.

That's worse, I think.

Well, I'm tired. I've got a headache.

I think you need to come to the coast. I need you, the book needs you. And I know it's work but you could have little holidays in the spaces between.

I've got Justine staying, remember?

Does she need you?

A lover's tiff, I snorted. Do you think she's my lover?

It isn't, of course, my business. Is she?

She's going back to Auckland in a minute.

Then you can come to the coast.

I'll phone you.

Soon.

Yes, Al. Bye.

I decided to go to David Jones to buy some bras. Nothing at all to do with anyone. I had this Latin teacher once called Elvira who reckoned you must buy underwear for yourself, not anyone else. Unlike my mother who thought you should wear decent knickers in case you got run over by a bus. I would have thought you'd be in such a mess by then that nobody could tell if your knickers were scruffy or not. Look at that poor woman, totally crushed. And I do believe she might have had a hole in her panties. That's not funny, Sandra, said Mum, you know what I mean. In case you faint in the street, then.

I've never fainted in my life. I much prefer the Elvira theory. Not that she was my Latin teacher when she propounded it, she was a glamorous businesswoman by that stage.

I bought two bras, fabulous French ones, and fabulously expensive, even on sale. One was ruby red with lilies in subtle shadow patterns of the ruby (yes, red can be subtle) and one was navy blue net embroidered with leaves. When I was choosing whether to have the lilies in yellow, or the blue and silver number, holding them up in front of me and looking across at a mirror, not too blatant but imagining myself in them, I saw the reflection of the shirtwaist woman. I turned round quickly, but she wasn't there. I looked back at the mirror to try to discern the oblique angle of its reflection but that didn't help. I ran about the underwear department a bit, surely she couldn't have disappeared so fast. I was standing in luggage staring about when an assistant said, pointedly, Can I help you, madam? I replied, In a minute, and then realised I was clutching handfuls of bras in the wrong department. So I went to the underwear counter, supposing shirtwaist woman was probably in a fitting room, and if I lurked about for a while she'd come out. I'm thinking, I said to the assistant, and so I was, these were hard decisions to make, you can't part with this kind of money without paying attention.

But though I considered my bras very carefully—and am still confident that I made the right decision—and then hung around the edge of underwear examining some lethal looking g-strings, she didn't come out, and I decided that she must have slipped away in that brief moment it took me to orient her reflection. Why did I want to see her? Curiosity, I suppose. It's why I do most things. Life is full of stories, unfolding all around you, sometimes it's good to pause and follow them for a while. It's one of the charms of sitting in cafés, watching the narratives happening all around, considering their ends and their beginnings, discovering, inventing.

I sat over a coffee and mused. What sort of underwear was shirtwaist woman buying? And for whose benefit? She wore dresses like my gran, so underneath could have been white, substantial, decent, pretty. But maybe hers were black and lacy, scarlet and skimpy, fast, Gran would have said, the kind I wear because they make me feel sexy, and you don't have to worry about keeping them sparkling white in the wash. I rinse mine through with hair shampoo in the bathroom basin, a trick learned travelling. Imagine how Gran's whites would have looked, after that.

He's a funny guy, that Dermot. I don't get him. He arrives to pick me up. I'm wearing a dark red silk camisole, the red lily bra mostly not showing, with a just-below-the-knee Easton Pearson black linen skirt cut simply on the bias, and sandals the same red as the top. He pauses on the doorstep, as if struck, and reaches out a hand and reverently shapes my hair. Doesn't touch it, it's a respectful gesture, but at the same time intensely intimate, erotic even. His face is ravished and solemn. My, he says. His vocabulary fascinates me. It's kind of archaic, I think. Maybe it's Irish. Maybe his accent and his vocabulary are an invention, his own version of some invented Irishness, or perhaps it's man-about-town glamour, excellent but not quite there, not quite authentic. Not parodic, he never allows an edge of irony that might suggest parody, rather and just faintly amateur imitation.

But he turns out to be fun, and I think I'm being churlish. The paintings are fabulous. He gets Holly who owns the gallery to put a red spot on a large and stunning one with a large and stunning price. I think of asking her to put half a spot on a small print in the Queen series, it's exquisite. I remember I'm not going to buy one. Maybe . . . I make a bargain with myself: if it's still here at the end it will be meant for me. Unlikely, it's one of the least expensive, it will go. Maybe the half sticker; after all, it's first refusal. I go up to Holly. Just a minute, she says, and walks over and sticks a whole dot on it. Problem solved. I feel annoyed.

You'll have to do a lot of looking at mine, says Dermot.

It's hot at Magpie. Though it's evening the weather is still stifling. The gallery is airconditioned but the lights stop it being cool. Even skimpily dressed as I am I find it uncomfortable. Dermot is wearing a slim-fitting black linen shirt over camel-coloured pants. He's a sharp dresser. Hot, isn't it, he says.

His car is one of those pretty little Peugeots that are convertible but he has the top up and the cooling on. I thought we might have a bite, he says.

I giggle at this. He turns and gives me a brilliant smile. It's all such a cliché, handsome man, fancy car. And me, wondering how soon I'm going to fail to act my proper part. Blow the whole thing.

He takes us to a Vietnamese restaurant which is a shopfront with a gaudy Buddhist altar at one end and plastic tables and chairs. He has brought a chilly bag with a Cloudy Bay sauvignon blanc, just about my favourite white but I'm too poor to buy it usually. The food's brilliant. It's also cheap, so when I say of course we are sharing this, and he refuses, firmly, I go along with him. He says I can return the favour, invite him to my place for a meal.

All these little sticky threads, winding out, netting me in a web of the future.

He sits there and gazes at me. As though I'm the most beautiful thing he's ever seen. He listens to the words I say as though they are sublime poetry. Think Cary Grant fallen madly in love in some fifties movie and you've got the picture. Am I doing a good job of Deborah Kerr? He tells me amusing things. He asks me about myself.

I think of telling him about Hotbaby. Not just because he'd be sympathetic, though that's an attractive idea. But he's a lawyer, he'll be able to make sense for me of the situation. I've got the words on my lips: A strange thing happened . . .

He says, You knew Tamara, didn't you . . . He stops, his eyes grow big, there are tears in them. Such a terrible thing, he whispers. Terrible, terrible. He shakes his head.

Yes, I say, terrible.

Such a brutal random thing . . .

You think it was random?

What else? There's a pattern to crimes, you know. A beautiful girl, and some sick character . . . he shakes his head again.

Did you know her well?

No. We moved in the same circles, sometimes. He smiles a wan smile. We were never an item, if that's what you mean.

This is the moment. A strange thing happened . . . But he's getting up to go, the moment passes.

I thought of that moment, later, often. If I had told Dermot my story then, how differently events might have turned out. How differently. But life is full of forks in the way, any one of which could lead to a totally other place. What if . . . what if . . . you say. If only . . . if only . . . with longing, or with horror. And hindsight is totally useless.

He doesn't come in. A busy working day tomorrow. But the weekend's coming up. He'll give me a bell. He sees me to the door, and kisses my hand, slowly.

He's clever. And I'm grateful for him not coming in, avoiding all those decisions about how intimate we might be.

I still feel the sticky thread of the web of the future. It's a courtship web. Oddly old-fashioned. Like Dermot O'Farrell. So well-mannered. Do I want to go to bed with him? Why not. Should I go to bed with him? Probably not. Will I go to bed with him? Not impossible. Not perhaps even unlikely. Down the track. But bedding is a game. It's play. Do you court people to bed? Maybe handsome lawyers do. I still feel the way I did when I first saw him, that this kind of beautiful man is not for me. With faint regret, perhaps, but mostly relief. The only mystery is, why does he think he is? If we were living in an Iris Murdoch novel it would be because he had fallen instantly and utterly in love with me and would probably be at home now writing me a letter telling me he couldn't live without me. I adore Murdoch novels but my world doesn't behave like hers. I can't think of any sudden fallings in love among my acquaintance. Liking, lust, bedding, that's the pattern. Maybe, rare cases, liking, lust, in love, love. I think of being in love. So long ago. So painful. So good to have left it all behind.

I'm in bed reading the latest A.S. Byatt and thinking, wow, this is a novel, full of ideas a lot of which I don't understand, genetics, physics, whatever, and wondering if there's a single Australian writer who could get away with this sheer solid intellectuality. It's hard work. But it makes you feel good. These ideas touch me, even if I am vague as to their meanings.

Justine comes in. I know she's all right because she telephoned this afternoon and sort of said she was sorry. She's been to dinner with the manuscripts librarian. She's had a shower and is still faintly damp, her skin looks burnished, I imagine I can see the long muscles moving under her skin like a beautiful golden beast, some big cat, slow now, but apt to spring. I'm wearing a thin cotton nightie and no bedclothes, it's still hot, suffocating, the air its now usual smoky self. She looks around the room with exaggerated swivellings of her head and eyes. No Dermot? she says.

My sigh is as exaggerated as her gaze. She gets into bed, grinning. Well, tell me all about him.

He would appear to be courting, I say, but I don't get far with my account. Justine is lifting my nightie over my head and teasing my nipples with her skilful bony fingers. Liking. Lust. Love.

Stay with me, Justine. Don't go home.

She laughs. And live happy ever after in your little house in the suburbs.

Yes.

Yes.

We both know she won't.

Chapter 8

I saw something once. Some years ago now. I was at the coast with Cleo and Paul. We were all staying at his parents' beach house. Cleo and Paul were already married, but it was before they had children. I'd just broken up with Bryce, after six years, six years which I had learned to believe were the beginning of a whole life together, maybe not marriage, but children one day, and constancy. Instead he's gone off with the usual bimbo, not saying he's going, no warning, gone, stomach-shrinking betrayal, and I was so miserable I didn't know what to do with myself. Come to the coast, said Cleo. Why, I asked, and she said, That's why, that you can even ask that question, the coast, Cass, holiday, pleasure, fun, and I thought, I suppose she's right, and I went.

    We walked, and swam, it was another hot summer, and took the rowboat out on the lake, fishing, and ate and drank and I did all these things and we laughed ourselves silly and had great fun but then I went to bed and was still the old misery who couldn't sleep and twitched and tossed in bed all sweaty and hot until the sheets were damp and creased, even so near to the sea the night was close, there was no freshness or movement in the air and I got out of bed and walked along the veranda, stretching my arms out so that my nightgown could flap out away from my sticky body. The house had wide verandas all round with French windows opening from the rooms. Mine was at the side, I walked round to the front that was only a short grassy slope from the water. I walked with my arms out and my head tipped back, my eyes half-closed, waiting for a faint breath of coolness from the sea. My feet were bare and I put them down carefully on the old wooden boards of the veranda.

There was a light on in one of the rooms and I looked in. The French doors were open but there was a screen door. I like to think I looked away again straightaway, as soon as I realised what I was seeing, but I don't know that I did, for I remember so clearly what I saw. Or maybe my mind was sensitive, like a film, and my eye was the camera which instantly recorded the scene, and there it was, captured, and I could look at it whenever I wanted.

There was a bed, and beside it a tall lamp with a yellow shade, which cast its light down upon the white sheet and illuminated the couple sleeping there. No nightclothes, no bedclothes. She was lying with her head on his left shoulder, her nose in his neck, his cheek resting against her forehead. Her left arm lay across his chest, her right hand held his penis nestled gently. His left hand lay along her flank and held her close against him, while the fingers of his right hand just touched her breast. Their legs were entwined. I knew that they had made love and settled into this beautifully habitual embrace and gone to sleep without turning off the light. He was breathing gently and she was very softly snoring.

I thought I didn't stop and look for any time but the image is still so clear in my mind's eye, like a snapshot, I said, but also like a painting, luminous and detailed, the white sheet, the lamplight on skin, hers golden, his pale, his straight fair hair meshing with the dark rippled mass of hers, his penis soft and curled in her hand, her nipple brown against his fingers. I always call this painting in my head The Sleeping Lovers.

I walked up and down the veranda for a long time that night, not again as far as their room. At some point the light was put off. I thought of how people talk about making the beast with two backs, with ribaldry and often disgust, it is meant to be an obscenity and a nasty joke in this phrasing, even though the act which it describes is such a marvellous thing, but then somehow how much more marvellous was their delicate lying together in this image of passion quieted into love. Sleeping together. I thought of Bryce, what else did I ever think of then, and couldn't recall ever sleeping with him quite like that. Plenty of sex. Plenty of passion, beautiful Cass, I love you, and then when he was finished rolling away to his side of the bed, king-size it was, quite a distance to be kept, he couldn't sleep when anybody interfered with him. Sometimes in the night he would put out a hand and touch me, but I soon realised it wasn't an invitation to come close, rather a checking up, making sure I was still there. I liked that, that he would want to reassure himself of my presence. But then I could have been a satchel or a mobile phone, a useful possession it would be a bother to lose. A person not knowing her place, or a naughty child running away. His reaching out not taking pleasure in me, but making sure I was to hand.

I have thought about this often since, and I see it as a kind of gift of Cleo's, however inadvertent, however painful to me. A small intricate image of love. I walked up and down that veranda until the sky started to lighten over the dark line of the sea's horizon, and the next day, though I was tired, weary as well as sleepy, I could see that maybe breaking up with Bryce wasn't the disaster I'd thought. I was sad, but not desperately miserable. My heart was sore, but maybe not broken. I went swimming in the sea, the waves were rough, and it was good. I was tumbled and pummelled and the pain of Bryce was all slapped away. It came back, but always more mildly, and then I thought, I've escaped.

At breakfast time Cleo said, Cass, are you all right? and I realised I was gazing at them, tenderly I think would be the word. Oh yes, I said, I'm just enjoying myself thinking what a shit Bryce is.

That's not news, said Cleo. And it would be even more useful to stop thinking about him altogether.

And now whenever I look with horror at Cleo's precise life, or think what a boring man Paul is, however can she stand him, I remember with a funny little illicit thrill in my gut how they lay together that night, and I think, there is love. I hope they are still entwined in one another like that.

And it's also a handy template. I put myself in Cleo's place, my head on the shoulder, my nose in the neck, my hand . . . And the shoulder? For it is the shoulder that really matters here. I've auditioned a few for the role, but none have fitted. Try Dermot? Somehow, I'm not hopeful.

Chapter 9

There was a bang on the knocker. I was immersed in one of the philosopher's sentences. I have never caught him out in an error of syntax yet, but it's hard work making sure. You have to admire him, not many people could control four principal and twenty-three subordinate clauses in one sentence. My room was still cool and very quiet and the loudness of the knocker made my heart jump. I went to the door but didn't open it, instead I twitched the curtain and tried to peer through the nearby window to see who it was. It was the colonel, and he saw me at it. You need a spyhole, he said. Just a minute. Take this.

He handed over a parcel with my tracky daks and T-shirt pressed as never before in their lives and went away again. I went back to the philosopher's sentences. Half an hour later he returned with a packet and a toolbox. Stand by the door, he said, might as well get it at exactly the right height for your eye.

And so he went on, drilling a hole to fit the cute little fish-eye lens that he'd bought at the hardware shop. Shall I make coffee, I asked, grateful for this; a spyhole seemed a desirable thing at that moment. I was in the kitchen when I heard an indistinct muttering voice, and the colonel's in reply. I realised how very clear and cold his voice could sound, very military, I supposed it was. He said: Lady of the house? There is no lady of the house. I heard more muttering, and the colonel again. No. No. Of no interest at all. Goodbye.

He shut the door firmly and came into the kitchen.

No lady of the house? What am I then?

Surely, ma'am, that's not an expression you would use of yourself?

Well, no. But you would.

Ah, but it is your house. Your territory, as they say.

True.

I don't trust these generic callers. No name is not a good look in this situation. If they don't know your name, have no truck with them. That's my rule.

I was slow, I know, but it only then struck me that it might have been Hotbaby.

What did he look like? Blue eyes? Short hair? Did he have a car? What colour was it? Gold?

Might have been. You know how thick your hedge is.

Was it a Monaro? An old one?

It did make an extremely throaty roar as it took off.

Yeah. So does the gold-coloured ute that keeps cruising around.

The man in the golden car, eh, said Al. So he is a friend of yours, after all? Not a pesky salesperson?

This time I did tell the story of the puncture and the business card. What a lottery life is. Yesterday that man, today this man, the most utter accident that I should tell one and not the other. Salutary, and fearsome, that our lives should be directed by such arbitrary, such peremptory, such idle decisions. I didn't think of this at the time. Only what a comfort it was to tell him.

The colonel was angry. We have to find out who he is.

How?

The car rego.

I thought it wasn't possible.

Not legal, but not impossible. I know a bloke who'll do it for a slab.

A slab . . .

Of beer.

I know that, I said, the context fooled me.

Of course you did.

I looked at Al. I suppose he got the information about me for a slab, too.

If it was him, he does seem to know where you live. But not your name.

I said: You don't think I should go to the police?

Maybe. We'll find out who he is first. The colonel was looking grim. Now I see why you were peering out of curtains. The spyhole is an even better idea than I thought. Where's your car?

Shut in the garage.

I have been feeling rather freaked. I could admit it now.

You'd better come down to the coast. I'm ready for you again, anyway. I've done a scorched earth on the whole manuscript, now, not an adjective or an adverb survived. And you'll be safe with me.

I can't yet, I said, remember, I've got Justine staying.

But Justine solved the problem by announcing she was going to Melbourne. She'd unearthed someone who'd worked on one of her treaties, someone she hadn't known about, and was keen to interview. And while she was there she'd do some work in the State Library.

I asked the colonel did he really think I was in danger from Hotbaby. He replied that hadn't somebody said that nobody ever erred by having too low an opinion of human nature? I said I didn't think that could be right, but he insisted. Oh yes, it could.

They've got that person in custody, I said. David Smeaton. The ex-boyfriend.

Yes, and if it's him it'll be all right. But we don't know that it is.

It's the pattern, I said. The rage of the betrayed lover.

If he was betrayed. Maybe he was betraying.

Such a terrible old desperate word, betrayal. And as much in currency as ever.

I googled the Holden Monaro. It said that with a full-throated roar the Monaro ushered in the golden era of the lion-badged V8. Poetic stuff, this car. It mentioned its sleek pillarless two-door boy-racer appeal, its long wide body and flared wheel arches, its sweeping roofline. It said it was a member of Holden's ambitious 'New Generation' HK range, in 1968. I suppose I could have seen all that in Hotbaby's sparkling relic, I just hadn't thought of it in that passionate way.

Dermot doesn't write an adoring letter in the manner of a Murdoch hero, telling me he loves me and cannot live without me, but he nearly does. He sends me an email: Oh what a wonderful time we had last night, we must do it again soon, do I like movies, he needs to know, of course he is sure I will, or maybe dinner, in a real restaurant this time, and what about a picnic, but no, not with the bushfires and the drought, winter will be better for picnics, what about the theatre, he can guess I'm a girl who likes plays, maybe we should pop down to Sydney and take in a couple. It's certainly flattering, and I feel bewildered as a virginal teenager in a Victorian novel: what am I to make of it? I am glad to be able to send, not too quickly, a reply saying I am away on business for a week or two, not even a lie, the colonel is business and who knows how long I'll be away.

Two dozen red roses arrive.

I ring up Cleo and get her voicemail. But she does ring me back, probably because I said it was urgent. I say I need to know about Dermot O'Farrell. Urgently? she says, crossly, and I reply, Too right.

Well, she says, handsome, prosperous, clever, charming . . .

Cleo. I'm serious. I need to know.

But the fact is, she doesn't know much more than I do about him. He's been with the firm some months, maybe a year, it's always longer than you think, came from Perth, she hasn't actually worked with him, he's commercial, not criminal, he seems to be highly thought of, isn't known to have a girlfriend, usually seen about with different extremely young modelish blondes (See, I interrupt, so why me?), looks as though he's got a promising future, maybe he thinks it's time to stop being a bachelor about town and settle down with a wife and family.

Oh yes, and I am so obviously the ideal candidate there.

Cassandra, are you telling me he's serious? Cleo's voice takes on that complicit note of gossip. Tell me, what's been happening?

Nothing, I say. Just . . . attention.

Attention? Yes . . .

But suddenly I've lost her. Someone's come in, she's got to go. I'm not sorry. I realise I am more disturbed by this attention of Dermot's than I like. I've got used to the idea of guys (and girls) who don't want to commit, who make it obvious the exit door is always open wide. That we're all free. Consenting adults having a good time. That's how it is, that's how you like it, if you've got any brains. That's how I've trained myself to be. Dermot is breaking the rules.

Next morning I was putting things in the car to go to the coast when Annie came past, on her way to Tilley's and her caffe latte. I once said to her, I see you're a member of the latte set, Annie, a good working-class woman like you, but she didn't get what I was on about and I realised I didn't want to explain that people say this as a way of sneering. It's a nice honest drink, she said. This morning she stopped. She's fond of a chat, Annie is. I think it is clever of her to have become a coffee-house habitué at her age.

Hello love. Going on holiday?

Hello Annie. Well, I'm going away. But it's business.

Ah. She nodded. Good idea. Get away. The poor dear lovely young woman. Dirty tricks—if only.

I realised the young woman was Tamara. I said, Yes, well, there's certainly been something very nasty going on.

The young women, they do want to be free, and it doesn't seem to be too much to ask but the world keeps saying it is and so cruel with it too. The poor dear lovely girl. Oh dirty tricks. Oh we need you.

You see, very sharp and sensible, but then suddenly odd.

Yes, she said, you save yourself.

The postman came past on his red and yellow motor scooter. Stopping to stuff my letterbox with its usual wad. Hello Mrs Tricks, he said, how's tricks? All the better for your asking, my lad, she said to him and he guffawed and went squawking off on his little bike.

He always says that, she said, thinks it's funny.

Mrs Tricks . . . Annie, is that your name?

Of course, dear. Annie Tricks. These sixty-five years. Ever since I married Hector Tricks. Not that anybody ever called him that. It was always Dirty. Him being a policeman, you see, everybody thought it was a good joke because he wasn't a dirty policeman at all, he was clean and very clever. He put fear into the hearts of criminals, did Dirty Tricks. We need him now, this murderer wouldn't still be around, doing in poor lovely young women. He was a good man, Dirty was.

And I could see she didn't just mean as a policeman. There was such passion in her voice. A good man, she said. I had him for forty years. Not as good as sixty-five but not too shabby.

Her face pinched up and she looked so sad I wanted to comfort her. But with a whiff of Chanel and a toss of her long mauvey chiffon scarf, which went prettily with her white hair and purple tracksuit, she set off. Bye love, she said, have a good trip. She has a slim figure, Annie, and seeing her walking down the hill, her feet moving smartly in her neat black leather trainers, I wish to be so lively and spry when I am her age. Mrs Annie Tricks, widow of Dirty. Not dirty tricks the ugly way the world works, but a person who could be counted on to foil them. What a difference the capitals make.

The colonel had offered to take me to the coast in his car, but I wanted the freedom of my own. I checked the emails, another enthusiastic one from Dermot, begging for an address, some contact, while I was away, maybe he could drive down and visit, we could go swimming. I decided to pretend I hadn't got it. I locked the house and set off in my little car. Hoping that my tyres would be safe from punctures.

Chapter 10

Don't take your usual route to the coast, said Al. Go north, on the Sydney Road. Turn into Sutton and wait fifteen minutes. Then go back to the highway and turn off for Bungendore and down the Clyde from there.

I laughed. Not a very funny laugh. Is that really necessary? Am I living in a thriller?

A murder mystery, I thought, said Al. But okay, look at it as a nice scenic drive, then.

Won't I notice if a bronze Monaro is following me?

Why should he use so obvious a vehicle?

I felt a flush of fear like heartburn in my chest. And a suffocating sense of plots, clever ones, cunning traps, that brought a breathless need to be smarter than they. Hot pursuits, and I too naïve, too uninformed, too innocent to escape.

It's a precaution, that's all. Not expecting it to happen, but in the unlikely case it does, you've foiled it. Trust me.

I did as the colonel advised. Turned into Sutton and waited, parked so I could see any cars driving into the village. None of them so far as I could tell was driven by Hotbaby. But it's hard to be sure, the way the light falls on windscreens, the dim interiors of cars; the people in them are shadowy figures at best.

At least I had no puncture, and arrived in the afternoon. Al was preoccupied. Make yourself at home, he said. A walk, a drive, a swim, a nap? I had told him I didn't want a daily payment, I was happy to keep accepting the whopping fee for the hours I worked, but otherwise, no. I'd brought the philosopher's book with me and was determined to get that done. It's fascinating stuff, I'm enjoying it, but just for that reason you need to pay attention. With him it's no more than a copyedit, more like proofreading really, and the best way to do this, so is the received wisdom, is to start at the bottom right-hand side of the page and work up, entirely back to front, that way you see the words exactly as they are on the page, you don't get seduced by the sense. Sense is the worst enemy of proofreading. That's why writers are mostly so bad with their own work. They read for the sense and believe they have set down what they meant to write, they don't see the odd dyslexias, the elisions, the typos. Friends at the Society of Editors who do a lot of annual reports, government papers, that sort of thing, reckon they are so dull you never get seduced by sense, so they are quite quick and easy to do. But how boring. With the philosopher I am interested in what he is saying so I have to keep checking he's really saying it. His copy is always very clean, but that's the dangerous part, you get lulled, that's when you miss the one error that's slipped in.

There are horror stories in the trade. A terrible one is a sad scene in a restaurant, when the heroine's teeth slid into her coffee cup, instead of her tears. Something like that can destroy a novel. A colleague told me a tale of doing a cookbook about Asian food, and throughout there was an ingredient called minced finger, which sounded gruesome, though it is something that cooks fear, but what could it possibly be? What it should have been was minced ginger, and what is remarkable is that one wrong letter in a word should change so completely not only sense but sound, and make such a mystery.

Of course these days there are so many spell-check errors. Especially bad are words of similar sound but quite different spelling, and unthinking journalists are worryingly prone to them. There and their and they're, all interchanged. Wether for whether, phased instead of fazed. (A mistake of the phuque-whitted I say to myself.) Maybe the language wants to abolish homonyms. That sounds strange, but I do believe language has a will of its own. And then there's ignorance: flaunt instead of flout, wrapped instead of rapt; they're spelt correctly so the computer doesn't pick them up. You wonder if some writers ever consider what words mean. She was wrapped in him, somebody will say; makes him sound like cling film.

Furthermore, there's writers being wrong and editors not noticing. P.D. James tells a story against herself, how she had a motorcycle reversing down a drive. She hadn't thought it out, and felt stupid, but neither had any editors noticed, till a whole lot of readers wrote to her and pointed out that motorbikes don't reverse, they just turn round. She laughed, it's a good story now, but it was mortifying. I think the person who should have been really mortified is the editor, it is the editor's job to know all these odd things.

It's the perfect excuse to bone up on popular culture, like reading women's magazines, all the trashy ones that people only ever see at the doctor's or the dentist's. That's what they tell you.

So I sat on the shady side of the balcony and worked on the philosopher, vaguely aware that the colonel was coming and going and carting things about. I wasn't reading from the bottom up, I'm not such a purist, and I ought to check his syntax, though I've never caught him out yet. The sea was an inky-blue colour, almost indigo, the exact colour of the colonel's eyes. I looked at it and thought about what I was reading. It's meant to be a sort of popular book, which doesn't mean that it's easy, but it's written for the thinking layperson who wants to understand how metaphysical ideas fit with other philosophical issues. Central to his thesis is the ancient distinction between the order of being and the order of knowing. Thomas Aquinas apparently it was who started us thinking like this. I feel ignorant, I should know more about philosophy. I like the way philosophers don't lose track of anything; they might disagree with past fellows, but they don't give up on them. They keep their backlists in print.

There was a good breeze from the sea, which had blown the smoke away. The air didn't quite sparkle, but it didn't have that apocalyptic tangible density that's been turning the sun into a sinister dim lightbulb in the sky, and makes you think that maybe messages are to be read in the heavens. It has certainly been a sky that says, we live in troubled times. My philosopher is offering to discuss various versions of the appearance and reality distinction, which is supposed to be central to the popular conception of what philosophy is all about. And so it is, he says, popular conception is not wrong, even if it does not always understand the different things that deserve to be called the issue of appearance and reality.

My conception fits in this category. It doesn't understand very often at all. Just as well I am being paid for the job and not by time, as I sit gazing at the blue-eyed sea and thinking, this is my life. Dermot. Hotbaby. Appearance and reality: where does truth lie? Get going, girl, read on, you might find the answer in the philosopher's book. Somehow, though, I don't think it's going to show me how to tell whether Dermot's for real, or not. Whether Hotbaby is a murderer, or no.

The colonel calls: time for a glass of wine. It has to be admitted, both he and Dermot have good taste in sauvignon blanc. Nothing illusory about that. The sun goes, the twilight lingers, Al cooks little red mullet over charcoal. Barbounia, he calls them, and grills Greek vegetables to eat with them. Greek, he says, but Australian too. Eggplant, or aubergine, courgettes, or zucchini, peppers, capsicums, poivrons. Thanks to the linguistic turn of twentieth-century philosophy, says my author, there is a tendency to reorder metaphysical questions as questions about meaning and language. The sea is darkly indigo now. What a pity, Al says, so many people have pinched Homer's wine-dark sea, you can't really use it anymore.

You just have.

But it involved a certain sleight of hand, he says.

Full of little red fish, garlicky vegetables, wine, I say: The idylls of ordinary persons. Aren't we lucky? We don't have to be kings to live like them any more.

Idyll, he says, repeating the word several times so it becomes strange, loses its being. Idyll. It would be a good name for a house. Maybe I should call this house Idyll.

You could never do any work in it.

Oh yes you could. Work can be idyllic.

Of course we have to look the word up after that. And find out that an idyll is actually a little poem, or more likely a piece of prose, and that it's probably going to be picturesque, or rustic, and so is the episode suitable for treatment in such a form. Especially a love story. Hmm. Lytton Strachey (this is a historical dictionary, my favourite kind, telling you of past uses) mentions happiness, love, simplicity. Two out of three is okay. It's from the Greek, *eidullion*, diminutive of *eidos*, meaning form, or picture. A form made of words, and not the thing itself.

I do so love dictionaries.

The colonel is in no hurry to start work. He tells me to have a little holiday, time for the manuscript will come. Sleep in, he says, and I do. It must be his habit of command. I wake late to a smell, rich and hazy through the whole house. The smell of hot sugar, oozing and syrupy, with the sharpness of fruit. At breakfast, which is even later, I say to him, So, is this the Apricot Colonel at work?

I think he blushes. Maybe it's the flush of his preserving activities.

How do you know about that?

I just smile.

The apricots are ripening, he says. In the little orchard in the secret valley. There is a moment, you have to grasp it.

Can I see?

Later, he says, when I am happy with my efforts.

The telephone rings, which I realise is a rare occurrence in this house. The colonel takes it out of the room, I can see him pacing the balcony as he talks, then he comes in and writes down some notes.

My man of the slab, he says.

I look at him.

He's got your friend Hotbaby.

The slab has bought a name, address, phone number and profession. Hotbaby is called Harold Perrot, he lives in McGregor, and he is a car detailer by trade.

Harold, I say. An unusual name, for somebody his age.

Quite handsome, isn't it. Who knows what his friends actually call him. Could have any sort of nickname.

And a car detailer, well, that fits. I'd have expected him to have something to do with cars. Not very grand, though, is it, not like a mechanic, not a real trade.

Meticulous, I suppose.

Mmm.

We sit silent for a while, until I ask: What now?

Now? Nothing. You're safe here. Later, well, strategies will suggest themselves. I'm a believer in inspiration in such matters. Leave it to me. You're the editor, I'm the strategist.

The colonel goes back to his preserves. I read yesterday's *Canberra Times*. Our prime minister seems determined to take us to war. He says it's not decided but of course it is. I skim through the articles, feeling rage like nausea in my chest that we are so lied to. The *Tampa*, the children overboard, the deployment of troops to Iraq—the truth is told about none of these, and do we care? Not nearly enough, not nearly enough of us. Voters say yes, they know the prime minister lied, but no, it doesn't worry them. How can you trust a liar? I wish there was somebody to appeal to our nobility, our honour, to ask of us that we behave well.

I cannot bear the meanness of this society we live in, and turn the pages in despair. I haven't talked to Al about this war that I can't believe but know we will end up in, I don't want to find him as gung-ho as our leaders.

There's a small article at the bottom of a page. David Smeaton, who was detained in custody over the murder of Tamara Sissons, has been released without being charged.

So the police don't think he did it, eh, says the colonel, when I tell him. Hmm. So there's Harold Hotbaby back in the picture.

After lunch we do a little work. He wants to talk me through his homework. He's done a good job on the adjectives and adverbs. The problem now, I say, is that it's a bit stodgy. Too dense. Too much information.

I point to a detailed account of the regiment, its personnel, their duties.

But that's important, he says. You need to know that. And it's really interesting.

To you. Not the average reader. People who like that sort of thing, they probably already know it. The rest of us, no.

But you can't understand it without that.

I can.

Not properly.

Enough.

You want me to gut it.

I want you to write a book that a whole lot of people will want to read. Not two specialists.

Fuck, he says. I used to think patrols were gruelling.

Here's what you can do. Take it out and we can put it in an appendix. Or an afterword. I'm not keen on appendices, and nobody will read them, but if it will make you happy . . .

It's really an essential part of the story.

No it's not. The narrative doesn't need it. It's a dead weight. Likely to make us jettison the whole enterprise.

Oh ma'am. You're a hard mistress.

The thing is, I say, we're good at stories. People are. I think it's part of being human. Give us the bones of a narrative and we'll hang flesh on them. You have to have faith in your readers. Trust me. Trust them. We've always done it—you mention Homer, but he wasn't anywhere near the first. I imagine people in a cave, the story of how we caught the mastodon. Even before language, when the picture scratched on the wall was the story: the animal, the spear, the hand of the hunter . . .

What's more, I say, there are some really meaty ideas in this morass of information. For instance, look at this, this is really interesting, where you say that the war was a very Prussian operation, militarily brilliant, but ultimately let down by politics, or politicians. I want to know more about this. And here, saying that Operation Desert Storm, and especially Desert Sword—that's the ground part, right?—were the most cerebral campaigns ever fought. Involving technology, surprise, operational skill, heuristic and academic training—you say they were above all the triumph of the intellect.

Well?

I want to know more about this, what it means. The fitting of the present into templates offered by the past, so the present makes sense in terms of the past.

Who's writing this book?

You, of course you.

Is he grinding his teeth? Look, I say, this war was a chunk of your life, but what's important is where it fits in the life of the rest of the world. See here: 'Saddam's misadventure in Kuwait'—that's a fabulous phrase . . .

Not mine . . .

I don't want to know about that, not now. I'll tell you about quotation marks some time. Any way, 'Saddam's misadventure in Kuwait is a cruel reminder to all of us that the post Cold War world may be more anarchic and more violence-prone than the preceding era' . . . that's potentially more interesting than who was higher ranking than whom.

So you're saying, more narrative, but at the same time, more ideas?

Two hours of this, and the colonel is restless. I've got to admire you, doing this for a living, he says.

We all do what we do. Seems to me easier than fighting wars. But that's your profession, as this is mine. I'm quite good at it, so it doesn't seem too hard.

He screws his face up and looks at me. There's this about him, he's good to work with, because he pays attention. Makes a fuss to begin with, resists, but then he learns fast.

I've got to go off, he says. Eden. Business.

Not being a wife, I don't say, At this hour? But he explains anyway. You've got to catch the fishermen when you can, he says.

Lock the doors, he says. You're perfectly safe here. But lock the doors.

He's left me a Thai beef salad which is very good, the meat pink, the sauce sharp, the lettuces crisp. It's like having a wife, I think suddenly, a loving wife whose concern is my comfort, who delights in concocting good things for my delectation. I sit on the terrace with a bottle of wine and a book but I don't read it, I eat and drink slowly and watch the evening gather over the darkening patchwork of fields, the sea colour draining to silver, the sky turning from pink to green to dim blue and the stars country bright. The curves and lines and dark crevices of the hilly pastures. Al's Picasso woman landscape; a lovely image, Picasso endlessly painting his at-that-time beloved woman and always seeing her differently and, however strangely, with love. I think of David Smeaton. Who was helping the police with their inquiries. Who has been released without being charged. These are forms of words that have their meanings, the most important of which is that they are not precise. That they in fact hide what they mean. A helper with inquiries may be a good citizen doing a civic duty, or he may be the most suspicious of suspects who will swiftly be indicted as certain evidence comes in. And the helper not being charged: the meanings here are multiple and impossible to discern. He has convinced of his innocence. Perhaps he has a tough alibi that will brook no breaking.

Or maybe because so far and only just not yet the crime cannot be pinned on him.

David Smeaton. A philosopher by trade. I expect he knows all about the duality of appearance and reality. Perhaps he told the truth and was believed. Or he lied so well he convinced the police he spoke the truth. I wonder if we'll ever find out. I wonder will we ever learn what happened to separate him and Tamara. There was all that anger, highly public anger, anger like an electrical storm whose reverberations are felt all around it. Anger suggests betrayal. And maybe somebody does know what went wrong. Which one fell in love with someone else. Which fell out of love with the other. It doesn't seem to be the sad separation where both agree in their oh so rational fashions that they should part but of course they will always remain good friends. That doesn't generate storms of anger. I remember Bryce, and my fury when he left, it can still bring a whiff of bile to my throat. I did think I'd like to kill him but not so far as planning to murder him. And now we are kind of polite acquaintances.

If David were guilty of the murder then that suggests it was Tamara who betrayed him and this his revenge. *Love to hatred turned.* David a philosopher, and you might think he would have the mental training to deal with such grief, but probably not. Philosopher, understand thyself. And he can't, any more than the physician can heal.

Perhaps. Maybe. Guessing. Supposing. The turmoil of this narrative. A bubbling cauldron, and you can fish out gobbets, of flesh or fish, fact or fiction, truth or lie. Newt-eye, frog-toe, adder-fork, dog-tongue. None very appetising.

It's dark, and the air chill. No moon, and the stars gone. Smells of bushfire smoke in the air. I'll go to bed and read my book. The doors are locked. I should have put on a light downstairs before night fell.

But then the morning comes, and its earliness is fresh with dew and the sun glittering as it comes up out of the sea. I go for a walk, and I do not find the valley and the secret orchard.

That is because it is hidden, says the colonel when he comes home at lunchtime. Tired, needing a nap, and so I spend the time in the philosopher's book, trying to read it as just a job with no meanings for me. And you know the good thing about philosophy is that it tries to be about truth, it believes that's what matters.

This house belongs to Al. Of course. But I mean in the way it warms to him, becomes vivacious in his presence. It is pleasant and calm when he is absent, but when he comes home it brightens up. Like a pet, or a wife. Make yourself at home, he says, and so I do. He goes off on one of his excursions and I work for a bit, but then wander. The cliffhanger, the great room, is a vast open space but there are things to be discovered in it, books, objects, paintings. Then there is the old house. His bedroom is here, it's got a Yale lock on the door and he always shuts it. There's another room he calls the library. It has only one small window and the rest is books, with a big table and a comfortable chair. I can see that sometimes you would welcome this calm enclosed space. The view from the cliffhanger is stunning but you don't want to be stunned all the time. This is dim, and very quiet, and I think I might come and read here. I wonder if he has read all the books. They are not bestseller new. I find a whole section of the children's books Gran had on her shelves, books that belonged to her kids, and that I loved. Biggles, and the William books, Swallows and Amazons, the Andrew Lang fairy books.

I didn't find the secret orchard but I did come across a garden to the side of the house I hadn't known was there, built on several terraces so it was flat and stepped, with drystone walls and enclosed with trees and shrubs, tall ones on the outside and the heights sloping in, so it was embowered, with just a space on the eastern side to provide a small view of the sea. When I was leaving I realised there was a Priapus at the entrance, a small wooden post of a figure with a smiling wreathed head and an enormous penis. He was carrying a basket of fruit. I touched him, that after all is the point of this massive erection, that you touch it, with respect. I even needed to bow a little, to reach it.

The wood was old, dense and hard, but old. Though maybe the statue was not. But touching it I knew that its substance was old, and powerful, and that was thrilling.

I walked back to the house, thinking of biological clocks ticking. They always make me think of that old James Bond movie: when the clock ticks down to all zeros then the nuclear bomb will go off. But Bond is cool as usual and works away neatly until it stops at 00:01. But biological clocks aren't like that, they don't count down to anything, no bang, nothing. Maybe the whimper. Not of a child but of a grown woman crying. Gran told me once, none of us are grown-up. You are, I said. No, she replied, I just do a very good imitation. After Bryce I gave up on the idea of children. Not immediately, but gradually. I tell myself that I am quite happy and I believe myself. Touching a Priapus has nothing to do with it. It's respect. Prayers for fruitfulness don't have to mean children.

I told Al I had seen the statue in the garden.

Did you touch it, he asked.

Yes.

He smiled.

Why?

He was opening a bottle of wine and gave that his attention. Then he said, I'm glad you know that's the right thing to do.

Not that I have any hopes from it. But I think we can perform pious acts for their own sake, don't you?

I should imagine it's the only way to do them.

Where did you get him?

Priapus, you know, was the son of Dionysus and Aphrodite. He's the protector of shepherds, fishermen, and farmers. He likes gardens. Just what we need round here.

He seems old.

He is. An ancient chunk of fig wood. Priapus has to be made of wood, and wood through which sap once flowed copiously. Not stone, that's a different cult, it's mortuary. For fertility you have to have wood.

Al poured the wine. He held the glass up to the light. I wonder what his old dad Dionysus would have made of this. Probably not resinous enough for him. We should get some retsina.

Not for me.

People say, when you get to like it, you love it.

Just one more thing to train myself into.

Or not. You can not.

It's a long way from home for Dionysus, I said.

He came with us, when we came, we brought him in our heads.

How does he get on with the Aboriginal spirits of the place?

Ah, that is a very good question.

I didn't notice at the time that the colonel wasn't answering my questions. But after that I often went to the garden, and always, it being the thing to do, touched the Priapus' thrilling phallus. I hadn't known about him being the child of Dionysus and Aphrodite. What a heritage. The colonel seems to know quite a lot of interesting things. For a military man. That sounds hypercritical, I suppose, not to mention patronising, but considering the literary people I mix with, most of them wouldn't have a clue. All those people educated in the humanities, and they don't know the stories of their own culture. Bet Dermot wouldn't know anything about Priapus. Of course he's a lawyer, I don't suppose that counts as a liberal education. It would have once.

Al came home with fishy parcels, and a newspaper. There'd been another murder.

Chapter 11

I'd just been thinking that it was time to get back to Canberra and real life. Dermot was still emailing me; the 'Cassandra is out of the office' message was flicking back and he was concocting a series of elaborate responses to this.

Out of the office and breaking my heart

Ah but will Dermot survive until she gets back to him???

Maybe she has gone forever and I am bereft

Heartless machine, send me some hope

How shall I pass this cruel gatekeeper? Am I her knight to take on the quest?

They were becoming wilder and wilder. Faux, I said to myself. I suppose their exaggerated antique despair was funny, I suppose it was meant to be, but I found it disturbing. Maybe he was using this jokey heartbreak to imply real affection? Maybe he thought that, being an editor, I needed to be courted with words, and that strange ones would be more valuable? Courtship again. I remembered Gran telling me how Jack admired her ankles.

Of course Dermot wasn't the only person emailing me. I do have other friends—Justine likes to send cryptic erotic

messages, which I reckon will get her in trouble one day—
and there were odd jobs offering. I'd just about got through
the philosopher's book, and Al was doing okay with his,
when he got down to it. It was time to return to the real
world.

But now. Another murder. Another young woman. I sat
down at the table. So, I said, they let David Smeaton go, and
now there's another murder. Sure looks like him. He must
be mad.

Al shook his head. He passed me the paper. No name,
few details, bare facts. A connection drawn to Tamara. But,
most importantly, a small piece of information: she had
been dead several days before her body was discovered.

David Smeaton was still in custody, said Al. So, if it is a
serial killer, that lets him out.

And puts Hotbaby back in the picture.

Maybe. Al rubbed the bridge of his nose, as though invisible glasses had pinched it. Maybe. But, it's possible . . . if it
was Hotbaby, and he wanted to kill Tamara because he
thought she was you . . . which doesn't seem very likely, do
many people kill women who won't put out for them? But if
it was you he wanted, why would he kill this other woman?

Rage, that I tricked him?

Unless he is a serial killer, and you just had the luck to
have your tyre changed by a psychopath.

People aren't very helpful on the road these days. Maybe
that's why he stopped, not out of kindness, not to be helpful,
but because he saw it as an opportunity to practise his hobby.

That's a pretty dim view of human nature. But, in that
case, you were lucky.

And Tamara wasn't. In that case, it really is my fault that he killed her. I put a psychopathic murderer on to her.

Hang on. You're running way off track. Even if all that's true, you can't feel guilty. Where serial killers are concerned, it's every woman for herself.

None of this makes me feel like going back to Canberra.

No, you mustn't, said Al. Not yet. Let me see what I can find out.

He shut himself in the library with the telephone. I wandered about. He'd left the bedroom door open, the first time I'd ever seen that. The room seemed curiously light, for part of the old house, which was dim compared with the brightness of the big room. I looked in, not very pryingly, after all he did usually have it locked and you had to respect that, but enough to see that the light came from above, that there was a spiral staircase leading up to another room which I supposed would have the same views as the cliffhanger. I'd wondered that he chose to sleep in the closed-in house, and now I knew why. I was surprised that I hadn't observed this attic storey, but when I went out the front and looked I saw that it was pretty much hidden by the large old pine trees. You could see it when you looked, but it wasn't noticeable.

Al was good at information. He found out that the second victim was twenty-eight, that she worked for an escort agency, and that her name was Jane Sutherland but she called herself Tiffany.

Tiffany, I said. That gives her the same initials as Tamara.

And she lives in O'Connor. In a fairly secure building, though nowhere is secure, really.

I suppose it was a client, I said. Or somebody pretending to be a client. Hotbaby . . . I suppose I should call him Harold Perrot, now I know.

She didn't work from home, said Al. And the agency that organised the business reckons it looks after its girls, it has these bouncer guys who chauffeur them about, so they're supposed to be safe. The clients don't know where they live.

The initials T.S. Living in O'Connor. Young women. But apart from that, random. Is that enough connection?

Oh, and there was a lot of blood. And *slut* and *whore* wrongly spelt written on the walls.

I felt sick. It has to be the same person, doesn't it.

It looks like it.

I have to tell the police.

Wait a bit, said Al. Let me go to Canberra and see what I can find out. You stay here. It's safe here.

But suddenly I didn't want to be here. However safe. Not on my own.

No, I said. I need to get back to Canberra. And I need to get rid of Hotbaby.

Get rid of . . . ?

I mean, take care of. Deal with. Tell the police. Have him out of the way.

I think you'd be better here.

No, I said, I'm too much in limbo, here.

First an idyll, now limbo.

I couldn't even smile. It's nothing to do with the house, or you . . .

Well, if you must you must. But don't go to the police just yet.

But the next morning he can't go. The apricots. This is their moment. The colonel has been to the hidden valley and they cannot wait. I ask him can I watch, and he says No of course not. But he may show me when they are done. He gives me an apricot to eat. I carry it carefully between two fingers and go and sit in the little garden, stopping and touching the Priapus rather longer than usual. When I look at his basket of fruit I see it as full of apricots, and I rest mine for a moment on its wooden images. They are weathered to silvery grey, smooth, finely carved. My fruit glows startling rosy-orange as if lit from within. Incandescent. I sit on a stone seat set into the dry stone wall, it is still cool here, in the shade, and a breeze from the sea has cleared the smoke, so it almost seems a normal summer, and I bite into my apricot.

There is the invisible drone of a wasp, maybe here in this garden, maybe far away in the Araluen Valley, maybe nearby in the secret orchard, piercing the flesh of an incandescent fruit. A sibilant drone, which is perhaps the air breathing, the wasp fluttering its sleazy wings, piercing the perfect globe of the fruit plucked by delicate fingers, the juice running in my mouth, sweet and astringent at once, complicated as wine. This apricot. I understand why ceremony is needed. It is a miracle. Tasting as apricots should taste, used to taste, hardly ever taste. A Garden of Eden apricot. I sit there with my eyes shut and the juice filling my mouth. Filling my mind. Here it is, our story, our history.

Maybe I dozed, maybe I dreamed. An enclosed garden, a secret orchard, a magic fruit: these are tales of enchantment.

The wasp droned, the air murmured, the juices filled my mouth, and so did my thought, here it is, our story. I have never lost the sense of that thought, though I have to puzzle over what it means.

When I got back to the house the colonel was not there. The air was hazy with sugar. I put out some bread and cheese but it was late afternoon before he appeared. He was . . . morose, taciturn, preoccupied, except that those are my words for him. I'm not sure he felt like that. But silent he was.

I said, That was a fabulous apricot.

The fabulous apricot. The fabled apricot. The apricot of fable.

This seemed unanswerable, so I said nothing.

Which of course it isn't. He walked about the room with heavy strides. It's a rose, you know. A member of the rose family. All these so-called stone fruit are. A rose by any other name . . . The Chinese knew about them four thousand years ago. But what narratives do they appear in?

Your jars?

Ha. You'd better come and look, I suppose.

We went down into the room next to mine, which I had never penetrated before. The air sugary and chill. One wall was the rock of the cliff, like mine, but the room did not have my expanse of window. There was a porcelain sink, two gas burners, two immense untinned copper pans. Shelves of bottles of fruit glowing in the dim light. On a bench were a number of tall cylindrical jars of apricots, the rosy golden globes of the fruit suspended in heavy liquid. It was like a laboratory in a cave, a treasure cave out of the

Arabian Nights. Do you need to say Open Sesame to get in, I asked, but Al frowned.

They are very beautiful, I said.

He was still frowning. No. They're not right. See here? A faint cloudy blur? The liquid should be utterly pellucid. You need perfect clarity before a judge will even look at them. It's unutterably hard, which is why you want to do it. No. I am afraid they will not do. So. Come on. Time to dine.

He made toasted cheese with tomato for our evening meal. Comforting childish food. Food that you ate in a time when the world wasn't dangerous, because you did not know it to be so, and eating it can restore you to that time, for a while.

Till Al said, after we'd cleaned up and were drinking camomile tea, to calm us, he said, I have been thinking. I shall go to Canberra tomorrow. Yes, I know you want to go, but you can come the next day. I am going to come and stay in your house, you need somebody to look after you, but I cannot do that tomorrow.

I mumbled. I did want to go back to Canberra, but then I had a picture of myself alone in my flimsy house, and could see the sense of Al's words.

Believe me, he said, his indigo eyes very dark as they looked into mine, it's the best way. I'm the strategist, remember?

I didn't much like the idea of another thirty-six hours in the cliffhanger by myself, but it did seem safer. Okay, I said.

Next morning he left early, putting my car in the shed and shutting the door. Nobody knows you're here, he said, but no point in advertising it. There's them as doesn't know what Private Road means.

I supposed this was the military mind at work. Guard against all eventualities. Don't take for granted you're as safe as you believe you are. What a way to live; I wanted my calm uneventful no-unexpected-eventualities editor's life back, when the biggest fear was an enraged author shouting from cyberspace.

I locked the doors and sat on the terrace. I'd finished the philosopher's book and could drive into Tilba and post it. Make a little excursion. But somehow I didn't want to. I remembered my first visit here when I had driven down the coast and sat on the hotel balcony and drunk beer, and looked at shirtwaist woman. I couldn't imagine doing that now. I felt as though I had eaten of the lotus and could not do otherwise than live its vegetable life. Was it because the killer had scared me into hiding, or was it some kind of enchantment? The hidden orchard, the secret garden with its ancient statue, the heavy haze of sugar; maybe simply breathing the air made you indolent.

The colonel, I noted, got away quite often. Maybe as antidote, recognising the danger, afraid of being trapped.

It was certainly time I got away, having thoughts like this.

Chapter 12

I had given Al the key to my house so when I got back from the coast he was already installed in the spare room. This gave me a small frisson until I remembered that I had stayed for days in his house and how was this different. He made coffee and sat me down with the newspaper, folded to the bottom of the front page. An item of late news.

It was titled: Amazon Attack? Underneath it said a man was in a coma after being mugged in an alley beside a Dickson nightclub. Harold Perrot, 43, whose bronze Holden Monaro figured prominently in the recent Summernats, had been injured in the leg and knocked unconscious late last night. He had been seen leaving the nightclub with a female companion. The police were hopeful she could help them with their inquiries.

Hotbaby. And Summernats made sense. The meetings of the mean street machines. Sally lives at Watson and complains bitterly all the time this huge meet is on, the first week in January, about the noise at all hours of the day and night. They go in for a lot of wheelies and tyre burning, and their engines and sound systems are in competition as to which can make the most noise, but I rather like to see the cars. They are so lovingly bizarre. They drive round town with the tops down and girls in T-shirts telling you how big their tits are—one year there was a pink Cadillac ute with a spa in the back and a girl in it wearing only tiny denim shorts—and it seems to me weird but somehow innocent fun, especially now the police have cracked down on drunkenness; they have to cooperate or they're banned, so they don't rampage as once they did. But then their games are only a distant murmur in O'Connor. Up close they're hot and noisy and smelly. Seems ironic to me; such beloved cars, polished and primped to gorgeous perfection, then they drive them to near-destruction and have to start all over again. Keeps them busy all year I suppose.

But of course Summernats aren't the point. Harold Perrot is. There's a description of the female companion. The girl at the bar said she was tall with dark brown hair, wearing a blue-green coloured dress with a tight waist and a full skirt, the top fitted and with longish sleeves made of something like feathers.

Struth. Remarkable powers of observation.

Well, said the colonel, I think the woman must have been quite striking. Memorable. The girl didn't see her face, her hair covered that.

He had a rather striking looking woman with him at the bushfire benefit, I said. If it was him.

So, does this mean the women are fighting back?

You reckon the woman did that to him?

Why not?

Maybe she was the front person for a gang?

What sort of gang?

Maybe a rival Summernats mob?

Maybe. But maybe he just picked the wrong woman.

And she worked out he was a serial killer and belted him before he could murder her? How did she know he was that way inclined?

Don't ask me, said Al. I only know what I read in the paper.

Which of course is the fount of all knowledge. I was silent for a moment. I suppose he made a move in the alley. It's a different modus operandi, but I suppose that's a good idea, change your habits. And it means . . . it really looks like Hotbaby is the one.

At least he's safely out of the way. For the moment anyway.

I have to go to the police.

I suppose so. Tomorrow.

There's always so much to do when you come back from being away you wish you'd never gone. A lot of messages on the answering machine. One from my mother, Am I okay for the bushfires. It sounds like a polite question, Have I got enough milk for tea? Though I suppose she means, not burnt out. I grasp the nettle and ring her straight back, no point in postponing. Yes, I'm okay, fires on the ridge but nothing devastating, not like the south and west. Not pointing out it's a few weeks ago, I'd have been ash if there'd been any problems. Good, she says. I did think I'd have heard if there was trouble. Mind you it's taken you long enough to get back.

I've been away, I say.

A holiday, I suppose. A holiday, how nice.

Edith—I think she's never forgiven Gran that name; the last Edith on the planet, she reckons, and no matter how often I say it's pretty and a fine old name and becoming quite fashionable, quite a few Ediths in novels and they'd know, it doesn't help, it's the dowdiest name, so uncool—Edith is driving to Melbourne and will call in to say hello. Won't stay with me. Some guy involved, as usual.

Anyone I know?

I shouldn't think so. I met him when he helped me with the car. He's a bit younger than me.

What's news, I don't say. What's he do in life? I ask this question to annoy her.

We thought we'd stay in quite a nice hotel, she says. What do you recommend?

The Hyatt. No question.

I'll let her work out if she can afford it.

There's also a message from Cleo. It turns out she wants to invite me to dinner. A repeat of her table for the bushfire benefit. Such fun, she says.

That's interesting, I say. I've got the colonel staying with me.

Cass! Is that wise?

Why ever not?

He's such a sinister character. These are dangerous times, Cass.

Aren't they always?

More so than most. This serial killer, and all.

What do you know—Cleo, you're not suggesting the colonel—?

Of course I wouldn't suggest. But you have to be careful. How do you know he's even a colonel? And what about his alibis for the murder times?

I heave a noisy sigh. Sometimes smugly married women give me the shits.

I just don't want to be saying I told you so to a corpse, is all.

Cleo, do you know anything about these killings?

I don't think anybody knows much, that's the trouble.

What about the murder weapon?

The police are keen to avoid copycatting, you know.

So discreet. It's discretion not truth you'll get from Cleo a lot of the time. Not always. But how do you tell? It occurs to me I should consult her about my adventures.

Cleo, I might know something. I should talk . . .

Cass, I'm so sorry, someone's at the door, I'll catch up with you later.

Dinner not organised, either. *Oh Cleo there's a man in the doorway with a long sharp knife and he says he's going to slide it between my ribs and press it into my heart.* So sorry Cass, something's come up, I'll call you later.

And then there's Dermot and the emails. Pretty soon they are going to have to admit, Cassandra is back in the office.

It's not as easy, going to the police, as you might think. No being whisked into the presence of the inspector all ears to hear what the sassy young woman has to say to him. Lots of waiting. Handed from one police person to another. Busy people, polite, listening, but how much are they hearing?

I had embarked for the fourth time on my story of lonely road, flat tyre, helpful stranger et cetera, telling it as it happened, getting to the point where I discover—I have to fudge this, it is illegal—the guy's name.

Harold Perrot, says the officer, suddenly taking notice. Harold Perrot? The guy in the coma?

I suppose so.

You reckon it was the same, changed your wheel?

Yes, and I gave him Tamara's card and . . .

Hang on.

He went away and came back with a computer printout. It was a modelling of the woman described in the newspaper. Tall, long-legged, brown hair in a fall obscuring her face. The dress, a rather lurid turquoise colour, tight-bodiced, full-skirted, and the sleeves look like they're made of some sort of swan's down, I think you'd call it.

Recognise her?

I didn't. There was some faint familiar air to her, but I think it was from Gran's boxes of patterns. Vogue Original, circa 1950-something. Probably the dress came from an op shop. The young are into retro clothes. Well, I'm not averse to them myself, you can get some gorgeous things, old designer dresses, or beautifully homemade.

The dress is retro, I said.

Is it? The constable looked across at the picture. How can you tell?

The fashion. It's not now.

I see.

There was a faint disturbance, somebody opened the door, called him away. I waited quite a while. Then someone else put her head round the door and said, Thanks for your help, Ms . . . We've got your details, we'll be in touch.

While I was waiting I'd put the picture in my bag. Not straight away, but waiting makes you irritated, and that makes you bold. It was just a computer printout, not like a photograph, and the details had been in the paper. I don't know why I wanted it; why not was probably the reason.

Edith comes in for a drink in the late afternoon; for a quick drink. They're going out to dinner. The guy is practically a toy boy, called Marcus, seems very charming, but then I suppose they are, do you ever see a surly toy boy? Not that I think he's a gigolo or anything, Edith isn't that rich. She's had decent jobs for a good while, since she and Dad split when I was five, starting off in a shop that sold household things, glasses, cutlery, china, it was a solitary dull outfit to begin with, but she got to be buyer pretty soon, then manager, and turned it into a small chain, very trendy, but not the sort of money that would buy a gigolo. I don't think. Not that I really mean to suggest she has to buy her men, though I reckon they cost. As do her clothes. She's pretty good for a putative sixty, slim, her hair a pale gold colour. It used to be dark brown, like mine, but it didn't go grey until she was fifty and it's been gradually gilding ever since. She's got a fine brown skin, the oily kind that doesn't wrinkle much, zits when you're young but rewards later, and this Marcus seems quite to dote on her.

The three of us sit around the study. I've got champagne, it's all Edith ever drinks, so she says. I hear about what she's been up to, and all about Linda, my sister, who's done the right thing and produced gorgeous grandchildren, and lives in Brisbane, which is a lovely place to visit. Not like Canberra, always too hot or too cold, Edith couldn't wait to get out of it, left the city along with my father.

So how're things with you, Sandra, she says. Oh my goodness, look at that. She's seen the computer image that I'd left on the table. Oh how funny. Oh, I so wanted one of those when I was a girl. And your gran would never let me. She pouts. A ming-blue shantung ballerina. With shoestring straps and a tight little bolero over. I reckon that's what that is, though it doesn't show. With bracelet-length sleeves. Oh, they were all the rage when I was—let me see —fifteen? Ming-blue or apricot were the colours. I wanted ming-blue. And Mum made me have cream organdie with little pink flowers. Oh, it was sweetly pretty, and I have to say it did look very cute, but it wasn't ming-blue shantung, like the with-it girls had.

She narrowed her eyes to look at the picture. A bit of a horror, really, isn't it. Maybe Gran was right. Who is it, anyway?

Maybe a suspect in a murder trial, I say. Best to be a bit brutal, if you want to get a word in.

Ooh. She drops the picture back on the table. Well, petal, we'd better be going if we're going to have time to freshen up before dinner. She smiles at Marcus, the kind of smile you wouldn't want to intercept. It has wattage plus a sort of buzzing of the eyelashes and eyebrows. You're meant to melt when you get smiled at like that. At this moment Al comes in. He is something of a shock for Edith. He has the advantage of knowing who she is.

Edith, this is Al Marriott. Colonel Marriott.

I know she'll like the colonel bit.

How do you do? He gets the smile, the tremulous version, including the eyelashes. He takes her hand and bows over it, not quite kissing, but the suggestion is there. Edith sits back down and we all have another glass of champagne. I feel my status rising in my mother's eyes, at the same time as my spirits fall. How can my main value be the man I attract? Especially as Al is a client, not a lover. Though I notice I am not telling her that, and despise myself for it.

But then Al says he is writing a book and I think she twigs. She gives me a squinty look. Nevertheless she goes on charming him, there may be the more reason, if he doesn't belong to me. She likes to have a collection of charming chaps available all the time. She is especially fond of military men because of their manners. I wonder what she'd make of the apricots.

I know I am not at my best when my mother is around. I know she thinks I'm a failure at the things she values. Like my father, I suppose. I expect I remind her of what a disappointment he was. He didn't disappoint me, nor I him. He died six years ago and I still miss him. I still think about him.

I don't know why this disapproval of Edith's should worry me, in most cases I've deliberately chosen not to be good at her kinds of things, but somehow I go surly and sharp when she's around, I turn into the expected disappointing daughter.

The colonel is telling her about the delights of being edited by her brilliant daughter Cassandra. She gives me another of her squinty looks: a beautiful man like this and all I can do with him is tinker with his prose. She gets up to go again, kisses me, kisses the colonel, I kiss Marcus. She says, Well, Sandra, you never know, Marcus may fall into your clutches too some day. He's a writer you know.

Really? I say.

Marcus grins. I wish.

No false modesty, angel. You know how fabulous that last thing was.

What do you write, I ask.

Oh, I suppose you'd call it ... But Edith has exited. There is to be no more chitchat. What, I say: epic poetry, advertising copy, the GAN? but they are out of earshot.

GAN? says the colonel.

Great Australian Novel. Like the Messiah, it is awaited.

Marcus is driving Edith's car. It's a BMW, not very new but impeccable. He toots the horn in a little tune as they drive off.

Back inside I fall flat on my back on the sofa. Edith drives me to extravagant gestures. I say: How can someone be one's mother and yet so utterly mysterious?

She's a glamorous woman.

And you don't get the chance to forget it. Sexy, too. That's why she left my father. I think that's what I'm supposed to think. Life with him was too quiet, in and out of bed. I'm sorry darling, she said to me once, but it was *dullsville*.

The colonel is smiling at me quizzically. I know, I say,

I sound bitter, don't I. But my father was interesting, maybe the most interesting man I've ever known, and, well, Edith isn't.

I find her interesting, says Al.

Oh yes, for a minute, as a phenomenon. Not as a person. And you can spend a lot of time wondering what are the answers to all the questions you ask, that she ignores, and why she does, and waste more time thinking it might all mean something. Whereas I think it might be a cross between a short attention span and malice.

You don't like her much, do you.

Not a lot. But I do love her. I worked that out and now I feel I can cope with not liking her. She's my mother, I love her. It's genetic, not earned. My father I liked, a lot. I'll be truly an orphan when she dies. But I won't be bereft as I was when Dad died, and Gran.

What did he do, I mean, his job—?

He was a public servant. Quite a modest one, I used to think, we lived in a perfectly ordinary house in Hackett, but then I found out he was actually rather important. In the days when such people were very much not the tools of government. I learned to read books from him; the house was extraordinary in that way, walls of books in every room. Edith used to say, Public *servant*, how servile, in a horrible sneering way; one day I said, Less servile than being a *commercial* servant, much more honourable.

You wonder if some way could be devised of bringing up children, without families, said Al.

People have tried, haven't they, and it was usually a frightful failure. The aristocracy with their nannies and boarding schools, and so on. A good family's a brilliant thing, and a bad, well, it's not always bad, and it can be salutary.

Salutary! That's a way of putting it.

I had a family, a good one. When Edith went off, Dad was our family. For me and Linda. And Gran. She was Edith's mother, but she loved Dad too. Edith said once, she left Dad for love, and I always thought how ironical that was, because Dad was the one who knew about love. She left Dad for love, she said, and I realised that she might have been searching for it, and doubtless that's why she left all the other blokes, too, but she didn't know it when she had it.

I poured the last of the second bottle of champagne into our glasses and settled back into the sofa.

Gran used to read me a story, I said, about a little girl who lived in a house on the slope of a valley, and every morning she would look across at a house on the other side of the valley, which had golden windows, and wonder about the people who lived in it, so lucky, so fortunate, to have a house with golden windows. One day she decided she would walk across the valley and see for herself, so she went down the slope and across the bridge and up the other side, a long walk, it took her nearly all day, and when she got there a little girl came out, and the first girl told her she'd walked from the house on the opposite hill, and the little girl said, Oh, you are the person who lives in the house with the golden windows. You are so lucky, it must be so lovely, to live in a house with golden windows.

And the first little girl looked back to where she had

come from, and there was her house, and its windows were shining, splendid, golden.

The colonel smiles, tentatively.

It was the sun, the morning sun, the afternoon sun ... I suddenly can't be bothered explaining, the point of a story is that it is that, a story, not a tract developing a moral. It is itself and it tells you.

So your mother never could see the golden windows in her own house.

And quite likely by then there weren't any. And there's another irony: Edith is boss of that chain of Homemaker shops, and, well, there she is, the original homewrecker. You know their slogan, on the telly? *Let Homemaker put the Heart in your Home.*

I sing it for him. I have to say, I always find it a comfort when life offers a great whacking irony like that. It almost begins to make it worthwhile.

Golden windows, said the colonel. So we all get our turn at them. But when we get them we don't know it, it's only other people that see them. Life is elsewhere.

It's a story, I said. Don't rationalise it out of existence.

I went and got a bottle of riesling out of the fridge. Edith takes me like that. I'd just poured us a glass when there was a knock on the door. I looked through the spyhole. Dermot. It had seemed time to let on that Cassandra was back in the office; this was the result.

So of course I invited him in and poured a glass for him and said, You two know each other, don't you. Both said Hi in rather surly voices. Dermot handed over a large bunch of crimson and orange gerberas. How amazing, I said.

They're rather sculptural, don't you think, said Dermot. Yes, I said, they are, and went to find a vase. I put them in a tall glass cylinder and they did look quite stunning. I think it's too hot for roses, said Dermot.

I always find roses something of a cliché, don't you, said the colonel. A dozen red roses. But then, like all clichés, they exist because we need them.

I took a mouthful of the icy riesling. The two men were sitting at opposite ends of my rather baggy sofa. Baggy, I say, but beautiful too, with a faded rosy chintz and puffy down cushions to sit on. I got it in a garage sale for fifty bucks. I wouldn't have seen myself as a chintzy girl, more sleek leather or perhaps a coarse no-colour linen, but this seduced me. It's interesting, being hard up; decisions made because they are such good bargains may take you on surprising journeys and even turn you into a different person.

I should say something to get the conversation going but am suffering from tired brain. I look at the two guys. Pity Dermot didn't turn up before Edith left. She'd have been impressed. Two chaps. Glowering rather. One with flowers. Edith would certainly recognise the gerberas as a fashionable flower.

Do you . . . begins the colonel. I imagine he's going to say, come here often, and start to giggle, but Dermot has grasped the conversation and is taking off with it. He says, I just called by on the offchance. I have to go away, he says. Business. So boring. And always when you don't want it. Changing one dull office for another dull office and a dreary plane trip between.

His voice has a petulant note. My brain isn't that tired, I realise Dermot is suffering from extreme disappointment. I thought, he says, we might have gone out for a bite . . .

Such a pity, says the colonel, but another time, I'm sure.

Dermot looks baffled. I take another swig of wine. So cold and good. I should be offended; how does Al know I don't want to go and have one of Dermot's bites? In fact I don't, I suddenly can't stop thinking it sounds like some bizarre sexual practice, and anyway I haven't got the energy for dancing round Dermot tonight. So I'm quite grateful. That would be lovely, I say. Some other time. And take another mouthful.

I'm usually good with wine. I love drinking it but I know when to stop. But every now and then something happens to my control mechanism, maybe I fail to pay attention for a moment, and I drink just a tiny bit more than enough, and then I'm doomed, I don't remember I should stop. I think, this is good, let's keep going, why not. So I do.

Al said that travelling for business was overrated, perhaps the most overrated act of modern times, and Dermot said, Yes, indeed that was true, and Al said, But at least you aren't going to a war zone, and Dermot said, I wouldn't be too sure about that. I thought of war zones and how Edith brings them with her, always has done. I remember the lovely rich peace of being with Dad, well if Linda wasn't in one of her states, and with Gran, and then going to visit my mother. I don't know if her guys felt like that. Feel like that. They are always second in command. Edith is the general, maybe she has the scope of the conflict in her head, they tag along obeying orders.

The Apricot Colonel

Dermot said he had to go so I kissed him on both cheeks and said, I hope you won't be terminally bored. He said Alas boredom was rarely terminal but not in the voice of a man making a joke. Al saw him out. He came back and said, We need some food. It's too hot, I said. He went into the kitchen—I say into the kitchen but really it's the same room, it's only psychologically you can go into the kitchen—and cut up a melon. Cool food, he said. Bring some more wine, I said.

He found some raw ham and put that on a platter with the melon, and there was a camembert and some rather dry Italian bread. He didn't bring the wine so I went and got it. Should you, he asked, which under the circumstances was a very good question, but not one I was prepared to hear. So I just glared at him and filled my glass.

I did think I ought to eat something so I cut up a piece of melon into small cubes and speared them one by one with my fork. Al spread some butter thickly on the dry Italian bread and looped the ham over it. Sinful, he said, but so good.

Families, I said. So what about you. Any children? And what about your bachelor state? You've met my mother. My life is an open book to you. What about yours? Isn't it time you told me about yourself?

Al took a bite out of the bread and ham. This tastes like France to me, he said. The countryside. Sweet butter. Thick bread. And this dense chewy meat. A mouthful, and I am in France. This ham is rather French, it's like French raw hams, I thought it might be, that's why I bought it. So I could be for a moment in France.

Where you have a wife and three children, I said. Or is it three wives and a child?

Once I used to think I'd live in France, he said. But now, I can't imagine living anywhere but where I do.

So, I said, you aren't going to tell me. I heard my voice sounding immensely sad. It made him laugh.

My mother had a saying, he said, she was rather fond of it, and I must say it enraged me whenever she said it. Ask me no questions and I'll tell you no lies, she'd say. So many questions I had, and I wanted answers, not this cop out. Once I said, I don't care if you tell me lies, just answer the question. She looked shocked. Lies, Alfred, she said, we must never tell lies.

I understand how you felt. It is enraging, when people refuse to answer. I'm enraged. Alfred—so your name is Alfred.

Yes. After my grandfather. What a burden that was. I turned into Al as soon as I could.

It's a noble name. Anglo-Saxon kings and all that.

It's all right to say that now. When you're a kid and the only one in the school with such a funny old fuddy-duddy name it's a different story, let me tell you.

What about Fred?

Freddo Frog? No better.

You could spell it Aelfraed, I said. It means elf-counsel, you know. And elves aren't funny little tiny fairy men, not at all, they're powerful spirits of nature. Look at Tolkien.

How do you know all this?

Reading my name book.

You looked me up?

It's one of my favourite pastimes. Some names are dreadful, they have sinister meanings. And Al, Al sounds like a United States marine.

Jesus no.

Maybe I'll start calling you Alfred. Or Aelfraed.

Would you? Mm. Would you really?

I had spoken out of mischief, in fact, so then I felt a bit mean. I nearly told him I wasn't Cassandra really, I was Sandra, but I was angry with his bland blind refusal to tell me anything about himself. Forgetting he'd have already heard Edith calling me Sandra. Maybe he thought it was a diminutive. I poured out another glass of wine.

Anyway, I said, Ask me no questions and I'll tell you no lies . . . Why not some truths? Why do questions have to be answered with lies? Why not, ask me a question and I'll tell you the truth?

I suppose my mother had her reasons. Children and their impertinent questions.

Oh, so my questions are impertinent?

I was meaning my mother and me.

And by extrapolation, me.

You're far too charming ever to be impertinent.

I snorted. Well, do you have any children?

An interesting question. One that all women and very few men can answer with conviction. All women know, yes they have, no they haven't. Almost no man can be sure—of some, yes, but can he ever say, with confidence, no, none? What about you?

So, are there any you're sure about?

Who's not answering questions now?

Words are war games for you, aren't they.

I think I'll make some coffee. Would you like some?

No thanks. It might keep me awake. I sat at the table, taking little sips of the wine, then called out after him, What about, Tell the truth and shame the devil?

He came back to the dining table. My mother said that too. But, I dunno, do you reckon the devil is that easy to shame?

I suddenly felt very tired. Tired brain, tired body. I'm going to bed, I said. Like a French general I took him by the shoulders and planted a kiss on each cheek. Sleep well, I said.

Chapter 13

I slept solidly and woke up early feeling tired. That's what drinking a lot of wine usually does to me. Not a hangover or a sick stomach, just tiredness. I lay in bed thinking. I wasn't suffering tired brain any more, that was zimming away energetically, if not frenetically, while my body flopped in a catatonic state and let it go. I told myself it was time to do some thinking. Things were disorderly. I needed to straighten them out.

The murders. The murderer was still at large. Of course if he was Harold Perrot he was in hospital in a coma, so I and any other potential victims were safe from him, at the moment. So I should *feel* safe. If he wasn't the murderer, and I knew I had no idea whether he was or not, just feared that he could be, might be, but if he wasn't then I didn't need to see myself in any particular danger. No more than any youngish woman living in O'Connor with a serial killer at large in the suburbs. He did seem to prefer women living in security blocks—I was assuming he—and that cut me out. On the other hand, and this was a new thought, he did seem to go after women with their own businesses, free-lancers, an IT consultant and an escort girl, so maybe that counted me in. Could you call an escort girl a freelancer? She worked for an agency, but so do most of us. Irregular jobs, needing a sequence of clients, susceptible to being contacted by strangers in the line of work (I thought of the colonel, a perfect stranger getting in touch); you could describe them in such a way that they had a lot in common. Different kinds of interaction, of course, some more hands on than others, or rather, the hands on different things.

But there was an order in which to set possibilities and perceptions. If it was Harold Perrot, we were all safe at the moment. If it wasn't I wasn't any more in danger than anybody. Good. So forget murder and get on with life.

Wait a minute. The colonel. Did he need to be here?

Yes, said brain. For a bit. Then see what happens.

Okay. That's settled. What about work?

I was doing the autobiography of some kid who had sailed solo round the world. A lone teenage yachtsperson. He'd written his story. Actually, his mother had written it for him, but we all went along with the fiction that it was his words as well as his journey. I doubt that was the only fiction in it. I know it'll sell a mozza. People love true stories. However lying and boastful. My job is to turn it into readable prose without losing the naïve charm of the eighteen-year-old boy/thirty-nine-year-old mother. Easy enough. Cut out the verbiage and the worst of the solecisms. *As a child my mother encouraged me* ... amazing how many people can't see anything wrong with that. Give them a more obvious howler of the same construction—*Walking round the corner the church came into view*—and they'll usually get it, but they have no problem with the child-mother's encouragement.

Anyway this is a simple commercial project. No writer defending her deathless prose to the death. Bestseller = dollar signs, not stars in the eyes. Should ask for a share of the royalties.

And of course there's the colonel ticking away. He'd brought me a chapter to read, and I must say, he's learned. Now he's writing simply, without his prose flashing its message in florid fluorescent colours, he's getting a really powerful narration. He's letting the matter do the talking. There's a lovely bit, a description of a news briefing given in February 1991 by General Norman Schwarzkopf, Stormin Norman as he was nicknamed, reminding everyone that the purpose of war was to enforce the resolutions of the United Nations, where the general talks about the Iraqi airforce as *he* and *him*: 'We knew he had very very limited reconnaissance means . . . we wanted him to concentrate his resources—which he did.'

It's so wonderfully surreal, I'd said to Al, the idea of the airforce as a single person.

Surreal? That's a good thing?

Of course.

The smell of coffee penetrates the bedroom. I remember I am still enraged with the colonel. It does smell good. It's getting hot up here. Downstairs will be cool still. My body is feeling a little energised by the simple smell of the coffee. A cup, two cups, I could wake up quite nicely.

Al had already got the paper. I don't take it normally. I could still be sitting in the kitchen drinking coffee and reading the personal columns at midday if I did, and there's nothing in it to read anyway—this is the paradox of the freelance worker, that you can spend all morning reading a contentless newspaper, on the grounds that you need to know what is going on in the world, the city, whatever. It takes a hell of a lot of willpower to resist the call of the newsprint, it's easier not to get it.

He'd also bought croissants, in a pile on a blue plate. They made me notice how hungry I was, after my dinner of three melon cubes the night before.

No news, he said. But he passed me the paper folded open at social page photographs. People at the ballet. Belinda Sissons. Andrew Sissons. Molly Vander-Browne. Belinda looks dauntingly handsome, all cheekbones, taut skin, hair drawn back, eyes enormous and violet blue, looking like some grand old iconic prima ballerina. She has the sort of face the camera loves, but that the human eye may see less kindly. Andrew beside her is a little pudgy, short, or possibly not, but considerably shorter than Belinda. Molly will be horrified at her picture, and will not be able to bring herself to believe she actually looks like that.

No mention of Hotbaby, said Al. Or of ming-blue woman.

I'd meant to be quite distant with him. Speak in rare cool syllables. But I am not good at this. Was always trying with Bryce, when I was annoyed with him. But then he'd say something interesting, I'm a sucker for the interesting. And actually my standards aren't very high, even faintly interesting will do. And suddenly ice-maiden Cassandra is in a conversation and enjoying herself.

So he might be out of hospital, I said.

I'll find out, said Al. But as he picked up the phone it rang, so he handed it to me. It was for me. A publisher. One of the grandest. A novel. The novelist one of the grandest. At one time, anyway. I hear some doubt, some faint hint of . . . it's hard to catch, nothing is said, but somehow I get the impression that this book might . . . a putative masterpiece, should be a . . . could be a . . . a great book . . . Here it comes: needs sensitive editing.

Needs sensitive editing. Don't they all. Of course I say yes. I'll knock the lone teenage yachtsperson over in no time. I even mention a fee. I'm getting bold. And remembering what I charged the colonel. A high fee. The publisher coughs. She agrees. Curiouser and curiouser.

Al was studiously not listening. I hung up and handed him the phone. Looks like I can go on eating, I said.

He went into the garden to ring. He is a private telephoner, and a pacer. If he were ordering a case of wine or a kilo of prawns he would go off and pace while he did it. Naturally secretive. I wonder how he'll find out if Hotbaby is still in hospital. I shan't ask.

No change, said Al, coming back inside. Still in a coma. His face purses up. Must have been quite a whack he got.

I can't feel sorry for him. But what if he's innocent? A car detailer whose hobby is souped-up old cars who just happens to have no social graces, but is kind? I don't actually know he wanted to jump on me.

The colonel's been sleeping at my place but he spends a lot of time in his own apartment, in a block of old government housing just off Northbourne Avenue. His pad, he calls it. Says it's quite spacious, as they were in the good old days, but basic, sitting room bedroom bathroom kitchen. I expect you've made it interesting, I said, and he grinned: Well, why not. He hasn't invited me there.

He'd got into the habit of disappearing and leaving me alone to work. It was still hot but downstairs stays cool. I've bought some solid metal flyscreens, of wrought iron like something out of a Moorish palace, so I can have the doors open but still feel secure; they muck up Elspeth's cat door so I have to get up and let her in, she's put out that she can't go and come as she pleases. I've taken to getting up early and getting well away with my work before the heat sets in. I polished off the lone yachtsperson and got on to the novel.

Wow.

The book is a large work by a very fine artist writing at the peak of their powers (yes, I know, the ugly plural, but I don't want to say his or her, just as I am mentioning no names, this is all highly confidential, I'm probably saying too much as it is, some people might guess) or perhaps not, perhaps teetering on that height, slipping down the other side. Writing with an edginess, yes, and a disturbing surreal quality, and I know that surreal has always been a mode with this writer, but here, the control is by no means certain. You can accept it, and go dizzy and dazzled along with it, or you can allow a cautious wonder, should this be so? Are we starting to tumble down that dangerously quick slope of the other side?

All this metaphor is a way of saying that the great writer is maybe losing it a bit. Is maybe a little bit mad. There are superb things, but does it really work? I read it through twice, not consciously thinking about it, trying to be a normal keen not-expecting-to-be-critical reader.

I've edited this writer before, several books ago, and always with the certain faith that what was on the page was what was meant, that it was absolutely right, though maybe needing occasional help from me to find its even truer expression. Now—I can see why the publisher agreed so undemurringly to the fee.

I decide to regard it as a masterpiece slightly out of control, not the dodgy result of a fine imagination in the process of losing itself. I need to be rather more handmaiden than usual. It makes me tense, it's exciting in a worrying way. Adrenalin stuff. You can cruise comfortably along with teenage yachtspersons but they're pretty boring. Nervousness and fear are so much more . . . fun, really.

The colonel came and went, we ate meals and drank appropriate amounts of wine. One morning he said: I think I should run down to the coast. There should be another crop of apricots. I'll go for a few days. Do some work on the book, I work better there. But I'll keep in touch with Hotbaby's case and whiz back if he gets out. Not that he'll be doing much murdering for a while, I think he's going to be pretty safely in hospital a while yet.

Hotbaby safely in hospital. He might die, might never wake up, might get turned off. But we can say safely.

I did think this break could be a good thing. I liked the sense of protection I got from Al's presence, but I was still in part enraged by his refusal to tell me about himself. Maybe a space on my own would be good. After all I couldn't live with him forever.

On Saturday I went to the peace march. I know I reckon the prime minister has made up his mind, will jump when Bush tells him to. But really concerted public opinion—I have to believe it may be taken notice of. My neighbour Mary was going so we rode our bikes. It's Mary who belongs to cat Elspeth, she's a schoolteacher and lives in the other half of my duplex. She has a teenage son, a nice boy who mows my lawns for me and waters if I'm away. We made a vague arrangement to meet various friends there. In fact, it was hopeless, there was a huge mob. But I did see a lot of people I knew, at varying distances. Cleo and Paul and the kids. Annie Tricks. Sally. Daniel. Useful bachelor Philip, with a friend, in matching shaven heads and oblong glasses. I thought I saw shirtwaist woman, but too far away. I almost expected to see Hotbaby. I wondered how this would have compared with the anti-Vietnam marches. It was impossible to pigeonhole people as old hippies or greenies or whatever, the kind of alternatives and ferals who can be dismissed as rent-a-crowd for any anti-government activity, or a ragbag of professional protestors nostalgic for the heady days of Vietnam. Plenty of the middle-aged and middle class. Lots of young people. Prosperous forty-year-olds with toddlers in pushers. Natty weekend-casual dressers.

There were speeches it was difficult to hear because the PA system couldn't cope with the vast crowd. After a bit we set out to walk around Civic. At the first corner a man with a camera and a woman with a microphone poked both in our faces. What were we doing here? Mary stepped back so I said swiftly and slowly: Protesting against the war. War is never a good idea.

We had not been among the first to start on the march through the streets, but when we got back to Garema Place the last had not left. I liked the idea of this continuous great plait of people forming a net around the city.

That night I saw it on the news, it went out on ABC National and there it was, from the air, that huge fluid teeming serpent of people winding its way round Civic, a perfectly circular movement, without beginning or end. It gave me a lump in my throat. And there I was, saying very clearly: *Protesting against the war. War is never a good idea.* I had been wearing a voluminous lemon-coloured shirt I'd bought in the Plaka in Athens, dark glasses and a big shady hat. I thought nobody would recognise me. But all my friends caught it. Bryce called, keeping civil as he has decided we should. The publisher of the grand novel rang. Even Linda in Brisbane. The colonel from the coast, full of admiration, though I did wonder how much he was teasing. The waitress at Tilley's said, Saw you on the telly. A split second, my short sharp words, and such mobs of people had heard them and seen me. I imagined the prime minister thinking, by golly, she's right. Yes.

Chapter 14

Cleo organised her dinner party for the Sunday after the march, and organised Dermot to bring me. He turned up early on the grounds we could go and have a nice quiet drink tête-à-tête first. I'd been at work on the novel. It felt a bit like Halley's comet, when people said you had to look at it out of the corner of your eye, if you looked full on you wouldn't see it. I was afraid if I looked too carefully at this I would fail to see it, but the fact is that's my job, I had to gaze at it with cold clear editor's eyes, and if I couldn't see it full on then maybe it wasn't there to see. I rather thought that with Halley's comet, too.

So I was wearing a singlet top and shorts and feeling sweaty and whiffy, quite enjoying this state because in a little while I'd go and have a lovely chilly shower and get all fresh and scented, but postponing it minute by minute and so leaving it a bit late as is my wont, I always believe I can be quick and take less time. I never learn by being frequently unready. I gave Dermot a bottle and a glass and went to get cleaned up.

I was in the shower when Marcus and Edith called, so Dermot let them in. I came down and found them all in the study, Dermot waving the wine bottle and Marcus saying No no he was driving, but coffee would be lovely and he could make it. Edith was eyeing Dermot as though he'd just blown in the window. I was pretty stunned to see them, Edith never comes without formal arrangement.

We had to call in, said Marcus, we'd been to this winery at Rutherglen and tasted this superb sauvignon blanc and I said we have to take some of this to Cassandra—wait till you taste it.

The bottles were on my little hall table. Edith looked as though they were nothing to do with her, as I'm sure they weren't. She's not given to presents. Clever Marcus, one visit and he'd worked out I was Cassandra and liked sauvignon blanc. My mother never had. I asked were they staying the night but Edith said they had to get back to Sydney. Marcus is a demon driver, she said, we'll be there in no time.

I showed Marcus the coffee things and went back to the room. Edith was staring at Dermot who didn't seem to be doing his usual Irish charm thing. I thought anything in a skirt rated this and Edith though clearly she isn't young, well, not that clearly, you'd never guess she's as old as she is, Edith is glamorous. I expected them to be flirting outrageously. But they were morose.

I was wearing my black linen Eastern Pearson skirt and a neat fitting little scooped top of pale green cotton. Edith squinted at me. You're looking very smart, she said, in a voice that would have been surprised if it could have been bothered. I always did scrub up well, I said.

Marcus was quite subdued too. I guessed at some argument over dropping in with the wine. It wasn't an

Edithian act. So why do it? Maybe Marcus wasn't the usual pushover? When he brought in the coffee Dermot excused himself and went out, coming back with a street directory of Canberra. Just checking I know the way to Cleo's, he said.

Haven't you been there before?

Oh yes, but you can't be too careful. You know the old Canberra torturous streets.

I refrained from saying, You mean tortuous. I do know how smart girls should behave. Dermot did look anxious. The roguish Irish charm, faux Irish it might be but lilting and truly charming, seemed to have vanished. His mouth pinched and he looked worried, turning his face away from the company and peering in a corner at the map.

I know the way, I said in the sort of gentle voice you use for talking to dim people. Cleo's my oldest friend, remember?

How is Cleo, asked Edith, and I said she was well. Three children now, I said. She's a clever girl, said Edith.

Marcus has a dark and wicked face, that you could call merry. He has a lot of black curly hair and eyes of a blue so pale it looks grey. His cheeks fold in fine pleats down to a sharp jawline, and his skin is finely stubbled black. I make these observations because we are sitting not talking, Dermot fiddling with his street directory, Marcus managing to look mildly diabolical as he sips his coffee, Edith holding her cup with afternoon tea manners. I offered Dermot more wine, but he said, better not, he was driving, he'd save up for Cleo's.

When I went to the kitchen to get a glass of water Marcus opened the back door and beckoned me into the garden. Maybe there was a secret and I was about to learn it.

I don't think Edith is terribly well, he said.

What? What do you . . .

Nothing serious, a bit of a cold coming on, I think.

I wondered if he meant this. I said: Maybe you should stay, not drive back.

She's keen to get home.

You could stay here, the colonel's away, I've got room.

She won't want to, said Marcus. But ask her. By the way, is Dermot all right?

What do you mean?

Oh, I dunno, all right. Doesn't matter.

Why wouldn't he be?

I just wondered how well you knew him.

He's a colleague of a friend's.

Ah. Marcus shrugged and went back inside.

He was right; when I asked Edith to stay she shook her head and said she had to get back, and I knew there was no pressing her. They got in her BMW and drove off, and so did we in Dermot's beautiful sporty job. I thought about Marcus; he seemed a nice man, and kind. Maybe Edith had found love at last. Maybe that was why she hadn't been flirting. But she should have been happy, and there was not calm or content in her. Maybe she wasn't well. I felt a twinge of concern. Surely Edith would be in robust health for years yet, so young and fit as she looks.

Dermot doesn't say much on the drive to Cleo's which takes about five minutes, but he finds the Irish charm. By the time he parks and zips round to open my door it's as though he's kissed the blarney stone on the way over. Handing me out, nursing my hand, looking down on me with doting eyes. Doing the gesture with his hand shaping but not touching my hair, the ravished solemn look, the barely breathed Beautiful. I have to say, repetition had rather robbed it of its oomph.

We were a bit late so the other guests had already arrived. They turned towards us and filled the air with funny little cries. *Here's the star! Will it be more than fifteen minutes of fame? I reckon it's an academy award. Bravo bravo. Wonderful performance.* It took me some seconds to realise they were talking about the peace march.

Good grief, I said. I didn't know absolutely everybody in the world watches the ABC News.

You were repeated a fair few times, said Cleo.

I didn't think anybody would recognise me.

Unmistakable, said Claude Vander-Browne.

It did occur to me that at least some of the people present were not likely to approve of the peace march. Cleo is much more left-wing than a lot of her acquaintances. I wonder how she can stand it.

It was good to have it said so clearly, said Philip the gay bachelor.

I said: It was very exciting. I don't see how the government can ignore us. All over the country, ordinary people saying, so loudly, we do not want this war. Government has to listen.

You think public protest can save us, asked Paul. I did feel moved when I saw such a seething mass of humanity. And, as you say, all over the country. You reckon they'll listen?

Governments can't ignore that kind of message, said Philip.

Andrew Sissons spoke. Howard has already made up his mind.

We all stared at him. You think so?

Yes. He has agreed with Bush that they will have this war. And this war they will have.

He says it is still not decided. Would Howard lie so comprehensively? This was Belinda.

Yes, said Cleo.

The troops are on their way, said Andrew.

Andrew is our man in Caracas. He speaks with authority.

A sad silence fell. The cute guy Cleo has in to help with parties brought round more drinks. Champagne mixed with mashed peaches.

Bellinis, said Dermot.

Heavenly, said Molly.

The cute guy looked at Philip, into his eyes. An odd thing for a waiter to do. But then he's not really a professional. Bill's a law student. Handsome. Wearing tight clean designer jeans and a white shirt. Slightly given to twirling. But why not add a little flourish to the scene.

There was a time when we couldn't go to a restaurant or a bar without being served by the children's friends, said Molly. But they do grow up.

And get real jobs. Thank god, said Claude.

Did your children do that, I asked.

Oh yes, said Molly. Everybody's children are excellent waiters. Yours will be one of these days, Cleo.

Come the revolution, it will be extremely handy, said Philip. But Molly gave him a look. You don't even joke about revolutions.

Belinda was wearing a straight blue linen dress the colour of her old profession. Bluebell. With a narrow piping of a sharp lime green colour. You knew by its arrogant folds that it cost a bomb. I murmured to Cleo, How's the London–Caracas axis? But she glared at me. We were on a terrace, under cloisters forming a U-shape round the swimming pool. The sea breeze had arrived and the air was cool. The bellinis came in flutes with long spoons to scoop out the last of the peach pulp.

In Harry's Bar, in Venice, where they were invented, said Dermot, they use spumante. If the peaches are very sweet, they use a dry one. If they're a bit sharp, a sweeter one. Very scientific.

Fancy that, said Belinda. Her voice was gentle, but I wondered if she was laughing at him.

Have we got the sweetness/sharpness right, asked Cleo.

He took her hand and kissed it. To perfection, as ever, he said.

I certainly didn't use spumante, she said. I know the Italian one can be delicious but here they are pretty universally disgusting.

Cleo's children came out to say goodnight, walking prettily among the guests, kissing cheeks. Caspar and Lily. Baby Pomona was already in bed. They took my hands and I went with them to tuck them up. I'm their godmother. I have made all sorts of wonderful but daunting promises on their behalf. I told Cleo she better not die and leave me stuck with keeping them.

When I come back we sit down to dinner, at a long table under one of the cloisters. Paul and Bill the waiter bring food. It's Middle Eastern, Turkish, the food of Cleo's heritage. Great platters, some hot, some cold, of gorgeous vegetables, and rice and barley, lamb and chicken, fat prawns. There is ginger and cinnamon, saffron and cumin, garlic and onions. Sticky brown raisins and quinces the colour of carnelian. The scents are so spicy and savoury they make my mouth water.

It's a banquet, said Claude.

I know where this food comes from. Not Cleo, though she could if she had to. Her mother. I shall have to kill you if you tell anyone, she once said to me, it's my secret. It's so brilliant, I said.

My parents weren't always office cleaners, you know. My mother knows how to do elegant food.

The old lady will have been busy for days in her own kitchen and then in Cleo's. Cleo reckons she likes doing it. I think she could have the credit. But it is part of Cleo's perfection to produce wonderful leisured food on top of everything else.

I ate a sheep's eye once, said Andrew.

How could you, shrieked Molly.

It was given to me in the sultan's own fingers. How could I refuse?

Bill went round filling glasses. I was glad Dermot was driving so I didn't have to count. The air was scented with jasmine and citrus blossom wafted on the faint breeze, mingled with the savoury meats and spices and garlicky vegetables. There was a gibbous moon, high in the violet blue sky, its reflection cobbled in the breeze-ruffled water of the pool. Gibbous is one of my favourite words. If you used it of a person, though I can't say I've ever come across anyone doing so, it would mean they were hunch-backed. Here it means humped, a moon more than half but not quite full.

This air, scented, fresh, not cold or blustery, or still and smoky as so often happens in Canberra nights; I think, Cleo can make even the weather behave.

You could imagine, said Andrew, beside me, that just over that wall was the Bosphorus. The Golden Horn.

Leander swimming to his Hero.

A displeasing concubine sewn in a sack and thrown from the wall of the Topkapi palace.

He spoke softly, in a sensuous voice. I shivered. At least, I started to say, women don't have to suffer those fates any more, but stopped myself, it was not a fortunate thing to say to the father of a young woman murdered. At least, I said, we can imagine the good bits and not have to worry about the cruel parts.

He spoke even more softly. Can I come and see you? In the next few days?

I stared at him.

On a professional matter. I have your card.

Of course, I said.

Dessert came. Little glass dishes of rosewater ices. Sweetmeats, fruits, nuts, Turkish delight, on green leaf-shaped plates scattered with rose petals. Sweet wine in tiny glass cups. People started to change seats.

There were faint murmurings and cluckings from behind the wall and then a sudden flurry of squawks.

Fox in the henhouse, said Dermot, with such a wry face that he made me smile.

Surely there aren't any foxes in Canberra, said Molly.

Oh yes, said Pedro, at my mum's house in Ainslie a fox got in and killed three of her chooks. She was very upset. They all had names.

A fox in the henhouse, said Cleo. Not that I wish any harm to the chickens, but the rooster and his dawn awakenings . . . I sometimes imagine a delicious *coq au vin*, with real cock.

Ah, real cock, said Philip in a dreamy way. Bill giggled.

Cleo took my arm. Come and see Pierre, she said, and slid her arm through mine and took me to the end of the cloister, where roses twined over a pergola, their long canes covered with luscious creamy pink flowers.

How's Dermot?

Where's Pierre?

Pierre de Ronsard. The rose. I've been waiting for years for him to flower like this. Come on. Dermot.

Courting, it would seem.

Cass! Oh how marvellous. It is what you want, isn't it?

I don't know about Dermot. He keeps wanting to see me, be involved in my life. I don't think I fancy him.

Don't you know?

Hardly had a chance to find out.

Courtship leads to marriage.

Yeah. I can't picture it.

Are you trying to be a confirmed spinster?

Why do all married women think marriage is what all their unmarried friends want?

Don't they?

I sigh. For a modern woman you sound like my gran.

Just go with it, says Cleo.

Cleo, can you see me married to Dermot?

Remember how unsuitable Mr Darcy seemed. Elizabeth Bennet thought she couldn't stand him.

Ladies and roses, said Claude, loudly. Ladies and roses. The sweet and the sweet.

I thought you meant prickly, said Cleo, and that was the end of our conversation.

On the way home in the car Dermot said in a thoughtful voice, Your mother is a beautiful woman, isn't she. And so is Belinda. I think my mother was, too. He spoke in an inward way, and I turned my face to him and waited for him to go on. After a pause I said, Was?

I suppose when you're small your mother is always beautiful. She left when I was still pretty young. Five, to be precise.

Like Edith.

I suppose so. She used to come and take me out sometimes, at the beginning anyway. I remember the first time she came, she gave me a kind of hug—you know how people have air-kisses? Looking back, this was an air hug—and then she said, straightaway, And how are my chooks? She said it sort of to herself. How are my chooks? How could I bear to go away and leave my chooks? Then she turned to me and said, Dermot, promise you'll look after my chooks.

And did you? It would've made me want to strangle the lot of them.

It made me wish I was a chook. I did look after them, as I recall, but not for long, my father got rid of them, and then it seemed to me my mother didn't come and get me any more. He said she had a new family now and that kept her busy. I wondered, if he'd kept the chooks, would she have kept on coming?

Dermot's voice sounded so desolate that I put my hand on his knee and smoothed it gently. I maybe don't know as much as I might about a mother's desertion, thanks to my father and Gran, but I know enough. He put his hand over mine and held it, until he needed that hand to drive.

It's a sad story, I said.

That's life, isn't it; a series of sad stories?

I felt a bit sad that so far I hadn't had to fend off any love-making from Dermot. I thought that maybe tonight was the night. When we got out of the car he pulled me to him, I felt his lean chest against mine. I kissed him on the lips, did a half turn and drew him through the gate in the hedge. If we were going to snog it needn't be in the street. His passion could take that much postponement.

Before I could put my key in the lock the door opened. It was the colonel.

Chapter 15

It's funny, when I stand beside the colonel he seems tall, I have to look up at him, and then when he's sitting down beside me he is shorter than I am. He is sitting beside me on my puffy sofa now, and I am looking down on him.

When he opened the door he said, Your phone's been ringing all night. Nobody leaves a message though.

Dermot said he wouldn't come in, what a surprise, though I can't say I'm as upset as I ought to be with the colonel mucking up my love life, and grumbled off in his beautiful little yellow Peugeot. There's a chick magnet, I say to Al. The car I mean.

Surely, a thinking woman's magnet, says Al. Along with its driver.

I'm thirsty, after all Cleo's rich food, and get some iced water to drink; he joins me. This is how we come to be sitting on the sofa when the phone rings. I look at him, down at him. He gets up and goes to answer it.

Now I see why he stands so tall and sits so short. He has extremely long legs. Like a supermodel's, they go all the way up to his armpits.

I'll put her on, he says. It's Marcus.

Cassandra? We're still here. Something strange has happened. I think it's strange.

What? Again I feel that flip of fear. Is Edith all right? She's okay?

As okay as can be expected.

Marcus, what's happened?

It's hard to say. We stopped off at the supermarket at Lyneham, just to get a few provisions, save having to run around at the other end, and all the shops would be shut anyway. So we did that, and Edith bumped into some old friend, and we stood around and chatted for a while, not too long, I didn't think . . .

Who?

What do you mean, who?

The friend.

Oh, Jan I think. Tall and skinny with iron grey hair. Anyway, then we got in the car, but after a short while it wouldn't go properly. Strangely bumpy. Wouldn't steer. I had to fight it on to the verge, nearly ran into a tree. And when I looked it had two flat tyres. Two. On the same side.

That's bad luck.

Luck, you reckon? I reckon it'd been tampered with. Two tyres, too much of a coincidence.

Who by?

Well, I don't know that, do I.

Maybe you ran over something, some glass, or something. And it pierced both tyres.

Maybe. Can't have them fixed till tomorrow. Should have some idea then.

Do you want to stay here?

We're at the Rex. Well, it was close. Reasonable. I just wanted to let you know. Edith's pretty shaken.

Marcus sounds rather shaken too. I say, If it was tampered with it's probably just kids. Idiots skylarking, thinking it's a fun thing to do.

If we hadn't stayed talking to Jan, if we'd got out on the open highway, the BMW gets to a hundred and twenty kays in no time, and they'd blown at that speed, we'd have died.

Oh Marcus. But you didn't. And maybe if you hadn't talked to Jan they wouldn't have been damaged.

The slashers might have been kids, but they just missed being murderers. If it was kids.

I hear Edith calling. Gotta go, he says. I'll ring tomorrow.

He makes it sound so sinister, I say to Al. Do you think it is?

Probably not. You look buggered. You should go to bed.

Thanks.

Strange things happen, says the colonel. Strange things are always happening. Then several at once, and you feel bothered by them, maybe even threatened. But it's quite likely just an unusually large number of strange things happening to happen all at once.

All just happenstance, I say. By the way, why are you back?

Hotbaby's out of hospital. Discharged himself.

Oh.

See what I mean? Strange things, no connection.

We hope. I thought for a moment. So, he's obviously out of his coma.

Yes. Several days ago. I didn't tell you, since, well, he was still in hospital.

Maybe Hotbaby let down the tyres.

Why would he do that?

He's a serial killer. They're mad.

Only to an extent. If he is a serial killer.

We've got to find out where he is.

Cassandra Travers, girl detective.

You say that, I may have to kill you.

That's not a proper thing for a girl detective to say.

Considering that so far I haven't managed to do a single piece of girl detecting, does it matter?

Which do you object to? Girl, or detective?

You know perfectly well. The whole thing's a put-down.

Next morning, when we were having breakfast, Al says: You're a sunny creature, aren't you.

What?

Sunny. You're cheerful, normally.

I think of all the times I've meant to be cold and taciturn and failed. Am I, I said.

A lot of women—people, I suppose—are naturally gloomy. Do you ever see the darkness of things?

I look at him. This is a hard question to answer at breakfast. Well, I say, if I am naturally cheerful, I could still see darkness, couldn't I?

I dunno. That's why I'm asking.

Why am I answering your questions? You never answer mine.

Because you are sunny. You don't naturally feel the darkness of things.

Rubbish, I say. But then I wonder if it's true. I have noticed I am optimistic. Equable. Certainly not good at icy silences. Or tit-for-tat bad behaviour.

When everything's normal, you're happy, says Al.

Isn't everyone?

The fact that you can ask! No.

I drink some coffee. Oh my god! Hotbaby. I've forgotten Hotbaby. Harold Perrot.

See. Naturally cheerful.

It's having you here. Bodyguard. Or, no, you're my worry doll. I feel no fear.

You're supposed to put worry dolls under your pillow.

You'd be too bumpy.

You wouldn't notice. You wouldn't be worrying.

It's not true, of course. I do feel fear.

Andrew rang and arranged to come in the afternoon. I had a morning appointment to have my hair cut, the ends were getting straggly, and when I got home Al had a message from Marcus. The tyres had been deliberately damaged, each one had a number of slits in it, consistent with having been stabbed with a thin sharp blade.

So they had been vandalised, I said.

Or tampered with.

What are you saying?

Well, said Al, vandalism's mindless, damage for the fun of it. Tampering has an end in view.

I admired this distinction for a moment. You think somebody was trying to kill them? How unlikely is that?

No, no, I'm not saying that. I'm saying, if you say tampering that's the path you're taking.

That's black. I'm seeing a terrible blackness there.

Ah, but you're standing in sunlight. You're not in the darkness.

Yes, but I have to fear that it might envelop me.

You don't, you know, you don't have to fear that.

Are the tyres mended? Have they left?

The tyres are done. But I think they're going to go to the police. Marcus left a mobile number.

I ring it but it doesn't answer. I thought of an old French movie I'd seen, 1970, *film noir*, long before mobile phones. I liked that, you knew where you were. In the *merde* mostly, but you knew it. No false hopes. And everybody was in the same deep doodoo. Reminded me of those novels where people killed themselves if they didn't get an answer by return of post. Early last century, and before. No thinking, maybe the mails are slow. You knew they never were. Nor were the correspondents. These days you'd have to wait a few weeks to be sure, and probably ring up as well, just to check it wasn't altogether lost, or the person had been too busy. Simple times, simple certainties. None of this electronic voice yapping on, your call is important to us.

Andrew Sissons came in the early afternoon. It was another stinker of a day. The kind of weather that sizzles your eyeballs. We sat in the relative coolness of the room and drank bubbly mineral water with lots of ice.

I feel I should apologise for the weather, I said. Still, I suppose, Caracas, you're used to the heat.

Hardly. Caracas might be in the tropics but its usual summer temperature is something like twenty-five degrees.

Oh, I said. How lovely.

And it's not so dry. Fresher.

I realise, I said, I don't know much about Caracas.

The capital of Venezuela, he said. Venezuela—isn't it a musical name—Venezuela means little Venice, after its water-dwelling people. It's on the Caribbean. The great river is the Orinoco.

The Orinoco. (I don't mention the Wombles.) Thank you, I said. I like useful information.

I'm not so sure about useful, he said.

I like useless information too. Any information, really.

Andrew in the newspaper photograph looked pudgy and short, but in the flesh he's quite tall and trim, with a solid body but not fat. He's a handsome man; I think Belinda could have married him at least partly for his looks. For his body. I wonder is her body why he married her. The only reason? *For only God, my dear, Could love you for yourself alone, And not your yellow hair.* I do in theory know I'm lucky not to have been born too amazingly beautiful; Yeats understood the problems.

Will you go back? To Venezuela?

I am due for more time there. It's difficult to think of the future . . . though that is partly why I have come to see you.

I opened my eyes wide and waited.

Tamara . . . Tamara had written a book. Ostensibly about her mother.

You've read it?

A quick glance through. Belinda doesn't know. Well, I don't know what Belinda knows. Belinda may or may not know, but she is behaving as if she doesn't. Refusing to know, perhaps.

So that explained Belinda's response at the bushfire benefit. I said, Do you know why? Why she's refusing?

He smiled a melancholy and anxious smile. I said it is a book ostensibly about Belinda. It is a book absolutely about Belinda. But it's also about Tamara, and me. As I said, I've just glanced . . . It could be a novel. A stranger to the events it describes would I imagine consider it a novel. They have that heightened, dare I say lurid, quality.

Not all novels are lurid.

Possibly not. This one is.

But you said, it's a biography. An autobiography.

Apparently. Perhaps she believed that is what she was writing.

Andrew was silent, and I waited for him.

My instinct is to destroy it. But my nature, my habit . . . I have a great respect for the written word. And it seems cavalier—cruel—foolish—to destroy the words of Tamara when we have so utterly lost her.

He paused again, and I waited again.

But then, will we lose her again, through this wretched book? He shook his head, like a man emerging from a diving pool, his hair plastered to his cheeks. I understand you are an editor by profession. Maybe she had already consulted you? I am wondering, could you have a look at it for me . . .

What do you want me to tell you?

I hardly know. What you think of it, I suppose. It's value . . .

You mean with a view to selling it? Publishing it?

No, not at all. With a view to valuing it, in the sense of . . . is it a document worth keeping? Is it of intrinsic value, to us . . .

Wouldn't you be a better judge than me?

It's rather painful . . . I would pay appropriately, of course. What do I want from you? That you should tell me it's rubbish, and ought to be thrown away? That it is a work of skill and honour and ought to be treasured? I don't know. I want you to read it and tell me . . . the truth, I suppose.

His smile now was rather cold. You will tell me I am a brave man, asking for the truth.

I couldn't do it straightaway. Not for a week or so.

Whenever. I know you are busy.

Is it on disk? On her computer?

No, that's an odd thing. There's nothing at all on her computer. It's literally a manuscript, a pile of printed-out pages.

She's probably got everything saved on disk somewhere. Some writers I know keep their disks in safety deposit boxes in banks.

Really?

Too many grim tales in the trade—I know of one novelist who was banging away happily on her third novel, had her computer stolen, no back up, appealed to the thieves, haunted second hand computer shops, no luck. She's never written another word.

What a cautionary tale.

I got us more bubbly water. Andrew said he'd deliver the manuscript in the next few days.

One thing I have to ask, he said. Absolute discretion. I'd like no one to know about this. Certainly not Belinda. But no one else either. He tapped the side of his nose. Our secret.

Of course, I said, in my primmest voice. Editors always work in confidence.

That's our story, anyway.

2003 was proving a very interesting year for work. And it was still hardly past the dead after-Christmas season. Love wasn't doing too well, but work was great. The teenage yachtsperson was pretty run of the mill, but all the rest, the colonel, the dazzling novelist, Tamara, had strange extra agendas. They weren't just words on the page, to be helped to reach their best potential, they all had secret narratives as interesting in their own ways as the manuscripts that hid them.

And fat fees as well.

Tamara's manuscript: her father was disturbed by it. Wanted to comfort himself that it was fiction. Her mother refused to believe or had persuaded herself to forget that it existed.

I sat very still. Tamara's manuscript. We were supposing she'd been murdered by a serial killer, that it was the random act of a psychopath who got some vile pleasure from it. But what if she, specifically she, had been killed for a reason? For what, perhaps, was in that manuscript?

No, that was a silly idea. If that had been the case the killer would have destroyed the document too. Its continued existence was evidence that it wasn't the reason for her death. Unless he hadn't known about it. Assumed it existed only electronically. Was there any evidence he had searched the flat, drawers open, clothes and books strewn around?

I needed to talk to the colonel about it. I know I promised confidentiality, but such promises are always contingent; my definition of confidentiality could be extended to the colonel, my adviser in current troubled times. The mystery of the manuscript might not have anything to do with the mystery of her death, but maybe I needed to be able to talk about both. I could trust the colonel to keep the secret.

I have a sudden thought: does the colonel ever lie to me? He has this habit of not answering questions, or doing so in riddles, but he said of that, ask me no questions and I'll tell you no lies, which would seem a fairly solid promise of the truth, that he won't answer rather than tell a falsehood. It is also a sign that he can keep secrets, irritatingly well. Have I ever caught him out in a lie?

He's a slippery character, but I think he is honest, moral, good, that he believes in right. Yes, I think so. I feel comforted, that I can report Andrew's conversation to him, and in the retelling of it perhaps make more sense for myself.

I forgot, at that moment, that our very first meeting involved a lie, a whopping one: the lie of a wife.

I rang Edith's mobile again and she answered. They were in the car, Marcus was driving. She couldn't wait to get home. She made it clear that this was a typical evil Canberra experience, she should have learned by now that she always had horrible things happen to her in Canberra. (Like marrying my father.) The police had been no use at all, of course they wouldn't find the vandals, wouldn't even try. They said they'd keep an eye on the shops, be on the look out for gangs of kids, but what use would that be? The damage was done, and you could be sure the perpetrators would never be caught.

I thought not for the first time that Edith must be awfully good in bed—what a thought to think about your mother, but I do—she's such a whinger at the world, the guys must notice.

The thing is, Edith, you're all right, that's the important thing.

We could so easily not have been. We've had a terrible brush with death. I don't know when I've been so frightened.

I was thinking that life is full of brushes with death and none of them matter, until the last one that grabs us and carries us off. But knew better than to say so.

Edith was speaking in a soft wail. I'm a mess of nerves. So much for a holi . . .

The car must have gone through a cutting because the phone cut out. I hung up . . . isn't it funny how the old phrases linger. I didn't hang up, I pressed the button. Like pulling the chain, that's a button to press now, but lots of us still pull the chain. And one-armed bandits, they're a button to press these days, too. And people have their own private buttons: If he thinks he can press my buttons, he's got another think coming. Horrible to think of someone pressing your buttons, so cold, so mechanical, so calculating. On the other hand, with Edith, I spend all my time trying not to press her buttons. Well, except when I can't resist a bit of mischief.

Al came in and kissed me on the cheek. We have become kissing friends. His skin smells delicious, it's fine and smooth, surprisingly so for a military man. When I say this he grumbles.

What would you expect? All cratery and poxy? Weather-beaten? Flayed by the winds of Desert Storm? Do you know anything about army life?

Only what I read in this great book I'm editing. I thought maybe they issued you all with Dew of Youth, or something.

My mother had skin like mine. Hers was very fine and silky. So's Edith's, I notice. And yours mightn't be bad.

So it's all in the genes, then.

An awful lot is.

I've got an epigraph for your memoir.

Yeah?

'The real war will never get in the books.'

Where did you get that from?

Desk calendar. It's Walt Whitman.

It's terrible. No good at all. It's the opposite of what I'm doing.

Is it? I dunno.

You think I'm writing a book that's a refutation of its epigraph? That's dumb.

It's a fabulous sentence.

Maybe. I'd like it to *mean* as well as *be*. 'The real war will never get in the books.' It bloody well will if I can help it.

How's it going?

Okay. But look at this.

He went to the cupboard under the stairs. Coolest place I could think of, he said. Put it there to rest. He came back with a tall glass jar of preserved apricots and put it on the table as delicately as if it had been a Fabergé egg.

I may have got it right. He squatted down so he could look through the jar at its own level. Remember what I said? Utterly pellucid? Perfect clarity? The last batch; three bottles. And driving it up that vile road; I thought it might cause it to cloud. But I think it's all right.

I squatted down to look at the jar too. It was full of a rich golden syrup that was perfectly clear, and in it hung globes of fruit that seemed to have their own luminosity. There was a radiance to this jar, the fruit hanging, suspended, filling the space, floating but filling it. Radiant globes, so sugary and secretive.

Aren't they beautiful? So beautiful. Charlemagne with his great cabochon rubies and emeralds and sapphires was not so content as I with my orbs of fruit. I should have brought champagne.

I'd never seen the colonel so simply cheerfully happy. Do you know, he said, I've just learned, that the fruit of the Tree of the Knowledge of Good and Evil, the fruit that Eve gave to Adam, and so brought all our sorrows upon us, it almost certainly wasn't an apple, apples are cool climate fruits. It was most likely an apricot. The Euphrates Apricot.

It was Eve made us human, you know, I said. We have to understand good and evil otherwise we can't choose. If we're good only because we know nothing else, it's worthless.

Yes? But we might be happier.

Only as vegetables are happy. Eve's curiosity—she was the one with the courage to choose knowledge.

And I have a jar full here.

The fruit of Eden. *Of man's first disobedience, and the fruit* . . . So it does have a fabled past, then.

Yes, I suppose so, how fabulous.

What are you going to do with them?

Eat them, in a little while.

What!

Have to try them. I have some jars at home for the show, but these we will eat. One day soon. Adam will feed the fruit to Eve, this time.

He sat on the chubby sofa, happily contemplating his work of art.

You know, I said, your apricots, and your book, the same words apply. Utterly pellucid. Perfect clarity. That's what you should aim for in your prose.

The colonel blew a puff of air between his lips. Did I mention how sharply carved they were? Quite soft and sensual, but with a fine linear curve to them. It's bizarre, he said. Apricots. Prose. Such utterly different things. And the same words can describe both. I think it just proves, words are slippery creatures.

Or all life is one, I said. But Al knew I was just being mischievous.

Suddenly I remembered my conversation with Andrew. I went and got a bottle of Marcus's sauvignon blanc and settled down to tell the narrative of Tamara's book.

Chapter 16

I've often wondered what it would be like to set down and write a novel. I can't imagine doing it myself. I can see how they go when they're done, how they can be fixed, made better, tighter, shapelier. But starting from nowhere . . . I'm full of admiration for those who do it. One of my novelists said to me once, You know Cassandra I've written seven novels and each time I start another one I'm filled with panic, I think, *I do not know how to do this.* That doesn't worry me so much as it used to, she said, I know the thing is to start and somehow it will work itself out. But it's a bit like setting off through wild country without a map, and hoping you can invent or find it as you go.

No wonder I don't want to be a novelist. Nonfiction writers I can understand, the Tuscan villas, the Provençal years, the Irish poverty narratives, there's the structure of the historical event, and mainly what you have to do is find good lively words for it, which of course isn't that easy, the writer of her own exciting life tends to find comfort in clichés. Or studies in philosophy where there are theories and information to order, and a certain scholarly precision in expressing them. And I know I say that storytelling is natural to us, it is part of our being human, and so it is, we all make stories of our lives, for our lovers, our friends, our children, and some of us are very good at this, but what we are all really excellent at is being told stories. There are never enough.

So maybe it isn't amazing that every single person in the whole world except me is writing a book. Even if it's only the one book they've got in them. Like Tamara.

Stuck on my filing cabinet is a cartoon of a man standing behind an X-ray screen showing his skeleton, with sketchy heart et cetera, and beside him a doctor saying, No, I'm terribly sorry, I'm afraid you haven't got a single book in you. Not a one.

I was reading the *London Review of Books* the other day, and it struck me, how the past of that country which is England lives on in the consciousness of the educated, the literate, the intellectuals indeed, but also of anybody who likes to read. Sam Johnson is still with us, really, his ideas are still around to be paid attention to, John Donne was writing just the other day, the fate of Kit Marlowe is still a worry—was he a spy, was he murdered—the questions aren't yet answered but there's hope they will be before too long—which might be another century or two.

I grew up so happily in English literature that I still think of it as mine. Austen, George Eliot, Gerard Manley Hopkins, Woolf, they are my countrypeople, they are the flowering of my civilisation. But they don't live down the road or round the corner the way they would if I were English by birth and habitation instead of by language and a distant inheritance. Instead I live in a country where we have to invent ourselves, and the place we live in as well. That is why I love novels, because that is what they do. They write us down and in doing so cause us to exist.

I've just bought a stack of new Oz novels, after all I have a professional obligation to read them, as well as being addicted. Besides, they're tax deductible. I went to Paperchain and indulged. I try to ration myself, but today I succumbed. Afterwards I was driving through Manuka and saw the colonel sitting at one of the outside tables at Verve, in ardent conversation with a young woman. She had long smooth shining brown hair and was bending her slender shoulders and tiny waist gracefully and eagerly towards him, looking limpidly into his eyes . . . I nearly ran into the car ahead of me, failing to see it had stopped for a pedestrian. I slammed the brakes on so hard that my eyeballs rattled. Fortunately the traffic crawls though Manuka. Well, why shouldn't the colonel have a shining brown-haired damsel gazing into his eyes? He's a handsome man, of course he would have a private life. I've got a good pile of books, even if they have shot out of their bag and strewn themselves all over the floor of the car.

I'm not sure there are many masterpieces among them. Too much of ye olde present tensie, as one of my authors calls it. It's a funny tense this; I remember some ancient critic saying it can only be used for comic writing, so unless you are a Damon Runyon you should forget it. Well, that's obviously a hopelessly wrong old-fogy stance, but still, if I'd been editing some of these novels I would have questioned their relentless present tense. The present tense is oddly enough the tense of urgency and at the same time of the eternal moment. Write a whole novel in it and it is terribly restless. But a bit is good. Less is more. Except occasionally, when more is even more and especially excellent. I am not sure how you work out how to do this. But I do know when you have got it right.

I wonder how many of these new novels I will actually read to the end. My house is littered with books bookmarked at some point, often embarrassingly only several pages in, occasionally perhaps a third of the way, that I intend to get round to finishing one day. Secretly I know I won't. I roam about looking for something to read, and think, ah yes, there's that one, but I don't pick it up and immerse myself in it, as I keep telling myself I will one day. That's because these books are about as appetising as week-old pizzas. No point in trying to warm them up, they will only go tougher and staler.

But a pile of new novels. Enthusiastically reviewed in the newspapers. Promising. Up and coming. Rare new talent. I look at them. Which one to choose? Every book with its scented pages and new stiffness is rare and full of promise. I have looked at their opening paragraphs, none put me off, I am hopeful.

The colonel wasn't back yet. If he was coming: he'd said he was. Maybe the brown-haired girl had other ideas. I'd done a good day's work. Reward time. I sat on the puffy sofa, looking out at the dusk in the viburnum hedge. The lamp cast its rich yellow light in a pool over my shoulder, into my lap. The sea breeze had come up, its brief coolness had not shifted the day's heat. I had my French windows open, my Moorish screen doors locked, so the air could blow through and clear out the tired breath of another long hot day. I'd chosen a book, a hard cover, the publisher must have high expectations of this new young talent, or was trying to make us believe that was the case. The opening was clever, maybe a bit too artily gripping, you could see it paying attention to the creative writing dictum, hit them with the first sentence and hang on tight. I prefer a bit more subtlety myself, creep your way in, wind your tentacles round, and you don't need to hang on, the reader is enmeshed. Look at that: metaphors. In the head and on the page.

There was a bumping noise behind me. A kind of concentrated thumping. Somebody was trying to get in through the screen door at the back. It shook, and hammered. I sat like a stone. I am the kind of person who when she is in bed and thinks she hears a burglar puts her head under the doona and hopes he will go away. But the thumping continued, rather more frenzied. The door should hold firm, it didn't sound like a very technically clever kind of breaking in, thumping away at a deadlocked door. But there was a window, what if they broke that and got in that way? And maybe they thought that the door was strong but the lintel wasn't; I had wondered about that.

I turned my head quickly, but the yellow lamplight shone in my eyes and I couldn't see anything. I should have time to get the phone and call the police before the door smashed in. Thinking of the serial killer, the blood on the walls. He didn't normally force his entry, the women seemed to have let him in, but maybe this time was different. Where was the bloody phone? I walk round the house when I'm talking, make a cup of coffee or tidy up a bit or something. Where the hell had I left it?

The thumping was stronger now. I got up out of the squashy sofa, difficult with the state of my breathing, and moved out of the range of the lamplight, squinting through the dimness at the pale oblong of the door. There didn't seem to be anyone there. Maybe already gone to the window? But there was the thumping again. I crept towards it, it was hard to make my legs function, they were trembling and didn't want to take this path. Another thump, a scratch and rattle. Then I saw.

It was the cat. She wanted to come in. She was used to coming in when she felt like it, now she couldn't because of the screen blocking her cat flap. Her solid little bullety body—it seemed plump and fluffy and it was that too, but hard underneath—was launching itself at the door. Oh Elspeth. I unlocked the screen and she came stalking in. I picked her up and sank back into a chair but she was offended and jumped down again. I sat in the chair with my eyes closed and waited until my heart started beating normally again. Elspeth made it clear that a little food would help her forgive me.

The mode of writing in the first person is an interesting one. It's difficult for novels of suspense. You could say the trouble with first-person narrators is you know they've survived. They've clearly lived to tell the tale—obviously the serial killer didn't get in through the screen door and do her in. Though I did edit a novel once in which it turned out after a couple of pages that the narrator was dead, she was lying on a slab in the morgue and telling you what was what. It didn't do madly well, clever but a cheat. Though not such an awful cheat as a thriller I read by a famous contemporary English writer, in which a whole section was narrated by a person who was killed at the end of it. Now that was disgustingly dishonest, because all the way you were thinking, well this has to work out because here she is telling it, this frightful fate she fears can't happen, then suddenly after about a hundred pages, kapow, she tells us she gives a shriek and a gurgle and it turns out somebody has stabbed her and she dies. Oh, I've died, she says, more or less. Though oddly enough that one did sell well; maybe because hers was a famous name she was forgiven.

The other thing that people are fond of talking about these days is the unreliable narrator. But is there such a thing as a reliable narrator? Ask Linda and me about our childhoods, or Edith and me about my father. Which of us would you believe? In the end it is the story you have to trust, and the reader knows when a story is trustworthy.

A paragraph may do it, a page, certainly a chapter; you'll know by then if it's got a good character. I start in on the second chapter of my hardback. Of course it may not be the book's fault, it could be the fright, but it's not grabbing me and it's not enmeshing me. I put in a bookmark and pick up the next, a trade paperback this, very handsome cover, even if we have had enough of naked sepia bodies for the moment. I think nostalgically of the great old Penguin no-covers, the orange and white bands, green and white for detective stories. They made you concentrate on the words.

Chapter 17

Al and I were sitting in the study doing a final edit of the first chapter of his book when there was a knock on the door. The postman, with a bundle of letters. This is service, I said. But he had another purpose.

That Mrs Tricks—is she a friend of yours? Only she isn't taking in her mail. Three days now it's been piling in the box. There's one of them things of perfume from her son. I knocked, but she doesn't answer.

Maybe she's away?

I dunno. It'd be the first time, she always tells me.

I'm not quite sure where she lives . . .

38 Baker Street. The postman handed over my letters. Maybe I should call the police.

I'll check, I said.

We went up in Al's car. Her house is one of those old Tocumwal jobs, that people are starting to admire, at least if you believe the real estate ads, with a tall row of camellias along the front. We knocked, and when there was no answer Al took out a little bundle of peculiar bent keys and in a minute had the door open. He gave me a don't-say-anything look.

I found her lying on the bathroom floor, her eyes fluttering. The Japanese, she said. They have pillows. Little logs of wood. Lucky. She sighed, and frowned. Little logs. Not like this. No pillow.

Annie, I said, Annie. Her eyelids fluttered again. Her voice was a barely audible wispy breath, painfully slow. The Japanese, she said, lucky. You wouldn't think they'd be comfortable. But they say they are. A log pillow—I wish I had a log pillow.

The colonel phoned the ambulance and I got a real pillow for her head and an eiderdown from her bed, soft worn old satin patterned with roses. Annie, are you okay? Does it hurt? Her eyes fluttered. What's your name? I asked, that's the question people always ask. What's your name and who's the prime minister, what a question to ask a sick person.

A little log, for a pillow.

What's your name?

Her eyes fluttered, and I thought she'd lost consciousness. I held her little cold hand in mine.

Annie, she said, after a long while. It's written down. Dirty Tricks always writes it down. Pith ink, he said. Her voice came out in little sighing breaths. The bathroom floor was hard, and the nights lying on the shiny tiles would have been cold. Annie can't be far off ninety. I thought I should keep her talking, keep her consciousness going. Her body hadn't looked bent, or twisted, but I didn't want to touch or move her in case something was broken. She didn't seem to be in pain to any great extent, more frowning and uncomfortable. I kept holding her hand, it was so cold, but perhaps not mortally. She was wearing a quilted dressing gown of some thick pink material, that would have helped, along with her pink sheepskin ugg boots.

Pith ink, I said, thinking this would be a wandering, like the Japanese log pillows. The colonel was kneeling beside her, holding her other hand, smoothing it tenderly.

Writing, she said. Write it down. Another silence. There on the paper. Suddenly it isn't.

Ah, said the colonel. Invisible ink.

In-vi-si-ble. You see it, then it goes. Each syllable a slow faint breath. I have never listened to anyone breath before, wondering if each exhalation would be the last.

But you can get it back, said Al.

Secret.

Secret—you mean there's a secret formula for getting it back? The colonel was asking these questions.

Comes back. You get the crim.

The ambulance people arrived. They spoke slowly to her, their voices loud, their hands gentle. A burly woman touched her thoroughly but delicately. You'll be right, love, she said. Looks like nothing broken. They got her on to a stretcher, wrapping her in blankets, doing up straps, loading her in the van, all with a slow and orderly patience, and drove sedately off. We followed.

What's all this about invisible ink, I said. Sounds awfully old-fashioned. School spy stories and all that.

Yes, said the colonel, you write it and then you seem to lose it, it disappears, but it's there all along, you can get it back—if you know how.

Come to think of it, I had a formula for invisible ink once.

Lemon juice was involved, as I recall. In some magic book. I never could get it to work.

I remember those magic books. People used to give them to you for Christmas. Always a disappointment, somehow. They never did turn you into a magician.

Invisible ink. Do you reckon there is such a thing, or is it a fiction?

Doesn't matter, really, said the colonel, rather absently I thought. It's a concept, that will do.

Will it? You mean the words exist even if the thing doesn't?

I was thinking more of the idea.

We drove out to Calvary. I was hoping this wouldn't be the end for Annie. Not so much that I feared she wouldn't survive her ordeal of nights and days on a hard bathroom floor. But, the perfume-posting son—it would be just the excuse he'd need to stuff her in a home.

We had to wander about, asking questions and waiting, for a long time. After a bit we went to the café and had coffee and a sandwich. Good coffee, a good sandwich. Al said, Hospitals will lose their reputation if they start serving food as good as this. Well, it is the café, I said, we don't know about the inmates. Do you know, he said, you get glasses of wine with your evening meal? If you're a private patient, that is. Is it any good, I asked. I don't think so, he said, but again, it's the concept.

I watched his long thin fingers cutting the sandwich and picking up each small triangle. His nails were rosy and nacreous, with a fine white line across the top, as though he had had a French manicure, but of course he hadn't, the pearliness was natural. I watched the precise delicate way his fingers moved, remembering him opening oysters, barbecuing fish, cutting melon. As though handling these foodstuffs gave him great pleasure, and he liked to slow the task and savour it. Giving each particular substance its due.

I said, You're not very bloodthirsty, for a soldier.

Don't you have rather funny ideas about soldiers? I think bloodthirsty is the very last criterion. Contra-indicated, even. Intelligent, disciplined, patient—they're the words. It's not the Hundred Years War, you know. Eating the hanged men because you're starving—did you know that cannibalism was much more rife in Europe than in so-called 'savage' lands? Though we like to kid ourselves that it wasn't. Well, not a Hundred Years War in theory, these days; maybe it is, after all. Intelligence is the real thing. At the top, I mean. Good minds. And intelligence in the spying sense too. But good minds are the thing.

Do we have those?

Good question. Among soldiers, yes. But of course it is governments that decide and the answer there is—as you perfectly well know—no. Neither intelligence nor compassion. And certainly not honesty.

So they will take us into this war.

No doubt. And I can't think of a single question to which war is the answer. Certainly not terrorism. War is quite formal, you know. It has rules—which is why, when they aren't followed, we have war crimes. War is the consequence of an ultimatum not complied with. Terrorism is none of these things. It's an abstract noun, for a start, and it's a crime, it should be puzzled out, solved by the best detective minds among our best policemen and the criminals suitably sentenced.

So Bush, declaring war on terrorism, is . . .

Dooming himself to lose. Which is why he is going into Iraq, to obscure that fact.

And Saddam Hussein?

Vile man. Appalling ruler. But going to war with him will do nothing to get rid of terrorism. Most likely the reverse.

Al looked so gloomy as he said this. I said, This is when we need Annie's Dirty Tricks. The good criminal-catching mind.

With the invisible ink. He was silent for a moment, then he said. The thing is, soldiers need their country to want them, to be glad of the job they're doing, otherwise it is too hard. Think of the Vietnam War, all those years of bitterness and anguish because the fighting men believed their country did not value what they had done. They were maimed and their heads were fucked and they thought nobody cared anything for them. And now, if this war is seen in the same way to be an unjust war, and one the country rejects, the same thing will happen.

What about the last Gulf War? You don't seem so critical of that.

It was a more proper war, there seemed a moderately noble purpose in it. Of course it was the result of a whole history of shonky deals over oil, but just at its moment . . . but maybe I just think that because I need to. It's my history too.

Mrs Tricks was under observation, they said eventually. Were we next of kin? No. And had no idea who was. True enough. I knew there was a son, but not how or where to find him. I wanted her to have a chance to get better before they could get hold of him.

Is she in immediate danger?

The nurse looked askance. We can really only discuss her condition with her next of kin.

Difficult at the moment. We are all there is.

Probably not, she said. She's sleeping now.

Can we see her?

Better not to disturb her. The nurse looked at us. She seems a resilient lady.

I don't think she'll need to go into a home, said Al as we drove home. Anyone can have a fall, and she doesn't seem to have done any real damage. Given herself a shock, probably. What she needs is one of those alarms, wear it all the time, and she can press a button if she needs help. We'll have to see about it.

Chapter 18

Waking up in the chilly dawn. The bed large and cool, the thin summer doona just warm enough. How I love my bed, its space, its comfort, its safety; curled up in it you feel free from all intent of harm. The harshness, the fear of the future, the concern for your own fate and the world's, are somewhere else. It even consoles you for the occasional nightmare. You'd think my bed a cuddly loving person in whom to trust, and so I do.

I have been dreaming of Gran, and when I wake she is still with me, but with a faint sadness, a faint reproach: I have let her go, I could have stayed asleep and still been with her. But the bed comforts me, and I think of her, those last days when I asked her questions and recorded her replies, I the family archivist, the word person who believes in writing it down. Before I drop off the twig, she teased, and I replied, Of course, suppose you carked it and left all this unsaid. She laughed, my gran, she was tough, she liked the truth to be spoken. Not to mention, I said, before you lose your marbles: a safe enough joke, she was as sharp as ever she'd been. I'd found some photographs for her to look at, taken in the thirties, willowy plump young women with soft breasts, in woollen bathing suits with little legs to them—no need for bikini waxes in those days—and webbing belts and deep plunging backs. Oh those terrible cossies, she sighed, so scratchy, and going shrunken and felty, and into holes all over your bottom, oh how could we have worn them. I think you all look gorgeous, I said, so shapely, so pretty, so female. They are at the lake, in the water, on the jetty, there's a rowing boat and in the background an old wooden house with verandas and oleander trees and finials on the roof. Gran remembered everything, the names of the people, where it was, who was there but not in the photographs. The fates of all those carefree girls, whom they'd married, what became of them, who was still alive: not many of them. I find photographs like this terrifying, that you can look at these long-ago smiling faces and know that death has claimed them, that this is what remains. Maybe alive a little longer in the memory of their fellows, like Gran, Lal she was called then, and in the different soberer recollections of their children and grandchildren, but soon just poignant images of light and chemicals. Ending their days in a box in a junk shop, nobody knowing who they are, another young woman looking at them and laughing, What weird swimsuits.

One day she told me about a dream she used to have, every so often she would have this dream, it was a dream of panic and fear, and still as vivid as if only last night she had dreamt it. She was in a small boat with her husband Jack and her three children and none of them could swim, except Gran herself. The boat capsized, sank, they were in the water and she had to decide who to save. Jack? Or one of the children? Which one? Of course, said Gran, I know that in real life I wouldn't have had a hope of saving anyone, it would all be accidental and fast and being able to swim wouldn't help, I'd drown too, but in the dream there's time, there's a choice, there's the children and maybe I can manage to grab two of them and save them. But then there's Jack and he's grown up and maybe I should save him. There'd be a chance of more children if I saved him. I'd wake up, ashamed, to think I'd be choosing Jack.

Jack, her husband, admirer of her ankles. He was a lovely man, she said once, with such longing in her voice, and I suddenly knew what she meant. I'd never thought of a lovely man before, but when Gran put the two words together, oh yes, I saw the force of them, I knew what she meant.

For years I had this dream, she said, and I was ashamed, because I knew I wanted to save Jack, I told myself if I saved him I could have more children—what does all this say about my subconscious—but the poor little helpless things, and of course I knew that other children wouldn't be these ones, I would mourn these for ever, but still I wanted Jack. But then they got older and learned to swim and there was only Jack who couldn't, so that was all right. But then the dream changed, and I couldn't save him, he was too heavy, I'd call his name but he wouldn't lift up his head.

I thought of Edith. Who would she have saved? Herself, was my cruel thought. But then if the dream had been true, maybe she would have drowned. Maybe she suspected Gran wasn't certain she'd have saved her.

I loved that time talking to Gran. It was as though the faint hiss of the cassette recorder hypnotised her, or liberated her, so she talked openly, freely, as she never had before, not to her granddaughter but to posterity, with all the necessity of truth and honesty and bearing witness.

I have a number of pictures of her in my head. There's the girl on the jetty at the lake, in a damp woollen swimsuit. There's the middle-aged woman who came to look after us when Edith left. There's the old woman in her bed, with her famous complexion, its rose-petal pink and white crumpled now, remembering her life for a tape recorder. But the most vivid pictures I have are the ones I never saw, of Lal in her heyday, the young married woman, Lal with her lovely man for husband, the figure from the paper pattern packets she spread on the bed, the Butterick women, the Simplicity girls, the Ladies' Home Journal, and Gran saying, that was so pretty, I made it up in fine lemon seersucker with a tiny brown sunflower, and this, blue, with a pattern of fine black roses, like an etching, and that was dusty pink moiré silk taffeta for your aunt Vera's wedding, a perfect circle that skirt was. Ah, that suit, tight and straight with its bias-cut peplum, that was wool, dark grey, very fine, like silk, it hung like a dream.

All those dresses, all those images, all those words, which Lal the clever sempstress sewed with such skill and care. I never saw her in this heyday, but the sharp ankles, the cinched waist, the pointed breasts, the bracelet-length sleeves, the stockings with seams, the shoes with stacked heels, the off-the-face hats with veils, the swoopy-brimmed shady hats . . . out of the sketchy covers of paper patterns this Gran, this Lal, walks with lively lilting gait, her skirts with their pattern of cornflowers and poppies on slithery art silk swirling.

Ah. Cornflowers and poppies. So this is where I am. My early morning sleepy daydreams have conflated Gran and shirtwaist woman. Again, and not consciously this time. Not really surprising, it's just the fashions.

I think I'd better get up.

Of course I have read accounts of and by children who have seen themselves as victims of their parents' consuming passion, parents loving one another so much they cease to be, or probably never become, parents. They remain the original fallen-in-love couple and have sense only of one another for all their lives. Better not to be the child of such lovers. Who was it said, the children of lovers are orphans?

Is this Edith? Is this why she is still searching for love? Because her parents were in love only with one another? Maybe she knew Lal would have saved Jack, not her.

By the time she was looking after us Lal was a widow, no Jack, the drowning dream had come true, though it was his own lungs that drowned him, so she said, the disease rattling and gurgling in his bronchi, slopping and slapping like a tide rising, until there was no air, no air at all, and he died. I did not know this at the time, it was in the recording days that she told me these things, and I imagined her telling bitter words over and over until she found the ones to express his pain and her anger and their misery.

He was far too young, she said. I reckon it was the quarry that killed him, day after day in all that dust, no protection, cutting the stone and the fine dust flying, but of course they never said, nothing ever happened, no responsibility, it didn't in those days. Of course there should have been compensation but how was I to know. And compensation doesn't bring your husband back. The tears ran out of her eyes and I turned the tape recorder off. I held her hand. At least you had him, all those years, I said. Still do have him. You're lucky, you know that.

She looked at me. Yes, I know that. And what about you, girl, what about you?

Gran. The shirtwaist woman. Her ghost, come to haunt me, tease me, remind me, elude me. Fortunately, or is it unfortunately, I don't believe in ghosts. And shirtwaist woman is no more my gran than are the sketches on the covers of the Butterick patterns; the ghost is taller, more broad-shouldered, and that blonde hair falling over her face would have been far too tarty for my gran. Hers was darkly shining brown, and cut in a shapely bob in the lake photographs, curved and falling silky as she bends over Peter the cat who died of furball, a hairstyle she kept all her life, though by the time I knew her it was striped with grey.

Chapter 19

When Andrew Sissons brought Tamara's manuscript I made him some coffee. He was edgy and walked about the room picking things up and not looking at them. I'll try to get it done quite fast, I said. I think you're not enjoying the suspense.

No, he said. He put three teaspoons of sugar in his cup and sat in a chair, visibly willing himself to relax. Gossip was his method of choice.

That chap, calls himself a colonel, what's-his-name, Marriott, I gather he's writing a book.

I was taken aback by this, and said with a certain indignation, Calls himself? He is a colonel. Then I thought, I don't actually know this, I just believe him when he says he is. When he calls himself colonel.

About the Gulf War, is it?

About his experiences in the war. It's very good.

Odd. There weren't any Australians in the Gulf War. A few navy personnel on boats, but no troops on the ground.

You'll have to buy it when it comes out, and see, I said. Though there were no guarantees that it would ever be published. I thought it was going to be good enough, that it would deserve it, but these are hard times in the world of books. It's autobiographical, which readers love, and there's quite an interest in military history, but still he didn't have a contract and that's the only guarantee in publishing, and even that's not absolute. You only know for certain when you hold the actual printed object in your hand, flip the pages and smell the gorgeous scent of new book. Writers say that only then does a piece of writing have its own life, not when it's a finished manuscript or a set of page proofs, it can't be said to exist until that final hand-sized form.

Oh, I doubt it's my sort of thing, he said.

I decided I didn't like Andrew Sissons. And that was a good thing. I could be brutally frank about his daughter's book. It couldn't hurt her now. He wanted the truth, he and his Bluebell wife Belinda would have the truth.

I've finished the grand novelist's book. The publisher said, Don't contact the writer, send it straight to me. This is odd. The writing of a book is a conversation. At all stages a book is a conversation. When it exists as an artefact, and is reviewed, if it's a good review then it's a three-way conversation between the reviewer, the writer and the potential reader. And finally there is what it exists for, the final luxurious intimate tête-à-tête of writer and reader. Even a journal, a form I'm not particularly fond of, is a species of conversation, the writer talking to himself. Solipsistic. But before the book exists the conversation of writer and editor is especially important because at its best it's creative, it is part of the ultimate making of the work of art. I like best the asking of questions, why this, what does that mean, why there, and a good writer listens and takes off into marvellous things that I could not have conceived, but that I nudged her towards.

As for good reviews, they're scarcer, much scarcer than good books. I've seen some shockers. Written by patronising ignorant nobodies who have no idea what a novel is (they talk about it as though it were a biscuit), who can't write eight hundred words of unclunky prose let alone the eighty thousand-plus a novel demands. I can't bear the way they are so cavalier with, so vapidly dismissive of, some of the novels I've edited. I just wish they'd remember it's someone's heart's blood they are dealing with here. Not always, of course, there're potboilers and calculated formulaic bestsellers, but mostly, where novels are concerned, it is heart's blood they are written in.

But I think I know why the manuscript is not to be sent to its author. Its author will probably never see it again. The novel is in fact marvellous, but its command of itself is fragile, it crumbles, it tears into frail pieces, into fragments and lost words. The most famous remark in editing is that of Beatrice Davis, legendary mentor of absolutely everyone in the grand old days of Angus and Robertson, a remark so famous it has become a cliché and you can't really use it any more, that an editor is an invisible mender. I had to do a lot of mending, and a lot of it was not at all invisible, not to anybody who knew the book well, like the person who'd written it. But I wondered if this person would ever see it, or recognise it if they did. I reckon this brilliant but flawed work is its creator's swansong. Not that I have any problems with flawed, I think that flawed is sometimes the most beautiful of all, it is where our poignant and difficult humanity shines through. In the Middle Ages they believed that there was nothing perfect beneath the moon, and so do I. We live in a sublunary and mutable world which breaks our hearts and yet still provides the only occasions of bliss we will ever know.

I felt tearful as I packed it up and sent it back to the publisher. I've done a good job, readers won't precisely see the cobbling, the patching, though they will be aware of loss. I keep thinking of Ophelia's words about Hamlet: *Oh what a brilliant mind is here o'erthrown.*

I will put Tamara's book off till tomorrow. I feel melancholy but that's nice, melancholy is good when there are grand and doomful things to be thought. The death of a writer: I feel a bit like an attendant, an acolyte, composing the limbs decently in the coffin, a good life, a long one, to be celebrated as well as mourned.

I decided to ring up Edith.

I'd had a small niggling worry about her ever since the visit with Marcus. Edith drives me round the bend, but she's the only mother I've got.

Oh hello Sandra, she said, in her bored voice. What's wrong?

Nothing's wrong. I had a minute so I thought I'd call and see how you are.

Can't complain. Well, I could but who'd listen.

How's work?

Don't talk to me about work. Busy as hell.

How's Marcus?

Oh, Marcus. I don't see Marcus any more.

What? What happened? I thought he was lovely.

Oh, Marcus, he was quite a sweet boy, but such a child. He's considerably older than me and I'm not a child. I've had enough of children. George now, he's a man.

George, is it. How old's he?

Ooh, I suppose he'd be getting close to fifty. He thinks he's older than me.

You should bring him down to Canberra. (This is mischievous. But talking to Edith is such hard work you have to have some fun.)

I heard her shudder. Oh darling, you know how I hate Canberra. Such dreadful things happen there. That Marcus would go, I blame him, really.

So, George's nice, I said, knowing she wouldn't say otherwise.

Of course darling. Quite gorgeous. Would I if he weren't?

There's a silence after this, as if even she has heard what she said, and remembered that her men are always gorgeous at the beginning and monsters at the finish.

Well, I said, I just wanted to be sure you're okay.

Can't complain, said Edith.

When I told the colonel that Marcus had bitten the dust—thank god I hadn't lived with her when I was young, the parade of stepfathers or uncles or whatever would have been terrifying—he said, You're not like that, are you.

You mean I don't have queues of men to choose from?

I mean, you aren't fickle. Not feckless. I liked Marcus.

So did I.

Of course Marcus might have wised up and given her the flick.

And along came George.

What a good idea postponing Tamara was. Maybe I wouldn't have disliked the book so much if I hadn't read it in the context of one by a real writer, the grand novelist whose powers might be flickering but still could shine, could dazzle. Tamara's book is extremely badly written, banal in the extreme, never does her prose sing. But it's not that. It's angry. Full of fury. She takes an axe to Andrew and Belinda so that their bloody hacked-up carcases litter the pages—and you might think that could happen only once but she resurrects them and hacks them to pieces again, time after time. And when she's not angry she's whingeing about how badly done by she is. I wonder if this is true. I wonder if Andrew and Belinda—she uses their real names—are the monsters she portrays. Did Belinda prostitute her daughter as well as herself? Was Andrew their pimp? Was their house in London a weekend opium den? Could he have bribed and corrupted people on such a scale? If a fraction of this stuff is true no wonder Belinda doesn't want to know about it. If it's not then Tamara must have been sick; maybe there's a very black irony in her death. Maybe it was the murder of one psychopath at the hands of another. If it was as we all assume a serial killer: the case isn't closed but you don't hear about it any more. I still feel nervous being a self-employed woman living in O'Connor.

It's not the drugs and the pornographic sex and the hit

men and the murders and the corruption in high places and the paedophilia, I've read plenty of thrillers where these things are the substance of the plot and no details are spared. But in thrillers and detective novels it's a kind of game, and a puzzle. How far can you dip into evil and danger and terror and come out the other side? Because we have faith that we the readers and at least some of the protagonists will come through; we'll all be safe, in the end. Whereas Tamara's isn't, it claims, a novel, and no one is safe. No one is rescued, no one is saved. Moreover, these are real people, a mother a father and a daughter. How could they do these things to one another? How could a family exist in such a state of complete lovelessness? How could one of them write it down? Because whether these things are true or not the ineluctable fact is this, Tamara wrote them down. Whether they happened or whether she made them up, she wrote them down, she gave them space in the world, and wanted to give them currency. That's how I came to have her red business card; she wanted me to edit her book with a view to publication. That is the ultimate act of lovelessness, positive awful lovelessness—I suppose I mean hate—to make it all public. Publication being—I think we don't always remember—a making public.

Certainly not written in heart's blood, unless what was in her veins was prussic acid.

I think of Edith. She's not affectionate. I am happy to see little of her. But I know from the way my heart jumps when I fear for her safety or health that I do love her.

I can't read much of this book at once. It sickens me. I shall have to read every word, that's my job. There may be a moment of redemption, but I have skimmed and didn't find it. I can't decide which is more horrible, the parents in fact doing these things or Tamara pretending that they did. And I am chastened that I have no idea who the victims are, parents or child. I have always prided myself on my ability to tell truth from falsehood by the nature of the writing, even when it's crap. This is crap, and I can't.

I don't want to see Andrew again. I shall pack up the manuscript, along with my invoice—I shall take his fee for reading this stuff—and a letter. Telling him to burn it. I never thought I would ever say that to anyone. Put it away. Hang on to it. Self-publish for your grandchildren. Embargo it for fifty years till everyone's dead. But not this, I never thought I would say burn. I don't know how much Andrew has read, enough, I suspect. I shall say it has no literary merit whatsoever, that its veracity is none of my business, and that the world does not need it.

I will not say, whether it is fact or fantasy it is morally indefensible. Andrew will never forgive me for knowing these things about him. I have to hope I never meet him again.

I saw him on the news that evening. He and Belinda, appealing for help in finding their daughter's murderer. Belinda was dressed in that soft bluebell colour that she favours—clever of her not to wear black, said Al—and appeared to have no make-up on but of course she did, you don't achieve that sculptured beauty without. He held her hand in a loving gesture, she leaned towards him. Please, they begged, if anybody knew anything, anything at all, that might help the police discover who did this...

unspeakable... thing... to their beloved daughter... Belinda dissolved into tears, Andrew held her to him, and on the screen flashed a picture of Tamara, that pointed-chin sideways-facing glamour pose we all try out at one time, her pale shining hair falling round her neck, her mouth slightly open, her eyes wide and looking just over our shoulders at whatever was waiting there. I shuddered. I hated Andrew for showing me that manuscript.

It's lucky the Sissons, mother and father, have an alibi for the time of their daughter's death. Otherwise this manuscript would make them prime suspects. But they weren't in the country at the time, very lucky, they didn't arrive until after she'd been murdered, they only came because she had been murdered.

That night we ate the apricots. They were okay, nothing like the fresh one I ate in the hidden garden, too sweet for my taste, the sharp luscious straight-off-the-tree Garden of Eden flavour of the original fruit has been made sweet and innocuous by sugary syrup. But that is how they should be, said the colonel. What really mattered was the appearance, the unblemished globes floating in but also completely filling—very difficult to get full but floating—their jar, the syrup of the right weight and density and clarity. Preserving fruit was important, he said, not everybody could eat fruit straight off the tree, and nobody could do it for very long, the season being so short. It was a thrifty and ancient act.

Lying in bed, considering the events of the day, I suddenly remember the Sissons' alibi. That we don't actually know for certain that they weren't in the country, only that they appeared to arrive later, summoned by tragedy. Andrew particularly took a long time to get here, I presumed because there weren't a lot of planes from Caracas. Maybe he came over, killed her, returned and then hurried back again after he apparently heard the news. That would show on his passport, of course. Unless he used a false one. The Andrew depicted in Tamara's book was capable of all that, murder, false passports, fake alibis, collusion with Belinda to commit crimes; it was the stuff of his daily life.

Of course, you had to think he wouldn't have shown me the manuscript if he had killed her, it was too incriminating. But then that could be the gambit of the double bluff. Expecting it would be found, he behaved as though it couldn't harm him, thus proving his innocence. Innocence. Ha. He is a very clever man, that Andrew Sissons.

And Belinda . . . I suddenly understood. The tall handsome Amazon creature who had hit Hotbaby. Belinda Sissons, the Bluebell Girl.

Chapter 20

I hadn't been to Tilley's for a while so when I went down to the supermarket I planned to stop off and have a coffee. There was a vehicle on display in the middle of the little plaza, one of the odder manifestations of the Summernats. I suppose nats is short for nationals, but I always think of gnats, irritating little insects. People were swarming all around this creature. Once it had been an ambulance, said a sign beside it. Now it seemed it might cause you to need one. It had one hundred and forty-six speakers powered by thirty-two amplifiers and produced 150dB of sound—slightly more than a jumbo jet taking off. I peered as best I could inside; I couldn't see much more than coils of cables, wire, hoses, grids and strange snorkelly pipes. However closely I looked I couldn't make sense of them. I suppose it was an idea, simply. It was something that could be done so someone had done it. It wasn't playing, if that was the word, no sounds came out; I wondered how and when it ever would. Driving along? The noise would destroy you. Parked several kilometres away in the middle of a paddock? Earmuffs on, set it going, and run. What powered it? I imagined looking back at it roaring out its music in the paddock and suddenly exploding in its own noise.

I thought, writing it down is enough. Contemplate it as an idea, as a description on a sign. Words for noise, not the noise itself. Like this exhibit.

There was nobody I knew at Tilley's—certainly not Annie still in hospital though back to her old fighting self and even more determined not to go into one of those dreadful old folks places, she just won't, and the social worker offering Al's suggestion, why not try an alarm, hang it round your neck for emergencies, that would solve the problem—so I drank my coffee and read the paper. When I went to my car in the small supermarket car park I saw Hotbaby parked in the next row. No mistake. The bronze Monaro, the object of desire, its great slabs of burnished metal, the oval windows, the numberplate with its name. My stomach flipped as though I'd swallowed a fish. I threw the groceries in my front seat and got in. The car was unbearably hot, like a small metal box for cooking in. The seat seared my bare legs. I started the engine and wound down the window to let hot air out. I put it into reverse, turned my head to check the way was clear to back out, and there was Hotbaby, the man not the car, Harold Perrot, shoving the top half of his body through the window. My foot slipped, the car leapt and stalled. He held on.

Put the brake on, he yelped.

Heart jumping, I did what he said.

Well. He settled himself in the window. The little blue buzzy-bee buggery car. And all its tyres nice and hard.

I leaned sideways across the seat, to get away from his face.

Why did you do that, he asked, his sneery voice changing to plaintive. There were no need to do that, all I wanted was a little fuck, a little kiss, if you wanted it too. You could have wanted it too. Girls do. It's nice in the Monaro.

Please, get out of my car. I tried to find the door-locking button, but his arm hung over it. I tried to wind up the window, but he was leaning on it, it wouldn't budge.

You're invading my space, I said, which was a sign of how upset I was, I hate that phrase.

Invading your space! I weren't invading your space when I fixed your tyre. Hello Mister Nice Man then. His tone changed again from sneering to plaintive. No need for the police. No need to hound a man. Just because I want a little fuck isn't to say I'd murder someone. Why did you think I'd murder someone?

My brain wasn't working well. His head and shoulders pushing into my car with the strong perfume of some deodorant underlaid with sweat and the powerful fruity aroma of a washing detergent, his breath acrid and minty . . . the smells were intimidating. I told myself I didn't need to feel afraid, this was Lyneham shops on a weekday morning, full of people, cars coming and going, I would only have to shout. I was also thinking the police must have talked to him, they must have told him it was me, I thought they wouldn't do that.

I wouldn't rape someone, not if she didn't want it, said Harold. I get plenty without that. His voice was indignant now. Last time I stop to help. The police. I never had no trouble with the police, clean as whistle. And now this fucking cow beats me up. I could of died.

But you're all right, you're not in trouble with the police now.

Well, I told 'em, didn't I. I told 'em. Iron alibi. But it's not the same as never having no trouble. And I might never be all right again, not my head, not my leg. I was in a coma, you know.

I had been bent sideways, and staring straight ahead, not looking at him. Now I saw that he was on crutches, that the bulky body he'd shoved through my window—a large window as they often are on these small cars—was held up by crutches, and that he was opening his eyes wide to stop the brimming tears falling. I remembered his ice-blue eyes, now they were wet grey like a rainy sky.

Your getting beaten up, I said. It was nothing to do with me.

It's the luck, he said, you set in a train of bad luck and it keeps going. You and the police, and then that fucking dog-faced bitch, that's two. Where's the third I want to know.

Of course there won't be a third. I paused. I am grateful for your help, with the car, but you frightened me, and, you know, women often have good reason for being frightened.

Not of me, they don't.

Well, I didn't know that. Now, please, get your head out of my car. I have to go.

A little sorry wouldn't hurt. You stuck-up bitches, you never say sorry.

I'm sorry you're having a bad time, I said.

I don't have trouble saying I'm sorry, I was sincere in this, he did seem quite pitiable hunched in the car, moaning over his woes, and I don't believe saying sorry is admitting guilt. But it should get better now, shouldn't it, I said. Thinking maybe if I was nice he would go. Immemorial female logic. The police are leaving you alone, aren't they?

Well, I had an alibi, didn't I. Police can't do nothing if you've got an alibi.

I suddenly felt happy. I am grateful for your helping me, I said. I did thank you for it, and I still do.

He looked a bit happier too. I said, How did you know it was me told the police?

Stands to reason. Course they didn't tell me. But you was the only person knew about the card. The red card you give me, the poor silly bitch who got herself murdered. Who else would know about that?

He heaved himself out of the car window, slinging himself up on his crutches. His hair was longer and floppier than the last time. He was wearing the same sort of dazzling white T-shirt, but his belly was flatter. He didn't look sinister. He looked ordinary. I started the engine, put the car in reverse, checked to see he was out of the way.

Last time I help some silly bitch on the road, he called after me. More trouble than it's worth.

As I finished reversing and was getting into gear to go forward I heard someone shout. Parrot! Hi, Parrot! How's it going mate? Another man in a dazzling white T-shirt was coming towards him across the car park. Parrot, eh. I knew he'd have a nickname. He wasn't really a Harold.

At the roundabout I had to give way to a Deux Chevaux.

I was quite pleased, it gave me a chance to look at it. Once I thought I'd have liked to own one of these comical French cars. Deux Chevaux, meaning two horses: they move rather like a horse-drawn carriage. This one was canary yellow. A good colour. As it wallowed round the circle I noticed the driver. I could have sworn it was shirtwaist woman. I thought of following her, but not fast enough, I was on my way, she on hers.

I sang in the car all the way home. Old ABBA songs, so corny, so good to belt out when you feel mindlessly cheerful. *Dancing queen, I am* the *dancing queen.* Not that my cheerfulness was mindless, I understood it exactly. Hotbaby had an alibi, Hotbaby didn't want to murder me.

Well, provided he was telling the truth.

I felt too light to settle to anything. The piles of now dog-eared and yellow-stickered manuscripts did not speak to me. Though an oblong of purple cardboard did. An invitation to a poetry launch.

Normally I avoid poetry. It can only get you into trouble. Poetry means a lot of difficult *p* words: poets, poverty, politics, pugnacity, puerility, passion, pig-headedness, poison . . . the list could go on and on. Not always all of them at once, but enough. And you could find yourself in a dark and bitter labyrinth of anger and despair and jealousy, and will you ever discover the way out? But I am fond of Colin Lake, whose occasion it is. He keeps on, writing poems, some good ones, very good. He has a nice wife who works as a nurse in intensive care so he can do this. Colin has tragic affairs about the place, falls disastrously in love, everything always going fizzingly wrong, breaking his heart, and then he writes some poems and recovers. His wife goes benignly on bringing up the children and feeding him.

I rang up Dermot. A cold voice said: Dermot O'Farrell. It didn't sound like him. Dermot? Colder and more impatiently the voice said: Dermot O'Farrell.

Oh hello Dermot. It's Cassandra.

Cassandra. The voice started its same cold self then warmed, found its music, as though he'd begun with a reprimand and turned it into a song. *Cassandra*—at least four notes it had—you've rung me!

Yes. I was wondering . . . I know it's short notice and you've probably got something better to do, but if you haven't, I wonder if you'd like to come with me to the launching of a book. Friday. And maybe afterwards we could have a bite, at my place.

Cassandra! What a lovely idea. Friday, let me see, oh no, no . . . yes, can fix . . . yes, yes, I'd be delighted. What time shall I call for you?

Dermot sounded very weird. I couldn't tell whether he wanted to come enough to postpone something or whether he didn't want to come but thought he couldn't get out of it. I didn't care. Time to get Dermot sorted. Now that Hotbaby was. My current light-heartedness showed that I had not convinced myself by logic of the undangerousness of Harold Perrot. Now I had seen him, and heard him speak, he had exorcised himself.

When the colonel came in we both spoke at once: Hotbaby has an alibi.

How do you know? we both asked.

I talked to him, I said, at the shops. I told Al about the wired-up ex-ambulance and him sticking his bulky shoulders through my car window. Al looked horrified. It wasn't nice, I said, but then when he talked I realised it was all right, that he had an alibi and it must be okay if the police had talked to him and not arrested him—mustn't it?—and that really he was a bit of a pathetic creature, with his fucking cow that had attacked him and injured him forever probably. Al smiled, with a pained face. How did you find out, I asked.

Oh, you know, the usual sources.

The usual dialogue, I said. I tell you, you don't tell me.

You have to protect your sources, you know.

You sound like a spy. Are you a spy?

If I was, my profession would demand that I denied it. If I say that I am, you would have to suppose that I'm not.

The usual bloody conundrum. All Cretans are liars.

What's that?

The Cretan saying, all Cretans are liars; if he's telling the truth then he's lying.

Al laughed. I said firmly, Friday Dermot's coming for dinner. You're not invited. You're positively uninvited.

Dermot? For dinner? The colonel stopped laughing. Yes. I see. Should be . . . amusing.

There was something weird about him too. I'm tired of men being weird. Why not lovely and simple? Loving and simple. Think of Cleo and her Paul. Think of Molly Vander-Browne and her Claude . . .

Well, yes. Weird. The lot of them. I suppose nothing is ever simple, with men in your life. Or women either, come to think of it. Consider Justine.

I had a great desire to stick to books. Only books.

It occurs to me. The colonel is jealous. No, that's not likely. You have to have a relationship with someone to be jealous, don't you? Maybe that's where Tamara's terrible book came from: jealousy.

I think I know who killed Tamara, I said to Al.

Yes?

Her father. Or mother.

Oh yes. The colonel has a nice way of listening, you know he is hearing you, not distracted like so many people you talk to.

Close to home, but the family, not the lover. I told him my theory about the fudged arrival from Caracas. I reckon if you checked alibis and stuff—not passports, he'd have false ones of those—you'd uncover some pretty cast-iron evidence. I reckon both of them were in it. In fact (and I have to say my voice was pretty triumphant at this moment) I reckon she's our Amazon. The Bluebell Girl is the tall mysterious woman who beat up Hotbaby.

Why?

It fits perfectly. They fit perfectly, both means and motive. You saw them on the telly, such partners, in life and in crime.

I thought, maybe, Justine . . . ?

Justine?

She's into kickboxing.

It's still a mad idea.

The colonel regarded me gravely. Sissons is a powerful person, he said. Catching him out won't be easy.

All the more reason. He's got something to hide, and the means to hide it. We have to expose him.

I was silent, and so was the colonel, considering my words.

Have you got any idea, how we might go about it? he said, at last.

Chapter 21

Cleo and I always give one another good birthday presents. This year I knew what I would buy her: a glass beaker from Magpie. Every time I see them I covet one, but they are far too expensive just to buy for yourself. This solves the problem; I can have the fun of buying one and then the fun of giving it away. They are a roundish chunky shape in brilliant colours, turquoise, orange, azure, vermilion, ultramarine, emerald. Colours as gorgeous as the names for them, with their ancient reminders of costliness and jewels. I think I fancy vermilion but will choose when I get there. They have patterns on them, chevrons, dots, lines like stitching. I suppose a rich person could have a set for water glasses. Cleo will like having just one, to take a glass of water to bed perhaps, or put flowers in, or pens.

I went late one morning to Magpie. Maybe the Shead exhibition would still be hanging. But no, it was almost dismantled. People had mostly collected their purchases, there were just a few unsold pictures left. And Dermot's, the big oil in the Queen series, the young naked woman looking tentatively out over her shoulder, the colours shining rose and golden against a dim background, like all good paintings so evidently and yet so mysteriously beautiful, you look and look with your heart as well as your eyes and marvel that it should be so. Her round bottom and girlish legs, the diamond crown in her dark hair. I was doing this when Holly came in. So Dermot hasn't picked up his painting, I said. How can he bear to wait?

Dermot, she hissed. Dermot. Don't speak to me of Dermot O'Farrell. He didn't last the opening night. Comes up to me all Irish blather, alas alas he can't after all. Forgive him, forgive him. I don't. I won't. I might have sold it if he hadn't stuck his lying red spot on it.

You mean, he bought it then unbought it on the same night?

That's right. I'd like to know what he thought he was doing. He may have charm but he's got no notion of commercial etiquette. You just don't do that sort of thing.

I could see that Holly was really angry. This was not just the rather excessive mode of gallery speak. I wondered why Dermot would behave so stupidly. If you're interested in art and sometimes buying it you're an idiot to fall out with gallery owners. The codes of behaviour are all the stricter for being tacit. I remembered him saying, You'll just have to look at it on my wall. I gazed at it. The queen smiled her sly sweet over-the-shoulder smile.

Maybe he's one of those people constantly plugged into his stockbroker, on his mobile phone, and just got bad news, frightful losses, whatever.

Likely, snorted Holly.

I felt a little light bulb pop over my head. Illumination. Dermot had pretended to buy the painting to impress me.

To tell me he was a man who could spend that many thousands of dollars on a beautiful painting.

No. That didn't make sense. Why would he want to impress me? And anyway if I ever did get to go to his house I'd know it wasn't there. Nevertheless, I had an odd sense that my little popping light bulb had lit up some truth. However imperfectly. The kind of bright idea you file away and forget, and one day the truth will reveal itself.

I spent a lot of time choosing Cleo's glass. But my first thought was right. The vermilion was the one. Brilliant and jewel-coloured but with something ancient and subtle abut it. I could imagine it cupped in the palm of a Byzantine prince, in a mosaic in Ravenna. Decorated with lines of crimson, like stitching, cross-stitch, blanket, satin, stem, running vertically down it. A beautiful object to hold. Holly wrapped it for me. You should have a look at the prints I've just hung, she said. Cecil Wander. A new artist. Young. From Wagga, the Wiradjuri people. Yeah, I know you've never heard of her, but I reckon you will. She's a good price at the moment—not for long, you can bet on it. It's a series, but she'll sell individually.

I stood at the door, thinking they seemed lush and linear compared with the rich planes of the Shead, which was what my eyes felt like at that moment. But I went and looked.

Gardens of Eden the series of eight prints is called. And quite suddenly I'm enchanted. One has in the foreground a plate with a fig cut open on it, showing its intricate inverted flowers. It's an etching, mainly quite a lot of black lines with some colour, the grapey mauves and purples of the fruit, dim foresty greens, a bit of blue, an occasional startling white. So luscious is the drawing, so vegetable with its trees and flowers and fruits, it takes a moment to see Adam sitting in the shadows stuffing a fruit into his mouth, a rather satyr-like Adam, stocky, fleeced with dark curls, dreamily greedily eating. And another moment before you see Eve, sitting with her legs crooked and wide apart, her own flowery parts as intricately drawn as the fruit's, holding a fig leaf over her face so it is completely obscured. It's called The Shameless Fig.

I'm entranced. Next is called Swapping. Again in the foreground a plate, an elaborate silver dish piled with a tangle of strange objects. You need to peer to decipher them. They're keys. A heavy iron one fit for a castle keep. Small bent skeleton keys. A Yale key with a top like a ziggurat. A key of St Peter, as in the Vatican coat of arms. The curly pretty kind you get in ladies' bureaux. One for winding up a toy. And an object scaled and scabbed in dark enamel colours, indigo, turquoise, violet. It appears to be a ring or fob with its own variety of keys hanging from it. Again figures emerge from the background. Curly-headed Adam. A tall person with wings and a cunning smile. Also breasts and a penis. A handsome muscular man who clearly goes to the gym a lot. Another sinuous figure partly scaled and scabbed in the same indigo and turquoise as the object in the dish. At first I can't see Eve, but then I find her, sitting right at the top of the picture, in a tree, lolling, her legs apart again, with her flowery pudenda blooming.

How clever, to call it *Gardens of Eden*, plural.

Another print has Adam curled up asleep on the ground

and the gym type bending over him, holding what looks like a lamb cutlet. Over his head are a number of circles like thought balloons, except they are perfectly round, rimmed in a gloomy red, like those signs forbidding smoking and such. In each is a female, crossed out. The spherical goddess shape of the Venus of Willendorf. The Winged Victory, with arms and a head. A Botticelli Primavera. Someone who looks scarily like Posh Spice. The gym type must be God, then. He's smiling thoughtfully but lasciviously and I suddenly notice he's got an erection. Not quite so grand as Al's Priapus, but impressive. I'm not sure what I think of this picture.

Fun, aren't they, says Holly passing by.

Confronting, I say.

Always a good thing in a work of art, says Holly.

I haven't been looking at these in order, exactly. The next to draw me in is a tree hung with enamelled leaves and dazzling rose-gold fruits, with Eve sitting cross-legged under it, holding out her hand sideways, palm flat, a rather oriental gesture, and on it a little pyramid of the fruit, already paler, less rich in colour. Beside her, curled round like a charmer's snake in the same scaled bejewelled pattern as the key fob, his head upright and his eyes bright and sideways glancing like a dog begging, is Satan. And suddenly Adam, twined around a branch, looking at the fruits in her hand. This one is called The Euphrates Apricot.

I should buy it for the colonel. He'd love it, its magic apricots of the Tree of Knowledge. But then I think, of course I don't buy him presents, we don't have that sort of relationship. I could buy it for me, and let him look at it.

I know I've decided to buy one for me, I've got that rather breathless feeling of anticipation that heralds such an exciting project. One needing time.

Cecil would like to sell most of the print run as complete sets, says Holly, popping up again. But she's prepared to sell a few singles. Holly knows I won't buy a whole set. She's letting me know how lucky I am to be allowed just one.

I see there's a print run of twenty-five. I don't think I want Euphrates Apricot. It's not my favourite. Swapping's nice. I did a book on wife-swapping once, the woman wrote it as a memoir of her first marriage. In the seventies. She wanted to call it Memoirs of a Misspent Youth. I said I thought a Misspent Marriage might be more striking. It was salacious. Far too much information about the men she got taken home by. The thing that struck me was the way everyone drove round stark raving drunk all the time. They'd go to these parties at one another's houses, swill down buckets of whisky, or gin, or rum and coke, the men would get pugnacious and fight with their wives and best friends, then toss their keys in a bowl for the women to lucky dip and drive home pissed as farts with the lottery of the evening. You had to wonder about the quality of their erections. The book ended with her bursting into tears one night and falling on her husband's neck and saying she couldn't stand it any more. What do you think, she asked me, is that a bit feeble? I'm wondering if I should go home with some cruddy bloke and when he's, say, pawing me in the kitchen I could stick a carving knife between his ribs. Or in the bedroom, with scissors? I thought this was a memoir,

I said, a record of what actually happened? Oh yes, it's that, she said, but you need a good story. As I recall she went with the scissors. Only wounding him. It was a prurient book, full of lurid details about the sex, the paunchy alcohol-breathing men with their sloppy kisses and groping paws and snoring after-sleeps, but while she dwelt on all their horrors she was moralistic about them, she the frail flower in the dungheap wringing her lily hands. Not well written, but it sold moderately well. (Why have I put a *but* in that sentence?) She wrote another but the publisher wouldn't touch it. The wife-swapping story was the one book she had in her—that always sounds like a tumour, quick get a surgeon—no use tempting fate, the publisher said. Nobody else wanted it either.

I walk slowly up and down, examining all the prints, and reading Cecil Wander's bio notes. She *is* young. Studied in Wagga. Works in graphic design. Already some handsome prizes. It would be nice to buy the set, but where would I put them? I haven't got room to hang them all. I'd like to think that she'll go on working and get even better. But if she doesn't, too bad.

Except I think she will. She sees so interestingly, and she knows how to disturb with what she sees. She shows evidence of an interesting mind, which is so important in writing as well as painting, in any art really, or maybe not music, I better not generalise there.

I think it's really the fig I want. Gorgeous shameless Eve, her face hidden, her intricate private parts so lovingly exposed. And the good thing is, I can have it straight away. Holly gets another out of a drawer, enfolded in acid-free paper. The grapey purples and tense blues are even richer in this print. I'll take it to the framer today.

Isn't it gorgeous, says Holly. It's my favourite.

I wonder if it is, really, or if she says this to everyone, whichever they buy.

Chapter 22

Although it was my invitation Dermot was driving us to the book launch. I'd offered, but I could tell he was one of those men who drive. Careful not to drink too much which of course is entirely admirable and desirable, as well as part of his conventional well-behaved nature. On the way I did proffer a warning. I have been to some very long poetry launches. A great many people make interminable speeches. Including the poet. Then he says he will just read a poem or two. Then he reads about a hundred poems. Your feet hurt and your back aches. (The National Library is killing in this respect, its marble floor is the cruellest surface I have ever stood on.) The cheap champagne is curdling to acid in your stomach. First of all you lose the syntax of the poem and then you realise you've forgotten what words mean. It might not even be in English except that you can't help feeling a foreign language would be more significant, it would have some mysterious musical idiosyncrasy so you could say, ah, Spanish, or Swahili, or Mandarin, and perceive why you couldn't understand it. You know for a fact that nothing will ever persuade you even to glance at the cover of his book let alone pick it up, and god forbid opening it, ever, ever. You know far more than you ever wanted about the poems and where they come from and how they were written and what they mean to him. They might be quite good poems, for all you know, but you haven't a clue, you stopped being able to hear them about three hundred poems ago.

I think you're exaggerating, Cassandra, said Dermot. Aren't you?

Understating, rather, I said.

I wanted Dermot to understand; I like poems. They're not my metier, but I like them. Just not endlessly read to a captive standing audience. Less is more. They are to be contemplated, savoured. One maybe, or two, could be good, but there is something about poets, the words titillating and tantalising aren't part of their working vocabulary, nor is teasing, or tasting. Leave me wanting more, I want to cry. What they are offering is not foreplay, it's rape.

You might think I'm being sexist here, making poets male. In my experience women have much more sense of drama. They know when to stop. Not infallibly, but generally. They flash a glimpse of poetry like Gran's well-turned ankles gracefully dancing in a flare of Nile-green crepe, so you are filled with desire to see the whole leg. Buy the book and you might get to look at the bottom as well, the private parts, the breasts, an eye, a smile, an ear.

This launch is set up in a courtyard outside the bookshop. There's a straggly sapling affording no shade and a market umbrella for the books. The drinks table is in a rim of shade under the eaves of the building, and sensible early arrivers are propped up against the rest of this shady wall, and along the window of the shop. All these people leaning against the plate glass, maybe it'll crack and snap. Great pointed shards of glass will slice down and decapitate, disarm, unman. How bloody that will be. The platters of cabanossi and cheese cubes are already puddling in grease.

Colin Lake, the poet, is standing in a group of fellows. He gives me a hug, and several kisses. I introduce him to Dermot. Dermot looks nervous. So does Colin. There are clots of people squinting, sunglassed, glancing up at the sky trying to guess how soon the sun will sink behind a building. This is exciting, I say to Colin, it looks fabulous, I can't wait.

I go and buy a copy, before any speeches or readings can put me off. He writes an affectionate message and signs it with his name and a small scaly fish. Colin always signs with a fish and I think it's now too late to ask him why. But Dermot does. Colin says, Because I'd like to be one. Dermot blinks.

The minister is there and he's introduced by the bookshop manager and makes a speech. Always a mistake this: long-winded and irrelevant. The minister rabbits on about how important poetry is to the health of a rich and multi-layered society, but try asking him for money. Poets are 'the unacknowledged legislators of the world' he intones, and every poet around looks shifty, it's been impossible to say that for more than half a century, he's using a dictionary of quotations, which doesn't tell you about fashions. We stand, glasses in hand, eyes vacant. I reckon not one of us is listening, except when a clanger like that hits the ground. Then it's the turn of the launcher, fellow poet Thom Vesty. They were *enfants terribles* together, at university, getting into mad scrapes and putting out arty little chapbooks, they've been bolstering and fighting and publishing one another ever since. Colin is tall, Thom is stocky, with hair like a head of hay and a frowning brow.

He begins with excitement and delight, then pauses, then qualifies this, and then qualifies the qualification. He is like a man sliding into quicksand, with each step he takes to extricate himself he sinks deeper. But why is he creating this quagmire out of his own words? He loves the book, he likes it, it's wonderful, he is quite sure readers will find it so too, if they like that sort of thing, which of course they will, a lot of them, most of them, people of judgment as they are, almost certainly it will speak deeply to them. Everybody is listening now, you can hear the ripples of concentration, the waves of embarrassment. Colin stands like an insect pinned, his grasshopper legs trembling, his long face bent over the book gripped in his pale-knuckled hand.

He's not launching it, I mutter in Dermot's ear, he's torpedoing it.

Except that torpedoing would have been quick, and Thom is slow. Step after step, deeper and deeper, stickier and stickier, the slow excruciating suck and slither of the bog. Finally he says, But you don't want to hear from me, when you've the man himself, and steps aside for Colin. Who thanks him for his robust words.

There is quite a small crowd now, and dense. It's still hot, but the sun has dipped behind a building and it's not so glary. Colin is speaking in the beautiful measured sentences that are his mode. There is a plop, he looks up surprised, then keeps talking about the poem he's about to read. Another plop. Another. Small greasy missiles are arcing out of the crowd and falling upon the two men. They fail to stop themselves flinching. Cubes of cheese and chunks of cabanossi, being thrown from somewhere in the crowd. Then hisses. Somebody says, Double Dipper. Somebody else, Charlatan. A counterpoint of voices: Fraud. Nepotism. Got the minister in your pocket. Teacher's pet. Two grants for one crap book.

Thom says loudly, Do I see a sad case of Schadenfreude, friends, and someone laughs raucously. Gloop is now flying through the air, the humous and babaganoush from the nibbles table, launched from carrot and celery sticks. The crowd ducks and parts, trying to avoid being splattered.

The bookseller shouts, I thought poetry was the art of civilisation, and there are jeers. Wrong! Wrong! In that as everything. What about the barbaric yawp?

Ah, so that's the past you're living in, sneers Colin.

Better than any future you might have!

The bookseller, alarmed now, steps forward. It's good to see poetry can arouse such passion, he says, clearly not meaning it. It's obviously alive and well and living in Canberra.

Over here it is. More jeers. Over with your lot it's the zombies. The unquiet dead. Get back to your tombs. Go in peace.

Thom jumps off the bench he and Colin are standing on and rushes into the crowd, his fists raised. People eddy, and the next thing I see he's lying on the ground, with several women squatting beside him. He looks surprised, not unconscious. Jeering voices shout, Fist-i-cuffs! Fist-i-cuffs! and three young men and a girl, very blackly dressed, run off arm in arm, their metal piercings glittering in the sunlight. Somebody mutters, Performance poets. Colin holds up his hand and reads a long poem in a voice that quivers.

It seems to be about a date palm, which has long curved clattering leaves like scimitars; they slice through the air and cut and maim and murder, without much discrimination. The date palm is a bitch goddess, she must be worshipped for her beauty and power, but she is cruel, however much devotion is offered there is no pleasing her, the blade-leaves are always likely to come whirling out. What's more, her sticky rich brown fruits are as like to poison as nourish you. It sounds strange, in prose like this, but it's a powerful poem, there's an intensity and rage to it that is chilling. The poet suffers, the sharp leaves slash and hurt him, he falls humiliated at the foot of this dangerous tree. But then he arms himself, I'm not sure whether it's with a real weapon, a long sharp knife that can slash in its turn, or whether it's with words that he performs his revenge.

It's a terrible poem, bitter, angry, vengeful. An anti-love poem. And so vulnerable you can hardly bear it. But why a date palm? What arcane symbolism is this, I am asking myself. And then I recollect. Tamara. That is what her name means, date palm. Colin would not expect anybody to know that, he thinks he can read out a poem about Tamara and nobody will know what on earth a date palm has to do with anything. Not expecting my obsession with names.

I remember Tamara saying she went to creative writing classes, that fits. Colin's fatal love affairs often come out of creative writing classes.

Fatal? Was the long sharp knife real?

I have to talk to the colonel about this.

Anybody would think I'm expecting him to solve this murder. These murders. Anybody would think that I think I might myself. Cassandra Travers girl detective. Well, the police aren't getting anywhere. Did Colin know Tiffany? Not his scene, I don't think, poor poets don't pay prostitutes. Not when they've got creative writing classes to hand. Maybe Tiffany took the creative writing classes. Maybe she wanted to write her memoirs too. Prostitute memoirs are a very successful genre.

Colin finishes the poem, stretched out beside the fallen body of the palm, his face buried in the sweet sticky juice that flows from her.

The launch is over, the official part. Quite a lot of people line up to have books signed. Trying to offer consolation, perhaps. Or possibly in gratitude for the spectacle.

Are book launches always like this, asked Dermot.

What a performance, eh? said a man standing beside me. Totally rehearsed from beginning to end, wouldn't you reckon?

You mean, they arranged the whole thing? said Dermot. The heckling, the food throwing?

I don't think so, I said, remembering Colin's and Thom's stricken faces. It's poets, you know. They're a violent lot. No money in it, so they fight bitterly for the prestige. Novelists can have a hope, even if it's entirely unlikely, that maybe one day they'll strike it lucky and make some real cash, but poets know they never will. They're famous for their wars, they've been going since the late sixties. Children of the revolution. Partisans, guerrillas, dictators, oligarchs, baby-killers, you name it, they accuse one another of it. Stilettos and bludgeons, bombs and poison. All metaphors, of course, I don't think anybody's actually killed anybody. Though there have been deaths, but mostly self-inflicted, drink and drugs. With honourable exceptions.

Jesus, said Dermot. And I thought lawyers were a tough lot.

Nah. Bunch of pussycats. They make money.

I once had the poets' wars explained to me by Colin, at a party. It was two o'clock in the morning and I was leaning against a doorjamb drinking red wine and he told me about them in his beautiful multi-claused sentences, even quite drunk Colin speaks lovely sentences. He was a protagonist himself, unwillingly he said, but people slotted you in and you couldn't do anything about it. It was suddenly as clear as a chart unrolled before me, Colin the skilful pedagogue with pointer, explaining; I understood the issues, the sides taken—not logical—the arguments and counter-arguments, the players and their roles.

Next morning I'd forgotten everything he said (Too much red wine, Cass, Cleo would say) but I still remember that crystalline moment when I understood. I cherish the idea that once, for half an hour, I knew what the poets' wars were all about. I didn't try saying anything of this to Dermot. He kept shaking his head and saying, Totally weird. It's only poems. Only poems. But poems can kill.

When I opened the front door for Dermot and me Elspeth slid in ahead of us. Dermot lifted his foot under her stomach and kicked her out. Scat, he said. It was a practised gesture, quite gentle, and I don't think it would have hurt her. Not her body, her feelings would have been deeply injured. Don't you like cats, I asked. Cats, he said, they're all right. But it's not yours, is it?

I'd marinated quail ready to grill when we got back and organised the makings of an exquisite salad to lay them on. Simple but elegant, was my intention, and of course delicious. When we sat down to eat them I did wonder what I'd been thinking of. The quail were brilliant, flattened out, crusty-grilled and succulent fleshed, but they were hard to eat. You need to suck the bones carefully to get any meat (I hadn't boned them, life is too short for boning quail, as somebody said about peeling mushrooms) and Dermot wasn't bothering, his pile of bones still had a lot of the flesh on them, and I wanted to lean over and say, Don't you consider that rather wasteful, for Gran taught us to eat up conscientiously, but I didn't think that would be very erotic and the point about this meal was to see if it could be, if Dermot could be anything more than pretty speeches. He's not good at flirting, Dermot isn't. Those speeches are not flirtatious, they're clunky, arrogant. I wonder is he any good at making love? I don't mean fucking, I mean making love to a woman. I think he might be gay. Anyway, I'm sick of pretty speeches. Let's get on. I wondered if my subconscious had been thinking of the famous eating scene in *Tom Jones*—the movie—where the lovers eat *at* one another, tearing flesh from bones with greedy nipping teeth and watching one another with lascivious eyes, getting grease everywhere. I certainly hadn't envisaged this faintly repelled fastidious picking and leaving. The *Tom Jones* bones were a lot bigger. The quail were very fiddly. I noticed his hands were blackly hairy-backed.

I said: You must be thrilled to have your Garry Shead home. (Yes, I know this doesn't come into the category of erotic conversation either but I was feeling bored.) Dermot looked appalled for a moment then his face went smooth as though he was one of those mimes wiping all expression off his face, only his hand was invisible.

Ah, yes, the Garry Shead.

Does it look fabulous in your apartment?

Well, said Dermot, the thing is. I made a space for it, where I thought it would look really good. Had to move some other pieces—my flats never have enough walls. But then when I hung it—he wrinkled his nose—the whole place suddenly looked dingy. This vibrant painting, then my dull as ditchwater room.

How strange, I said. I would have thought, with it being so vibrant, you wouldn't notice anything being dingy. Dingy would disappear.

Yes. Well, it didn't.

I'm remembering your promise, since I can't afford one, I can look at yours.

Ooh, to be sure. We'll have a grand occasion. When I've had the place painted.

I was getting somewhere. The original consolation had implied, you'll be at my place so often you'll have a great many chances to see it. You'll have a version of ownership, through frequent gazing upon. Now it was a grand occasion, when . . . I somehow doubted that I'd be around to need another excuse for an unbought painting.

I wondered if Dermot's wiped-clean face now had a slightly hostile expression. I expect you have quite a collection of art, I said, with girlish admiration.

Ooh, modest, modest. I tend to buy infrequently, but well.

And of course it's such a good investment.

Yes, I suppose so, but one doesn't think of that. One thinks of the pleasure one gets from daily living with good stuff.

I took a risk: Do you think one becomes a better person for looking at good art? Contemplating it every day?

He leaned across the table, took my hand, kissed it, and looked up at me with narrowed eyes.

I do think so, he murmured.

I looked at him and thought of handsomeness. He was so beautiful, those smooth chiselled planes to his face, the dark curls and blue eyes. I had always thought him rather too handsome, but maybe that was to do with unattainable. I wondered what it would be like to wake up with such beauty on a pillow beside you. What if I reached out now and touched the crisp curls?

Do you see much of Marcus, he asked.

Marcus? Edith's Marcus?

Yeah. He seemed a nice guy.

Maybe that was it. Dermot was gay; it was Marcus he fancied, not me.

I'll probably never see him again. Edith's dropped him. It seems to be George now.

Dermot seemed quite pleased to hear this. Gay, it did look like. Still, we'd see.

I'd planned to have coffee on the sofa. I put Diana Krall on the CD player and nipped off to check my face, rubbing my lips with a new coral-coloured gloss so they looked pink and tremulous, though they tasted of false strawberry which I found rather disgusting. I manoeuvred Dermot into the corner of the sofa (by saying, you sit there) and I sat in the middle. Poured coffee, and some Grand Marnier that Justine had brought duty free from New Zealand. There was a plate of chocolate truffles. I let myself sink rather horizontally back into the puffy cushions, turned towards Dermot and took a bite of truffle, arching my lips so as not to disturb the gloss. I let one hand lie negligently in the space between us. To me it was shrieking out to be picked up and held, not kissed, kissing hands is what French politicians do, kissing hands would be a cop out, at this moment. Lovers hold, stroke, squeeze, there can be passion in holding hands. Dermot was busy sugaring and stirring his coffee. I wasn't drinking coffee, I didn't need the distraction. I leaned forward and took a sip of Grand Marnier, leaned back a little closer to him. He drank his coffee and sipped some liqueur, turned his face to me. I half smiled at him with parted lips and wide-open eyes, letting my hair fall in a sweep against the sofa back. He put down his cup and glass. I looked at him and waited. He looked at me. He leaned over and picked up my hand, stroking it, looking at it as though it was unfamiliar. He put his arm around me and held me tight to his chest, his eyes gazed down into mine. Unfathomable was a word that came to me, deep and far away and full of a kind of anguish, it seemed, anguish and perhaps adoration at the same time. He murmured my name, slowly savouring its syllables. He held me tight, I could barely breath, my heart was beating rapidly, my chest felt tight to bursting. How wrong I was thinking that I would find no excitement in Dermot's embrace. His nearness, his intensity, the yearning power of his gaze made my breath flutter, and my mouth pouted open ready for his lips to press into mine. This may be it, I thought. Not gay at all.

I didn't find out if it was. There were heavy stomping feet on the stairs. The colonel strode into the room, then stopped theatrically short. Oh, hi, hi, he cried, with booming cordiality. He sounded like a bad actor in a bad American comedy. Oh my jeeze, I hope I'm not disturbing anything . . . I just felt I had to have a little hot drink. I'll be quick. A quick hot chocolate and off. Don't mind me. Just . . .

I was so exasperated I couldn't speak. Dermot stared after him. Hot chocolate, he said. Does that guy live here?

No. He's a client.

Dermot smiled a rather nasty smile and raised his eyebrows.

I edit him, I said, my teeth clenched. Thinking that edit him was what I'd like to do. Chop out, abridge, slash with a blue pencil, delete. Reduce by half and then reject from the slush pile.

Oh good lord, is that the time, said Dermot.

You needn't go, I said. The colonel will have fixed his nightcap in a moment.

He looked down at me with a little sad smile. Another time, he said.

I walked to the door with him. An enchanted evening, he said, his hand air-stroking my hair. Not only beautiful and charming but a good cook. With a reluctant glance he stepped out into the darkness.

Good night, Dermot, I said, and shut the door. The colonel came out of the kitchen. You can clean up, I said. I'm going to bed. I stomped up the stairs. They're wood, uncarpeted, it's easy to bang your way up them. I would never speak to the colonel again. Ever.

I hope you're not in love with that guy, the colonel called after me.

I wailed. I couldn't help it. It started off as a low-pitched scream that I prolonged for a considerable time, quite to my surprise, a long low wail that ended in a kind of choking croak. It felt wonderful. It felt so good I wanted to do it again, but didn't; a second time might not be so good, it would be a pity to spoil that one glorious perfect sustained and sustaining superb wail. Unlike poets, I know when to stop.

Chapter 23

Saturday morning. The colonel came running into the room and grabbed my hand and pulled me after him. Hurry, he said, and I did, not questioning or holding back. I wasn't talking to him since last night's stomping down the stairs and invading my sofa party but it seemed pointless to say that and I've already remarked I'm not good at not talking to people. *Hurry.* He so clearly meant it. Out to his Land Rover, his foot heavy on the accelerator, forcing it fast to maximum speed, braking hard at crossings and traffic lights. What, I asked, what, but the rapid screaming drive, the bursts of speed and sudden urgent stops shut me up.

We got to Cleo's street. Now suddenly we were slow and quiet. The colonel turned off the engine and we slid along the gutter till we were outside Cleo's house. The square was hot and lazy in the summer morning. A man washing his car, veils of foam running down the paving stones of his drive. Some girls playing pole tennis, the pock of the tethered ball against their racquets muted in the dense air. A boy wobbling past on a bicycle. Children in some invisible swimming pool, calling like birds summoning up the dawn. Gingerly he opened his door. Stay here, he murmured, and clicked it softly shut. He came round and opened mine in the same way. Can we get round the back? he breathed.

One side of the house was garage as far as the fence, the other had a high stuccoed wall, with a door set in it, locked. The wall was covered with a trellis twined with star jasmine. Using the handle of the door and the flimsy trellis Al drew himself up with leaps of his long legs and sat on top of the wall, then pulled me up after him by the same means. I heard the trellis crunch and splinter but he had my weight. On the other side were garbage bins and we got down that way. Normally I would not expect to be able to do any of these things, but in the silence and tension of the colonel's presence they happened. This side passage was a place for compost and garbage bins, a wheelbarrow, bamboo stakes and gardening tools leaning under the eaves. We crept slowly along. At the other end was another fence, made entirely of trellis, and a gate with a latch inset, that did not seem to have a lock. I could hear Cleo's voice speaking, softly, urgently, fluently, with a kind of mesmerising pent-up energy. My first impression was of beautiful cadences. Lovely rhythmic patterns of words, persuading, I thought she must be practising a speech to give in court. Until I got the sense of them.

I am appealing to you, as a fellow lawyer. A fellow human being, yes, indeed, but a fellow lawyer, a colleague, who understands. Who knows what our profession means. You do know that this won't work, it can't work, you will be hunted, you will be marked forever. Give her to me, Dermot, give her to me, and all will be well, you will be safe, you can go and nothing will happen, you will be free and there will be no penalty, no problem, no fear. I give you my word, as a person of honour, as your colleague. It's so easy, Dermot, give her to me, she will be safe, you will be safe, we will never speak of it again.

Quietly we crept to the lattice fence and peered through. There was the calm cloister of Cleo's back garden, trellised with roses and jasmine, the tiled terrace surrounding the pool, dark green and secret in the slanting light. There was Dermot, holding a knife with a long thin shining blade in one hand. The other held Pomona.

The baby was wearing a swimsuit with straps across the back and Dermot was holding these gathered in his left hand which was stretched out across the pool, suspending the child above the water. Pomona was waving her arms and legs in a parody of swimming, her neck was red and her mouth was open as though she was getting ready to yell. Cleo was standing just out of knife's reach, in a bikini and transparent short kaftan, the colour of her Pierre de Ronsard roses. Such detail I saw, every detail of the scene, a chair tipped over on its back, a curly metal table with a jug of fruit juice, a plate with peaches, a mobile phone. The rug with toys where the baby had been playing. The shards of a vermilion glass beaker on the paving stones.

No, said Dermot, and I heard his voice more strangely sinisterly Irish than ever, there is no way for that, no way for my safety in your way. It is too late for any of that, now.

No Dermot, it doesn't have to be. Cleo was standing very straight and leaning slightly forward, vibrating with alertness. Dermot took a measured step forward. The knife held her at bay; every attempt she made to reach for the baby was met by its slashing arc glittering in the sunlight, like a slow hypnotic ballet. You can go away and be safe. What you have done is not so bad, and almost no one else knows. Fiona and I, we will simply forget.

You don't know, said Dermot. It is too late for all that now.

No, Dermot it is not, it is not too late. Give me my child and I will never say a word.

Dermot smiled. She drowns, he said. The hand holding the child dipped toward the pool. So easy for a child to drown. The mother is distracted for a moment, the child crawls, falls in. Too late. The everyday banal suburban tragedy. The helpless child drowning in the swimming pool. And nobody to know she was held under. In a strong hand there'll be so little struggle.

But I will have seen. I will have seen and I will have stopped it happening.

And that's the other sad thing. A young woman, pretty, clever, slashed to death. The serial killer strikes again, the police will say.

Cleo whispered, The serial killer?

The baby started to wail, her face went red and she opened her mouth in a series of long sobbing whoops.

All this time, it seemed a long time, the colonel had been watching intently, as though this was a play and all it needed was watching and listening. Now he motioned me to stand back. He took his hand out of his pocket and there was a gun in it. Gently he lifted the latch of the gate then suddenly flung it open and stepped on to the terrace. He raised the gun and spoke slowly.

Give the baby to her mother.

Dermot turned around. He saw the colonel and the gun and looked at them for some seconds, unmoving. The colonel raised the gun slightly, taking aim. Cleo stepped forward, and Dermot turned to her, swinging the arm that held the baby across in front of him, then slowly placing her in her mother's arms. Cleo gathered Pom close. The child's sobs faded to hiccupping little snorts.

Drop the knife.

Dermot held his hand out and gradually opened his fingers. But only partly, then he swiftly closed them again and with his left hand grabbed Cleo by the short tufty hair on the back of her head and pulled her round in a quarter circle. He held the thin blade pressed against her neck.

Now you drop the gun, he said.

But Cleo moved. She ducked violently back and down, pulling her cropped hair out of his hand and jumping backward into the pool. Dermot teetered on the edge and the colonel stepped forward and smashed his fist into his jaw, lifting him up in the air in a soaring arc. He came crashing down again into the pool, in his turn. I rushed forward to help Cleo, who had kicked out to the shallow end. She was standing up, shaking and crying and holding the child close and high against her cheek, I had trouble persuading her to give her to me so she could climb out.

Maybe he'll drown, said Al, watching where Dermot had sunk. But he came up, thrashing and spitting and choking. Just stay there, said Al, pointing the gun at him, and using the phone to dial the police.

I can't swim, gasped Dermot.

Neither can the baby.

Cleo sat in a chair holding Pom tight. I wrapped them both in a towel and put my arms round them and held them close. Dermot kept going under in clouds of panic and bubbles, Al's punch had sent him well into the deep end, until he worked out he could hold his breath and walk the few paces to where it was shallower, and there he was when the police came and arrested him.

How did you know, I asked the colonel. How did you know that was going to happen?

I didn't, he said. I feared it. When my mole in Cleo's practice . . .

Is that *true*? Did you really have a mole?

Of course I did. Al looked surprised. You didn't think it was a joke, did you?

Maybe . . . a lie . . .

He looked hurt and just stared at me. Well? I said.

It took him a moment to take up the narrative: My mole in Cleo's practice . . .

I interrupted again. Is she young?

Moderately.

Pretty?

I suppose so.

Does she have long smooth shining brown hair?

Well, yes . . .

And did you meet her at Verve?

Once, I think.

Aha.

Aha, what's aha?

What's she called?

Fiona.

Fiona. And she's just a mole.

Well, she's an auditor, actually. Her business being fraud, particularly. The firm called her in.

Not a—special friend?

Cassandra! She's a very nice person. But, well, I said, she was my mole. She worked out that there was something tricky going on, and she also worked out that Cleo was suspicious too, and talked to her, and then she realised that it was Dermot and he would have worked out that they knew . . .

It was my turn to shake my bewildered head.

So, you see, said Al, I guessed Cleo could be in danger. And when I found out this morning that Paul was taking the older kids away for a night's camping, and that Cleo had been talking about having a nice quiet time just her and the baby . . . but it was guesswork. Though I did realise Dermot was losing the plot, he wasn't any longer the calm clever operator that he had been . . . I knew I couldn't take any risks.

We had to talk to the police, when they came. They were interested but sceptical when Al told them that the angry man in the swimming pool was the killer they were looking for, and then Al drove along the river to find Paul at the camping place, since his mobile phone was out of range. I rang up Cleo's mother to come over.

And here is the story. As told by the colonel, later in the afternoon, to Paul and Cleo and me sitting round the table in their dining room. Like Poirot at the end of an Agatha Christie novel, I said, and so it was.

You know, said Al, how people tell you things, a story, an adventure, an account of an event, even a piece of gossip, and you think, there's something wrong here, something's not quite right, not everything, most of it is okay, but somewhere there's a lie, a falsehood. Maybe it's something left out, a lie of omission. A number of times I had this feeling, but I mostly put them out of my mind. Things have a way of becoming clear, eventually.

The murders. Quite early on I decided that Harold Perrot wasn't involved, not his kind of thing. He's car mad, he's not a murderer. Then I started to wonder if we were dealing with a serial killer at all. Tamara's death, and Tiffany's: what if it was not a case of random acts by a psychotic, but a careful plan. In other words, what if the actual killing was a carefully planned act, absolutely necessary, as he—or possibly she—saw it, to the killer's well-being. What could be a reason for somebody's wanting Tamara dead?

It's usually something a person knows. Has seen, has deduced, has understood. Something that makes that person dangerous.

Here a number of these vague disquiets came into focus. And the person who gave me the vital clue was Mrs Tricks. Annie Tricks. After she had her fall and was lying on the bathroom floor her mind was wandering a bit. She mentioned invisible ink. You can write something in invisible ink and after a while it fades and disappears completely, and then with your secret formula you bring it back again and can read what is written.

Ironing it, said Paul.

Pardon?

Ironing it. You iron it and the message reappears.

The colonel bent his head. Yes. Well. I thought of Tamara's profession. Crashed computers. Where what is written fades and disappears. When it appears to be utterly lost. Tamara's profession was uncrashing them. Making what had seemed irretrievably gone come back. Perhaps she had made appear what somebody did not want ever to be seen again.

One odd fact may have supported this. Andrew Sissons remarked that Tamara's computer was completely blank, and that there were no back-up disks or CDs to be found. Wiping his victim's computer and stealing all back-up does not seem like the act of a random killer. It might even be someone's motive. The question was, who? Who would be afraid of what Tamara had understood? A client, is a logical answer.

Dermot did not at first come to mind. But after a while it became apparent that there were a lot of things wrong about Dermot, false impressions, false seemings, falsehoods. Why for instance would he pay ardent court to a beautiful young woman like Cassandra but not follow through by making love to her? Yes, I know, I was listening, upstairs, but I did have a good reason. (I could feel my face burning hot with blushes.) I too wondered if he was gay. It was evident he wasn't what he seemed.

Marcus provided a clue there. He's a smart guy, Marcus, I've had some good conversations with him. Yes I know, I didn't tell you. I had to talk to everybody who might be of any help. That evening when he and Edith called unexpectedly, Cassandra, and you were in the shower, so Dermot had to let him in, Marcus recognised him. Only vaguely, he'd met him in Sydney at a party, and afterwards there'd been some trouble, something in the paper, though Marcus didn't mention that part to him, just said, Oh hello, we've met before, haven't we. But Dermot vehemently denied it. No, no, he was from Adelaide, it couldn't possibly be him.

He told me he was from Perth, said Cleo.

Exactly, said Al. Anyway, Marcus let it slide. As you do, on polite social occasions. But he thought about it, and later when I was questioning him, he remembered it, he said he'd been a bit worried about what sort of person Dermot was, so I said I'd keep an eye on him.

He didn't mention it to me, at the time, I said. Except, I suppose he did ask me was he all right.

Well, he didn't want to make a fuss.

The car tyres!

I think so. That same long sharp knife—he gestured faintly towards Cleo—when he went out to the car to get the map. Marcus didn't draw that conclusion, otherwise I don't think he'd have worried about making a fuss. You could see that as the beginning of Dermot's unravelling, his failure with Marcus.

He tried to kill him—and my mother—because Marcus had recognised him?

Once you've done one murder, the rest seem to follow—no reason not to keep on, you've killed for safety, safety keeps demanding it. Anyway, I remembered your mentioning that Tamara had done some work for Cleo's firm.

I wondered if perhaps someone had caused their computers to crash deliberately, in order to cover something up. As I said, with computers not much is ever utterly irretrievable. It is to the layperson, who doesn't have the skills, or the money to pay someone who has. It's expensive because it takes a long time. I think Tamara became suspicious and found what the person wanted hidden. She was a conscientious but also an impassioned worker, she suspected something wrong and persevered until she found it.

Fraud, said Cleo. A complicated and clever siphoning off of funds.

That's where my mole comes in. Fiona. As I said, actually an auditor. And with advanced computer skills. She briefed me as well as the firm.

Why? I said.

Because I asked her to. You'd be surprised what people will do when you ask them. She worked out that Dermot had been comprehensively defrauding the company, that the crash would have been to cover his tracks, and give him time to make it all seem perfectly proper. Unfortunately, Dermot realised she knew, and that she had told Cleo.

The colonel had turned pale and was looking quite sick. I think Fiona would have been next, after Cleo and the baby. You see, and I blame myself—he shuddered—when I think . . . Cleo and Fiona of course didn't know about the connection with the murders, they thought it was just fraud.

That's why I thought I could talk him out of it, said Cleo. It seemed such an overreaction, murdering a baby . . . And then he mentioned making it look like the serial killer, and

I knew . . . I thought I'd been afraid before, but after that . . . She put her hands over her face, and Paul wrapped her in his arms.

I should have warned . . . taken precautions. Because of course Dermot was by this time quite mad. He'd killed two women, with precise planning, and he was going to go on killing people until he was quite safe. He thought that no one would ever suspect him, handsome clever wealthy Dermot. But he'd lost the plot, he was careless, he had no alibi, he did not understand how easily he would be caught. Which wouldn't have helped Cleo, of course.

Why Tiffany? said Cleo, but I could see she knew.

To make it totally random. He had to admit having known Tamara. Killing someone with whom he had absolutely no connection removed him from the scene. So Tiffany—victim of her suburb and her initial; that randomness had a kind of mad logic.

Maybe, also, Al went on, because she was an escort girl, he thought she was dispensable. Even deserved it.

I thought the girls were safe. Driven around by the bouncer . . .

Sometimes they moonlight, they don't go through the agency, saves the rather hefty fees; they make an arrangement with the client . . .

I was glad I hadn't had time to tell Al my theory about Colin and the creative writing classes and the vengeful lover, though as a possible narrative I do think it was very elegant. I blushed when I remembered my Andrew Sissons scenario. I caught Al looking at me in a worried way. Andrew Sissons, I said.

Ah, yes, that was a good theory. I knew by that time though that it wasn't right. I just couldn't tell you—he shook his head, and frowned. His eyes were pleading.

Cleo touched Paul, and he went off for a moment. I knew he was checking the children, even though Cleo's mother was with them. I wonder when I'll feel safe again, she said. I know Dermot can't get to me, I know logically everything is as it was. But I don't feel safe any more. I can't forget that moment when I realised it wasn't just fraud, that he was a killer.

I still think it was clever, how you worked out it was Dermot, said Paul, coming back and sitting with his arm around Cleo, who snuggled close.

Well, to tell you the truth, it was pretty arbitrary at the beginning. It started off because I couldn't stand the bugger. I thought him a vile slimy creature with nasty habits. So I was prepared to see him as a multiple murderer, to be perfectly frank. Nothing would have surprised me. But I did go after him in the beginning with more emotion than evidence.

And I thought he was a nice young man who might be good for our Cass, said Cleo in a mournful voice.

Matchmakers have the strangest ideas, said Al. But what you did was believe the persona he offered.

You mean I was a sucker for the Irish charm.

False Irish charm.

Do you think he was gay, asked Paul. Is gay?

I've wondered about that. I know he didn't fancy Cass.

How do you know? I bristled.

I know how it is when a man fancies a woman. I know he

didn't fancy you. But he wanted people, and you, to think that he did, and why that should be is an interesting question. But as for gay; lots of gay men like women, they're great at flirting with them. Not all, of course. I think Dermot doesn't like women at all, hates them, fears them. That syrupy charm, it's a mask, it's designed to keep the world at bay. And I think it's not just women—Cass and Cleo, those model girls he's been seen with—I think he's a kind of outcast, that he hates other people, men as well.

And children, said Cleo.

You'd need to be a forensic psychologist to get to the bottom of all of that murk. I did wonder if he intended to harm you, Cassandra . . .

Last night?

When I hid upstairs. Logically I didn't think he would kill you, he'd be certain to be caught, known to be with you, no alibi, et cetera. The other murders were minutely planned—the police didn't have a clue. But I certainly wasn't going to trust to logic. Psychopaths do tend to go from cool planning to a sort of deluded frenzy; murder has worked and so now they are gods or anyway supermen who can get away with anything. And I was right, as we see with Cleo; he was quite mad, taking desperate risks, a moment of logic would have shown him he couldn't make that work.

I was blushing again, remembering my behaviour on the sofa.

I wanted to come down and smash him up, said the colonel. I've never heard anything so vile. I wanted to come down and punch him to death.

I remembered Al's feet stomping on the stairs, the faux

jaunty manner. I was laying a kind of trap, I said. I never fancied him either, really. Far too handsome. Far too weird. Though I was prepared to think he might have been interesting. But I did want to find out what he was up to.

You weren't . . . hurt? I mean, heartbroken, or anything?

Heartbroken? You've got to be joking. Dinted pride, maybe.

I should have had faith, I suppose. I mean, I did, that you'd eventually . . .

Let's not talk about him any more. I shivered. It's like having a slug in your life, leaving slimy trails all over everything.

At least we can wash them off, said Al. It's disgusting while it lasts, but we can wash all traces away.

On the outside, said Cleo. But you can still shudder, even when it's all washed away, you'll never forget its filthy tracks on your body.

Paul held her close in his arms.

This wasn't a social occasion. The colonel had told his story, it was time to go.

In the car the radio came on when he started the ignition, announcing that Australia was at war with Iraq. Al pressed the button and turned it off.

Chapter 24

Of course, that is not the end of this story, as it would be were it an Agatha Christie novel. There's a lot to tell yet.

How Al and I went back to my house, for instance.

He drove the Land Rover at a leisurely pace, so different from the mad dash to Cleo's that morning. My brain was still sorting and slotting the things he'd said, fitting his jigsaw pieces with mine. I remembered Andrew Sissons saying there were no Australians fighting in the Gulf War, no troops on the ground.

So, I said, the moment of truth. A lot of moments of truth. The end of the play, when everything is resolved.

Everything?

Why not. Big and small. One thing . . . I repeated Andrew's claim to Al.

He was silent for a while. Did you believe him?

I paused too. I knew my answer was important. It had to be true, and it had to not hurt him.

You know, there was a moment when I thought your whole book was a mighty work of fiction. That you'd invented the whole thing, using the facts of course, like a historical novel. Only a moment. Then I knew it was fact.

I'd always believed in it, I knew what you were doing was true, but then I saw that it was fact as well. Did I believe Andrew? Hardly. I stored away what he said to ask you. Having faith that you would make it clear.

Andrew's is a common misconception, he said. The thing about that man is that he knows a number of things quite certainly but he speaks as though every thing he says is absolutely so and people believe him. Such men are dangerous—always only a portion of what they say is to be believed, and you never know which. I can tell you: nine Australian Army personnel served with the British Forces fighting Operation Desert Storm, and some were in the thick of the battle. There were four majors two captains two lieutenants and one sergeant.

No colonels?

I wasn't a colonel then.

It was quite early when we got to my house, too early to go to bed. Cleo had offered drinks but we'd refused. Let's have a glass of wine, I said, some nice fresh cold white. But there was none in the fridge. The housekeeping had totally packed up. Al went to get a bottle out of the car; far too warm. He hunted the kitchen cupboards looking for an ice bucket, and finally found a tall tin flower pot. He emptied ice cubes in, added water, and set the bottle in it. There, he said, give it ten minutes. I put peaches in a bowl. We stood by the kitchen bench looking at the bottle chilling. Then at one another. I lifted my face to his and we kissed, a gentle loving slow kiss. I put the bucket in his hands, picked up the glasses and led the way upstairs.

It was hot. I opened the windows and turned the fan on. He put the bottle in its flower pot on a chair. He slid his hands down my arms, ice-cold against my hot skin. I gasped. He pulled my dress off, me gasping again as his cold hands touched me, shuddering with delight. My hands are too cold, he said. I'll warm them up. No, I said, I like them like that. His hot body, and mine, and his ice-cold hands making me shiver with desire. Ice-cold hands and desire: the pattern imprinting itself on my senses.

It wasn't too early to go to bed, after all.

Sometime before dawn I floated almost out of sleep. I was faintly aware of the dogs barking, their mournful plangent notes filling the night with that strange discordant music, which made you feel they saw things and felt things that were too sad to be grasped. When I opened my eyes the moon was flooding the room with a brilliant cold light, bleaching out the colours, turning it into a mysterious other place. Al was lying half on his back, I on my side with my head on his shoulder, his left arm holding me gently close to him, his right hand resting on my hip. My left hand drifted down to hold his penis, and I slid back into sleep. The image of the lovers lying together which I had carried like an icon in my mind for so long had gathered me to itself, it was my face that slept blissfully within the picture.

I had found my shoulder.

In the morning when I drifted to the surface of sleep I was lying on my side, with Al twined close behind me. Loving spoons nestled in a drawer. You see, he murmured, our bodies have danced together all night, asleep and awake. His body enfolded me, I curled further back into him. We dozed a little, until our bodies woke thoroughly up.

The next day passed in a haze. More lovemaking, food—not the bottle of warm wine floating in its tin bucket—the conversation of lovers. When did you . . . at what moment . . . what made you . . . what was the first . . .

When did I begin to fall in love with you? said Al. The first time I saw you. You were such a surprise, so beautiful, and so sharp—I loved the way you took me to task. I find intelligence incredibly sexy. In a sexy person. What about you?

I wasn't so clever as you. I didn't notice for quite a long time.

You did have Dermot to distract you.

I felt a huge crimson blush suffuse my face and neck. Please, I said. Al laughed. Even your breasts go pink, he said. All right, I won't mention him again. Though I have to say, that scream—I wanted to come up and hold you tight, then . . . but it was a good scream, I hope it worked.

Oh, the scream—it was Dermot, a lot of it, but it was also all the times you enraged me so much I determined never to speak to you again.

Did you? I don't think I noticed.

I pummelled his stomach. Gently of course. It was hard. I loved looking at his body, lolling beside me on the bed. I traced the elegant line of his pelvis, with its little pouches of muscle. I love that line in men's bodies, and so do sculptors, they carve that pelvic girdle so lovingly. With the little hollow cups of tender flesh beside it.

He slid his fingers along the curve of my waist. You're so soft and plump and cuddly. So smooth.

Less of the plump.

No, more, more. His fingers caressed my skin. I've always wondered, he said, why people say skin is smooth as satin. Satin's quite rough, compared with the living softness of your skin.

We didn't say anything for a while after that.

I thought I liked having you round because you made me feel safe, I said, after the while.

I'll have to show you how dangerous I can be.

I did know how much I like talking to you. Though I didn't think about it, I just kept greedily doing it.

And so on. And on.

And that's still not the end of the narratives. Now I have to tell how Al and I went to his house.

Shall we go to the coast, I asked, next day. I wanted to see the steep green paddocks again, Al's Picasso woman landscape, and the way the late yellow sunlight sifts thickly across it, I wanted to sit on the terrace and look at the sea, to walk in the hidden garden. I wanted to make love in that house.

Soon, he said, there are things, first.

Will you show me the secret orchard?

Yes.

Maybe all that respect I paid to Priapus had its effect. Priapus the son of Dionysus and Aphrodite; to think I never knew that. Patron of gardeners fishermen and shepherds.

I'm pleased to see, he said, that you are properly respectful towards me.

Only if I want to be. Maybe it is because you are also the child of wine and love . . .

That was the end of conversation for a bit. Then Al said, I know I made you angry because I wouldn't tell you things. I think I ought to now.

There's more?

More.

He arranged for me to meet him at his apartment. I didn't ask him why. I'd decided to enjoy his games. Maybe I always had? Especially now that I trusted that explanations would follow. He gave me a key: Let yourself in and I'll come to you.

The apartment is on the third floor, no lift. The stairs are concrete and echoing, like a fire escape. The building did begin life as public housing, though in more generous days. Al said it was spacious for its size. I expected that opening the door from the drab and draughty landing would be a revelation. I wondered if it would be pale, or jewel colours. As it was it was some time before I noticed anything about the room I entered, apart from . . .

The first thing I saw was an open cupboard door and hanging from its top edge, on a coat hanger covered in loops of crocheted pink silk, was a dress. A ballerina of ming-blue shantung, with shoestring straps, and a bolero made of swansdown, with bracelet-length sleeves. The skirt was long and gathered full.

I closed the flat door carefully behind me. When I turned back to the room the dress was still there, splendid, ugly.

The fabric felt slubby and ever so slightly rasping to my nervous fingertips, it rustled when I touched it, swinging from its coat hanger. The skirt was lined with layers of stiff net petticoats. I remember Gran saying that girls used to dip them in a thick syrup of sugar and water to make them stiff like that.

I knew it had to be the dress worn by the woman who beat up Hotbaby. Didn't it? What was it doing here? Was its owner living here? Was she sleeping with Al? I felt a stab of jealousy so sharp I wanted to vomit. And another slower ache: disappointment. I had thought us so happy together. I put my hands on the table and lowered myself into a chair. I felt old and very frail and my brain wasn't working. I gazed at the dress. A vintage model, indeed, or else a careful reconstruction. My eyes moved from the dress on the door to the cupboard itself. There were other dresses hanging in there. One was art silk printed with poppies and cornflowers and ears of wheat. Its long flared skirt was Dior late-forties New Look. It was the dress shirt-waist woman had been wearing at the hotel by the beach when she had been drinking Pimms, and I had named her after it. Was it shirtwaist woman who had walloped Hotbaby, then? And what was her connection with the colonel?

There was the sound of a key in the door and Al came in, looking pale and quite tense, the smile he gave me tentative. My head was full of pain and my eyes and all the lines of my face heavy and dull with it. I had so many questions to ask I couldn't think of one. After a while he began to speak.

You said I didn't tell you things. You were right. Partly because it's my way, but much more because I thought you were safer not knowing, and a lot because it was too hard. Now I want to tell, I have to tell you, and I'm terrified.

That dress . . .

You recognise the dress. I thought it would be a good place to start. Show and tell. His smile was a kind of grimace. It's mine. All the dresses are mine.

You mean . . . you're the woman who beat up Hotbaby? You're shirtwaist woman?

Shirtwaist woman? Oh, the poppy dress. Is that what you call her? How did you know about her?

I saw her, at the pub at the beach. And in DJ's underwear department, I think. She fascinated me—I suppose it was the vernacular of her clothes—my gran, she had clothes . . . My voice trailed off. I was trying to think what this could mean. At least I was pleased she wasn't another woman he was sleeping with. But that made him the other woman . . .

Vernacular—that's good. I call her Alfreda. I think of her as quite grand, she has quite an arrogant walk, don't you think? Of course she's me, but me being someone else. I'm not gay, you know, you do know that, and I'm not trans-sexual, and I don't have ambitions to be a drag queen. Sometimes I need to be someone else, and I do it by dressing in women's clothes.

He darted little glances at me as he said this, to see how I was responding.

You dress as a woman to be someone else.

Yes. Being me isn't always . . . I dress as a woman and I can leave fears and failures and all that debris somewhere else. It's Al that suffers all that. Alfreda is free. Al is suspicious, constantly alert. Alfreda notices nothing. It's such a good feeling.

Couldn't you get that by being another man?

I've thought about that. But all my failures, all my burdens and baggage, they're to do with being a man, I couldn't ditch them in the same way, being another man.

So it was you that beat up Hotbaby?

Hotbaby? His face darkened. Yes. It's the one thing I'm not proud of. It did get out of hand. I wanted to find out—I grabbed him and he went for me—I hit him. It was the falling rather than the punch that did for him, the narrow lane, the gutter. I was angry—him trying to rape you.

It wasn't exactly rape.

Near enough. Slimy little bugger that he is.

Pathetic, rather, I said.

Don't sentimentalise him. He's not a nice piece of work. I'm sorry I hurt him, but there it is, I did.

He looked at me. What about Justine?

Justine. Who you tried to make me think was Hotbaby's nemesis? That was truly wicked.

Yes. But I wanted to sidetrack you from Belinda. After all, what connection could she have had with him?

Oh, I said, mortified. I hadn't thought of that.

So, Justine?

She's in Melbourne.

Are you in love with her?

No. I'm fond of her. I love her, I should say. But I'm not in love.

So you aren't—lesbian?

What do you think? No. Justine knew I wasn't. It was a game, a lovely game full of pleasure. Pleasure—it's something.

It's a huge great thing. You're such a sensual being.

I suppose I am. All by myself, mostly. A solitary sensualist. Sounds like those late nineteenth-century decadents, all those corrupt flowers and stuff, and loving one after their fashion.

Why am I rabbiting on, I asked myself. I wanted to cry.

Shall I make some coffee, he asked. He hung the dress in the cupboard—for the first time I saw, on a high shelf, wooden milliner's heads with brown and blonde wigs designed to fall half across the face—and shut it in, then opened some big louvred doors beside the clothes closet. For the first time I registered something about the flat. Behind these was a kitchen. Small, but perfectly formed.

Remember, he went on, our conversation the first day we met? When you so utterly charmed me?

I didn't know that, I interrupted.

I didn't want you to. You know it is in my nature to be secretive. This talking to you now, it's a kind of liberation, and it's bloody painful. A bit like having a dislocated shoulder and someone manipulating it back in, it hurt like hell before and it hurts like hell now but after it will be good, you hope. I don't think I'm going to make a habit of it. In my case it's what, my heart, my mind, my spirit? that needs shoving back into the right place . . . Anyway, that first day, you said, could a person be a bachelor again . . .

When you lied to me and said you were married.

It's the only lie I ever told you—and it was brief, I almost immediately untold it.

I think I believed you didn't lie to me. You didn't need to, you just clammed up.

You made me think. I was a bachelor again. I was married. Once. As you suspected, not many people get to my age without being married. We had a child, born while I was away at the Gulf War. Imogen. She was months old when I first saw her. My wife was angry at being left alone for so long, she said I didn't love her, but after a while it was all right, we were happy. Fairly happy . . . my wife . . . remember what I said about darkness . . . how some people somehow live in darkness . . . She didn't much like my being in the army, but it was okay while we could live together, even if it did mean moving around a bit. Imogen was a beautiful sunny child, she was a joy. But then I was sent to Somalia. My wife was furious, she wanted me to get out, to take a pension, I could have done that, but I saw it as my duty to go, I wanted to go.

You've doubtless heard a bit about what it was like there, the horrors, the miseries. The starving children. The massacres. I wish I hadn't seen them. And while I was away my daughter contracted meningococcal disease and died. I couldn't get back in time.

My wife left me. You know how the death of a child can destroy a marriage. And shortly after that my mother died, drowned in the sea. She was a good swimmer, for fifty years she'd swum in that sea, so I have to wonder if her drowning was accidental, if she didn't somehow arrange for it to happen. She was lonely, my father had died some years before, she'd wanted me to leave the army and come and live on the farm, it was hard for her to manage, it would have been idyllic, all four of us, plenty of room, the farm running the way it ought. When Imogen died and Sarah left I think she'd had enough.

And I . . . I realised that life is not elsewhere. Too late, of course, stupid man, I realised that life was where my wife was, my child, my mother. Now that they were all lost to me.

I know Alfreda recreates her. Her clothes. My mother was a tall woman, stately, shapely, with a bit of help her clothes fit me. And then there's her striving for the perfect bottled fruit. These things are a kind of homage to her. All too late. Too late.

Maybe you've been a bit mad with grief.

You think there needs to be some irrational explanation? That otherwise it's all too disgustingly odd?

I sighed. No wonder the colonel had found all this too hard to tell me. I was finding it too hard to hear. What year was your mother born?

1919.

A year after my gran. Does that mean you're old enough to be my father?

Certainly not. I doubt I'm even a decade older than you. I was the child of her later years. So it was described at the time. These days—he looked at me—it's more the norm. But back then, I think they'd given up hope, it was a surprise when I turned up.

He took my hand. My thought was to pull away, not to let myself be touched, but my hand felt otherwise, it opened to his and held it tight.

But I have learned. I know that life is not elsewhere. It's here, it's to be grasped. I remember your story about the golden windows ... Maybe it is not too late for other things.

He was silent for a while. We weren't holding hands any more. Al's were clenched on the edge of the table, and he leaned towards me with such intensity in his eyes, his sea-blue eyes, his indigo eyes, that I couldn't break his gaze. I stared back and found that I too was clutching the table. I felt like a person standing on a cliff looking down into the sea and wanting to step over the fence and tip down into it, feeling the irresistible pull of that vast mesmerising water. I hung on harder to the table as though it were that fence, the only thing between me and the plunge.

I would marry you, he said.

Would?

I would marry you. Wish, want, need, to marry you. Utterly.

I had not thought of marrying, I said.

No? Then please think now. But—you needn't tell me. Please think, and say yes. When you are ready. Take your time. Please don't say no. He unclenched his hands, his eyes let me go. There had been a spell, and I don't think this broke it, just stretched it, made it more spacious. He glanced around the room. Now you can tell me what you think of my pad.

I hadn't even looked at it. Now I did I saw it was beautiful. Painted and furnished in a range of milky colours. It's you being a dairy farmer, I said, all the dairy colours, cream and clotted cream and milk and yoghurt, it's your heritage.

He laughed at that. The floorboards were creamy too, limed white, and the curtains were thin linen, pleated, the light sifted gently through them. There were rugs on the floor, faded to pinky brown, and a lot of paintings on the walls. One was a Garry Shead from the Kangaroo series, playing with the idea of D.H. Lawrence living in Thirroul, writing his book there, and evoking the Kangaroo as a big poignant guardian angel. Guardian beast. There was a tall press full of worn blue and white china. You do good rooms, I said.

I thought to myself that *Euphrates Apricot* would look terrific in this room. Perhaps I should after all buy it for him. As a saying yes or a saying no present. Which?

Chapter 25

Reader, I married him, says Jane Eyre at the end of the novel named after her. Notice she doesn't say Dear Reader, she is not buttering us up. It is a stark statement. Take it or leave it. A lot of people have been critical of this ending. They say poor Jane, plain Jane, couldn't have the lovely man in all his glory. She has to take him after life has battered him, when he is blind, and broken. They suggest that Charlotte Bronte ought to have ended things differently, giving her Mr Rochester in the full flower of his beauty, or else making Jane refuse him, giving her power if not happiness.

But the thing is, and I think Charlotte Bronte knew this, there is no such thing as a perfectly beautiful man. Much of the glory is false, or flawed, or more ordinary than it seems. Mr Rochester in the full force of his glamour was not in fact an attractive figure, not when you knew him, knew about him. The glamour was only one flat and tricky surface of him. The underneath was murky, a mad wife in the attic, intentions of bigamy, it offered a pure young woman a terrible lie. The maimed Mr Rochester is the classical paradox of the blind man needing to lose his eyesight in order to be able to see. Jane marrying the broken man was accepting the real, the honest, the true Mr Rochester. The human, properly dimensional man. She liked honesty, did Jane. She did not mind hardship, if that was the price of honesty.

Al wasn't broken, but he was flawed. A sensible woman could have done a balance sheet of debits and credits.

Tender with old ladies

Likes to dress in women's clothes

Owns and can use a set of skeleton keys

Not to mention a gun. How? Legal?

Bottles apricots

Good talker

Wounded by his past

Very sexy

A loving lover

Was a soldier

Is a soldier

May be a spy

Good cook

Secretive

Sometimes portentous

Organising

Arrogant

Knows about important things like Priapus

But which, in that list, are debits, and which are credits? And who wants sense at a time like this?

So. *Reader, I married him.* Jane said that. *I* married him. Did Cassandra? Could Cassandra cope with the knowledge of a whole man? The danger of him? I walked around the beautiful pale room and looked at the paintings. The small

Shead with Lawrence and Frieda making love, watched over by the wise Kangaroo. I knew what I wanted. I wanted him to put his arms round me and hold me. I wanted to take the plunge into the sea-blue depths. And that's what I did. I walked back to where he was packing our coffee cups in the dishwasher and put my arms round him and was gathered into his. Yes, Reader, I married him. Of course I did.

I should add a postscript. The apricots, so serene and perfect in their heavy syrup. They won first prize at the local show. They didn't do so well in Sydney, only a runner-up. Al was philosophical. Next year, he said, next year we will surpass ourselves.

Acknowledgments

Thanks to Margaret Connolly, Rosanne Fitzgibbon, and Sue Hines, for turning my pages into a book. And John Stokes who encourages me.